THE WHOLE
OF THE MOON

DON'T ALL TEENAGERS WATCH PORN?

Anna Perera

For Cy

CONTENTS

'I heard to-day for the first time the river in the tree.'
– Emily Dickinson

ONE

Please understand Evan's not weird. He just went into a massive meltdown in the car on the way to school.

Mum was singing along to some rock god, smiling in a girly way and it was one of those mornings where everything feels possible and amazing things are just waiting in the ether for me to grab with both hands and when that kick of inspiration to live a big, extraordinary life, hits me between the eyes, I feel so excited it's hard to breathe.

The old, brown microwave was on the front seat of the car and I was kind of dancing my way to the edge of an unpredictable adventure in the back. Happy as anything until Evan kicked my leg to stop me bouncing around.

I punched him and his iPad sprang out of his hands to my feet.

My mouth fell open at the vile video of a girl's bare ass, an implement of some kind and two guys.

It felt like someone stepped on my head and kicked me down to earth.

Evan grabbed the iPad and the look on his face nearly finished me off but I had to tell and shouted, 'MUM, Evan's...'

With storming pain in his eyes, Evan mouthed, 'Sh - ut - up. Sh - ut - up,' slowly and calmly and I'm sure he would have choked me to death if Mum hadn't been there but she was.

When a skateboarder in school uniform clacked onto the road in front of us, the car braked, Evan leapt out, leaned back in and said, 'I wanna rape a girl, kill her, then kill myself.'

The rock god effect vanished even though the music was still playing. Mum froze, expressionless. When Evan had gone up the school steps, she shook her head unable to take in what he said.

Rooted to the spot, I hesitated but told her, 'He was watching hardcore porn.' Needing to immediately separate my having watched low-level screwing in movies from Evan's obvious evil addiction.

'I don't understand,' she said.

'You were going to get a thing on the internet to stop us getting that stuff?'

The car behind beeped.

I clicked open the door, got out and looked back for an answer but Mum just nodded slowly to herself.

'Have a good day, sweetie.' And drove off.

TWO

Evan was the cutest kid in the whole world when he was little but now he's turned into someone else. Someone I don't know.

What you've heard about kids sexting, assaulting and abusing each other is worse than people realise. Even some of the geeks do it. There are plenty of ten-year-olds at it and younger. No one takes much notice unless a compromising picture of an underage gets posted on Facebook. To stop parents checking what their kids are up to, new apps have been invented to make it harder for them to spy, but horrible, unbelievable suggestions, insults and photos are always doing the rounds.

I can't tell you the number of times I've told a guy I'm not interested in seeing another dick pic. The first time was in primary school when bully boy, Vernon Wood, shoved his phone up my nose when we were waiting to go into the hall for gym.

'Ugly, fat face,' his friend jeered and I smiled. No resistance to stupid words, no fight, is my motto after what Vernon did to my friend. There's no remedy for that kind of behaviour so I ignored it and pointed my chin so high in the air, I could almost see through the window as far as the school gates, which is impossible for anyone with an ordinary neck length like mine to take in at the best of times.

The thing is, Evan's eighteen months younger than me and in the middle of GCSEs. Academia suits me down to the ground. He's different. He hates school. We're related but you'd never know. He's short for his age which upsets him while I'm tall for mine which I love, and I have to admit I can't remember the last time we had a real conversation about anything other than Dad's girlfriend, Shell. We guess that's short for Shelley but neither of us have bothered to find out for sure. It's not that we don't like her. It's just that we don't want to meet her.

Anyway, back to that evening; the warm kitchen smelt of pineapple from the two for the price of one pizza we were eating at the kitchen table. A voice from the TV announced: 'Figures show a child sex offence is recorded in Britain on average every ten minutes. Offences rose to more than 55,000 last year,' and none of us blinked an eyelid, because we were all in our own little worlds.

I was already in my red pyjamas, reliving the half smile I exchanged with Watty at the bus stop. More about him later. Mum must have been wondering how to bring up the comment Evan made this morning, and, he was (I imagine) lusting over the girl, the implement and whatever the two guys were up to on his iPad.

Mum glanced at her phone. 'Dad's on his way over.'

Evan pushed his plate away and jumped up. 'I've got to do tectonic hazards. Yeah, I have. For Geography.'

'No, you don't.' Mum shook her head. 'We're having a family meeting about this.'

'About what?' I was thinking of gorgeous Watty not asking a question. As I said, more later.

Mum gave me one of those 'I'm not in the mood for games' looks, and tried and failed to squash the twelve-inch pizza box in the undersized bin beneath the sink while Tickle, our bad-tempered black and white cat, sprang onto the table to finish off the crumbs.

'I'm not hanging around to talk to Dad.' Evan stormed out, leaving Mum and me staring at the open door.

'Evan. Come back here. Right now.'

Silence.

Mum ripped the pizza box to shreds, stuffed the lot in the bin, the door bell rang and I ran off to answer it.

'All right, love.' Dad kissed me on the cheek. 'Bit early for bed isn't it?'

For a second I forgot about him not living with us anymore, to watch a gigantic lorry squeeze into the side street but there was a bunch of cars in the way. It scraped past and I turned back to Dad. 'Just 'cause I'm dressed for bed doesn't mean I'm going.'

We walked to the kitchen arm in arm and he took one look at Mum's face and raised his eyebrows. 'What's up?'

'Do you have any idea what Evan's doing online?'

'I can guess,' Dad shrugged. 'Is that what all this is about? For goodness' sake, Tessa, all boys his age watch porn.'

For a tense second I thought Mum might throw him out but she said, 'Marya, tell him what happened this morning,' and turned her back.

'Uh, oh. I'm in trouble already.' Dad sighed and I was like, trying to make him feel better by putting the coffee on and Mum sat down with her head in her hands and started crying. It wasn't the best time to come face-to-face with Jeremy, the lodger, who lives in the back extension with its own shower. A nurse in the local, hard-pushed hospital, he's probably already worked a hundred hours this week and not sure what to do, Jeremy glanced at Mum, nodded at Dad and vanished.

I put my arms round Mum's shoulders. She dried her eyes. Dad made strong coffee and that was as far as our family meeting got.

THREE

You can imagine my frustration when Mum woke me up at 7.00am and launched into a speech before I'd even opened my eyes.

'Pornography is a global industry worth more than a hundred billion dollars. At the last count there were more than 400 million internet pages with 70 million search requests for it daily. Daily, I tell you.'

Bleary eyed, I watched her flip open the white blinds.

'Porn's massive growth is calculated years ahead by legitimate, mainstream businesses with marketing teams, accountants and investment managers.' Mum glared. 'Big hotel chains earn millions from selling distorted views of sex with violence that are considered normal.'

'STOP.' I leapt out of bed and edged her backwards out of my room.

'It's out of control, Marya,' she said as I closed the door. 'Your grandfather had a stash of magazines in the shed. They had pictures of naked women that were pathetic compared to the stuff that's around now.'

'Thanks for that,' I shouted but she hadn't finished.

'Kids don't know what they're getting into. It's not real sex.'

I muttered something but she carried on ranting behind the closed door.

'Kids' natural awareness and preferences are being stolen by money men and no one cares.' She paused, maybe realised she was talking to herself, gave up and went downstairs.

I got dressed in peace.

Ten minutes later Mum left for work and Evan was still asleep. I banged on his door to tell him to hurry up. I don't know why I waited for him but I did.

We didn't speak most of the way to school and Evan looked miserable as we headed down Fairfax Road. How am I going to become a Nobel Prize winning something with all this going on?

Everyone says I'm really grounded and sensible. The least messed up of anyone they know because I never lose it. Well, I felt like losing it now. Felt like screaming and swearing because porn has hijacked my little brother. Stolen his normal reactions, changed his behaviour and the noise of cars, smell of petrol and even the cracks in the concrete under my feet made me desperate to yell my guts out, but then, I'm not a screamer so I just kept walking.

'What's your problem?' Evan said at last.

'I'm not the one with the problem,' I huffed. 'I don't watch hardcore porn for fun.'

Evan pulled a stupid face, threw the rest of a satsuma at me and was hyper-annoying until he caught sight of radiant, confident Shula Hanan, who has the ability to mesmerise anyone within a five-mile radius of her goddess body and huge twinkly eyes. If you don't know who Shula is then you don't live in Lewisham or South East London.

I swear Evan blushed as she crossed the road. Everyone at the school gates turned to look and Shula sailed up to us like Cleopatra on a golden barge. Big smile blaring her sugary white teeth.

'Hi Marya. Have we got English first thing?'

'No, after break. The supply teacher has a dentist appointment at nine thirty. Remember?'

'Was it today?' Shula flicked a gloss of black hair behind her ear and blinked at bully boy, Vernon Wood, my only nightmare, walking towards us, babbling to an older bloke who must have been one of the relatives in the paving company where his whole family work. Big-boned and strong, it was hard to walk past without remembering what he did. His hard, nasty face ricocheted off the pavement and opened up the desperate ghost house in my mind where I was forced

7

to remain silent about something I still can't swallow. Even the solid ground beneath my feet felt under attack as Vernon ignored the beeping cars to march across the road with the same stupid 'what do I care about anyone but me?' grin, from six years ago.

'Wish our proper teacher, Miss Chandros, would hurry up and come back,' Shula said.

I looked at her, took a deep breath, let the horror go and said with a bang, 'Yeah, but it's not like she's going to give up maternity leave to make us her priority when her premature baby is only about five days old. By the way, this is Evan, my brother. He watches hardcore porn for fun.'

Shula frowned. 'Where's the fun in your sexuality being manipulated by actors working to a three-line script?'

Evan had no intention of answering and fell behind while I gazed at Shula with admiration. How did she come up with that perfect reply without hesitating for a single second?

I turned and caught the back of Vernon Wood disappearing into the newsagents opposite, relieved he didn't stop to gaze at Shula because then he might have noticed me and maybe said something vile. I felt sick and the sick was guilt. He was over there, out of the way but his face was in front of me, rattling the street as we walked and I wished I could tell someone but I can't.

The moment we turned the corner I was myself again but didn't ask Shula what she meant by a three-line script. What is that? Being a member of Mensa must have something to do with her all-round brilliance. I feel more intelligent just talking to her and frankly, if I have an idol, it's Shula Hanan, and I'm like a hundred and ten per cent straight.

When we started chatting about *Othello*, why he couldn't see through malicious Iago and how we'd like to shout out the lies he told about Desdemona, Evan was nowhere to be seen. Later, when I saw him on his own in the playground, I wished I hadn't shown him up like that. I didn't mean to. Didn't want to. It just came out.

FOUR

I caught up with Evan in his bedroom when I brought him tea and toast because Mum had to work a double shift and asked me to make him something because he didn't have breakfast, has two more exams to go and looked dead pale this morning.

Of course he didn't bother to look up from his iPad when I plonked the tray on the white bedside cabinet.

'Sorry, I showed you up in front of Shula. Sometimes my big mouth runs away with me.'

He just looked at me and reached for the mug. 'This tea's cold and so's your face,' he said, brown hair flopping over his eyes.

There's no way I was going to leave the room until I'd had it out with him so I added, 'You really upset Mum, you know?'

'How?'

'How?' My jaw dropped. 'Since when have you been so stupid? You were watching porn on the way to school.'

'No, I wasn't,' he bluffed. 'That was just a silly picture someone sent round and I was laughing at it.'

'Don't lie. It was a video and you were glued to it.'

'Huh. You're insane,' he said.

His SparkNotes for *Lord of the Flies* was open on the scruffy, unmade bed where he was lying and I thought, *Oh, yeah, well — that couldn't be more appropriate, could it?*

Evan lunged for the toast with iPad face down in his lap. 'What's the point anyway?'

'…Point?' I was prepared to be patient and hang around for his brain to kick into gear with another lie even though his stinky socks were on the floor next to a crushed packet of crisps and empty bottle of fizzy orange, because now I was really worried. If he can't admit

9

he was watching porn then what hope is there for sorting the problem out?

'Nothing's going to happen.' Evan looked at me like a small child woken in the middle of the night and told to get his things.

It turns out I'd walked into the middle of one of his deep thoughts and had, not only to be patient, but to enter another realm of existence. 'The future is hard to know. Yeah?'

'What are you on about?' Evan said.

'Me? What are you on about?' I said.

'All my mates have had sex except for me,' he muttered with a mouth full of toast.

'No.' I was shocked. 'Even Jez with the big, twitchy ears and Alex the moron?'

Evan half nodded.

'I don't believe it. Boys are boasting liars and anyway sex shouldn't be about competing. There's nothing wrong with waiting.'

'You don't understand how desperate boys are. It's never going to happen.' His voice was all shaky. 'No girl's ever fancied me.'

'That's not true. Jolene used to follow you around last year.'

'Yeah, but she didn't fancy me. She was new and no one else would talk to her.'

'How mean. Kids are cruel. Who have your mates had sex with then because I bet it's none of the girls I know?'

'Three of them have done it with Yolanda,' he said.

'Oh my god. You shouldn't have told me that. She's what? Fourteen?' The conversation was getting out of hand. Next thing Evan would be asking me who I'd had sex with and that was something I didn't want to get into with my brother but what could I say that would straighten him out? What could I really tell him? It seems honesty can get you into trouble and I was beginning to regret I'd started the whole thing.

His eyes went slightly wild. 'What difference does a couple of years make? In some countries the age of consent is fourteen.'

'Yeah?'

'Look it up.'

'I will.' Now I was horrified as well as shocked. 'Yolanda's out of her mind to even look at the losers in your year. She'll get a reputation.'

'So.' When Evan stops talking there's nothing to do but be patient and wait for him to start again. Sometimes it takes a few minutes. Sometimes a week. However legendary the subject, it can be dropped with no explanation if you interrupt. That's how he's always been.

He turned away. I waited and instead of my mind spinning with Yolanda's antics, I managed to bring myself back to the messy room to keep the conversation going. 'But then it's not my business. As long as she consented?' I said.

'Obviously. Girls are mental but not all boys are. Everyone saw Yolanda go after them. I was pissed she turned me down.'

I was going to ask why obviously and tell him off for calling girls mental but realised how upset he was when his eyes went really sad and hopeless and he reached for the SparkNotes for *Lord of the Flies*.

Time stopped.

I looked out of the window.

It was raining and there was no one in the street.

What he wants felt impossible. He hardly ever leaves his room and his big chin, weird, sunken eyes and spots on his nose made it hard to imagine any girl ever fancying him.

'Is that why you watch porn?' I said.

'I wasn't watching porn.'

'Yes, you were.'

'Prove it,' he sneered and I stole a corner of toast, crammed it in my mouth and gave a lecture based on *Lord of the Flies* instead.

'The central conflict in the story refers to the part in all of us that either chooses to do the right thing for the sake of the group or give in to evil and gratify our worst instincts. Rape and killing are evil and I get why you said that, Evan, but it wasn't right to threaten to do what you said. You haven't failed at anything, and just because Yolanda turned you down shouldn't be a reason to sacrifice your own goodness by even thinking such things.'

Inspired by my own smartness, I paused for a second but Evan acted as if my intelligent comparison between his situation and the biblical theme of the book was a severe blow to his head.

'NOT NOW,' he yelled, covering his ears. 'I've got stuff to do.'

I went and sat on my bed and stared at the grey sky through the white blinds. At the paisley duvet I couldn't be bothered to straighten. At the ancient Twilight poster beside the mirrored wardrobe and listened to Evan talking to himself next door. 'Get over it. You idiot,' he said.

The light was still out when Tickle pushed my door open. In the darkness with slivers of moon coming through the open white blinds, he looked at me with half closed eyes, miaowed through his hairy face and almost outdid his own shadow when he shot onto the bed to settle in. When I stroked his soft ears and patted his neck, he twisted sideways and yawned and I thought, *There's nothing in that little brain apart from the need to stretch,* and then he started staring. 'You're just a cat, you don't understand,' I said, but sometimes I know he does and I'm back in the nightmare from six years go with the music still playing. Running down the stairs, crashing into the handrail in a rush to get to Mum in the garden. Pushing the other kids' smells and flesh out of my way and out of existence but they hung there like the old, grey moon.

FIVE

After school the next day we went straight to Wolf's Winery where Mum's the daytime manager Monday to Thursday but does the early evening shift on Friday. I can't tell you the number of times we've sat at the wonky oak barrel in the far corner where sawdust on the wooden floor, a few mirrors and the whiff of grapes and vanilla is supposed to make it feel like a real winery.

Due to Mum, who's always rushing around, the main course is half price for us on Fridays and Evan and me have got into the habit of ordering two separate dishes and sharing them. Tonight it was Shepherd's Pie and Lentil Sebastopol. Risky, I know, but believe me the resulting stew was memorable and I can understand why people say food porn is just as addictive as porn porn.

I was about to congratulate myself for wiping my plate clean in record time when Dad walked in and screwed up his eyes as if he couldn't see us properly. I spotted him first, nudged Evan and we both stared, hoping he wasn't with Shell.

'Was just down the road,' he said with a weird, sheepish smile. We looked past him. There was no sign of a female so our gobsmacked faces quickly fell back into place. He said hi to Mum who was checking a wrongly charged bill behind the counter and pulled up a chair.

'Everything OK?'

We nodded.

'Can't stop,' he said. 'Just thought I'd pop in to ask if you want to come to lunch tomorrow at the new rented flat.'

'The decorator's gone?' I said.

'There's some finishing off.' His smile went over our heads. 'Still

13

smells of paint but it's better than the last crappy place.'

'I'm not coming if Shell's going to be there,' I said matter-of-factly. Something I've told him several times before.

'No. No.' Dad seemed distracted. First he started patterning the sawdust on the floor with his black sneakers and smiled for no reason at the cool young guy with navy headband at the next barrel who was munching smashed avocado on toast. A particular favourite on Friday afternoons. Then Dad took the *Evening Standard* from under one arm, shoved it back under the other and got up.

'Your mum says you haven't got anything planned. Need to get a move on to collect little Freddie from his gran's so I'll see you tomorrow.'

Just so you know, 'Little Freddie' is Shell's son.

At sixteen, Dad left school and started working for a charity that trains ex-prisoners for employment. He studied for qualifications in the evening so now he's a probation officer who does his best to keep them out of trouble. With a large caseload, diminishing funds and tons of paperwork, Dad's often stressed.

We think he met Shell on the number 43 bus when he was cracking up from dealing with an offender who was a substance abuser and a bit of a murderer but we're not really sure.

At the time, Mum said Shell was an out-of-the-loop, bored home worker with a three-year-old son, who has since bought into a mobile dog grooming business with her sister. Her husband designs exhibitions and Mum once talked to him on the phone when it all blew up.

'I don't want anything to do with any of them,' she said afterwards. 'And if your dad wants his freedom he can have it.'

Shell's not on Facebook so we don't know what she looks like. We found out later she was on her second marriage when they met. Maybe she's a romantic dreamer? One of those people who believe true love is out there somewhere and doesn't have a clue about real life. Well, that's what Mum says.

On the way home, going over the image of Dad messing up the sawdust, smiling at the cool guy for no reason and shifting the newspaper around, led me to grasp the entire situation. Dad's riddled with guilt because he watches porn, too, which is why he couldn't look at Evan who sat there gently invisible. There's nowhere to go with a thought like that so I left it alone and went back to thinking about the many things Dad should have said to Evan. 'How are the exams going?' would have been a good start.

For ages I thought it might all work out. Mum said it would. It hasn't and that's after nearly a year. Poor Evan.

I'm never getting married.

SIX

D ad's new, rented flat is on the top floor of a Victorian terraced house in the dead-end street that loops round to the primary school.

Kabira, who came up with the George Elliot Summer Reading Challenge we're all doing, lives on this road, but I don't know which number.

Kabira is going to try for a campus university next year while I'll have to study in London to save costs. She's great and I wanted to see her but hoped she wasn't around because how do you explain to someone you've known for years that your dad has moved here with his married girlfriend and her son when she doesn't even know your parents have split up?

Panic-stricken, I half expected Kabira to jump out when Evan pressed the door bell and I ran the whole way up the stairs to the top floor and collapsed against the wall with a burning head, totally grateful for the stink of paint coming from Dad's flat and no sign of my friend.

When he caught up, Evan gave me one of his *'The sooner this is over the better'* looks, and we put on our suspicious half smiles.

The carpet in the flat was beige like the walls. There was a white mirror over the fire void and a small photo of Evan and me as little kids on the marble mantelpiece. In pride of place was a big, silver-framed picture of the new, happy, smiling family: Dad, her and Freddie. It felt like Dad had made a new movie and fired the original actors. Us. I tried not to look at the photo but couldn't resist and I know Evan was doing the same when we went in with Dad behind us.

'The new sofa was supposed to arrive this morning but never mind, the spare kitchen chairs will do for now.' Dad plonked himself down on the old, blue armchair that used to be in our house and we took the pine seats opposite. With nothing to look at but the photos it was weird. So weird.

When the front door clicked, it was obvious what was going to happen next. Evan glanced at me but I was too annoyed to react. How many times have we told Dad we don't want to meet Shell or Freddie?

They appeared two seconds later and it felt like someone pulled a plug and every breath emptied out of me in a sudden rush. There was nothing left as I took in Shell's young, podgy, smiling face which is far less attractive in real life than the picture on the mantelpiece.

'Hi, Marya and Evan,' Shell said quickly with stern little Freddie beside her. Evan didn't react. Unable to be rude, I sort of nodded before turning to face Dad who jumped out of the armchair to peck her on the lips.

'Of course they haven't got back to me about the sofa,' he said.

'Oh, no,' she said, a bit over emotional.

Silence.

'Did you put the pasta on?' Quick-moving Shell undid her navy trench coat and patted her grumpy son on the head. 'OK, I'll do it. No. It's fine. Come on, Freddie.' Off they went with me impaled on the pine chair and Evan locked into a sudden lip twitch.

Dad got his phone out, walked up and down the springy beige carpet to speak to the furniture company, complaining about the amount of time it was taking to get through then off he went, pans knocked together in the kitchen and we sat there fuming.

Luckily, Shell remembered she had to sort out something with the mobile dog grooming salon. 'See you later,' she said and disappeared with Freddie without a single word passing between us.

Dad called us into the kitchen and placed bowls of pasta with tomato sauce on the table. 'Here you are.'

The plunging sound of the washing machine sloshed around as we ate and I pretended not to notice the brand new, slimline iPad on the chair that Evan couldn't resist taking a closer look at.

'That's Freddie's,' Dad said.

'Just want to check something,' Evan said.

'You'll wreck it. Give it here.' Dad held out his hand and Evan put it down. The pretence that everything was all right instantly vanished. There was Dad beaming like a kid while us miserable kids half choked on soggy, overcooked pasta, unable to play happy families for a minute longer.

With slow movements, Dad wiped cheese crumbs from the edge of the plate and licked his fingers one by one, and the moment he finished, I said I had to meet a friend, washed up and we left.

'What a fucking idiot.' Evan kicked the low wall as soon as we were outside. 'I'm never going there again. I hate him.'

'Dad's lost it,' I agreed. 'Apparently it's quite common for men his age.'

Angry as hell, Evan stuffed his hands down his pockets and looked up and down the busy road for the bus as if he was a badass in *Game of Thrones*. I was about to tell him the several ways that parents often go crazy during their kids' teenage years when the famous Yolanda who's slept with far too many boys in Evan's year, turned up behind us. With tons of make-up, brown hair pulled back in a pony tail and dressed in white leggings and cool, grey sweatshirt, you'd never guess she was only fourteen.

'Hi,' Evan blushed.

'I'm his sister, Marya,' I said with a slightly evil eye.

'Yeah, I know. What you doing?' Yolanda grinned and cracks broke out in her pink concrete lipstick.

'Waiting for the bus.' What did she think we were doing? Getting our ears pierced? I was annoyed she carried on standing there while images of her doing it with stupid boys like Jez and Alex swam round my head.

'Right.' She looked away. 'Me, too.'

We all stared at the busy road and I was tempted to talk about underage sex when I realised that being with Evan was making me crazy. Then, loaded with shopping from Tesco, a middle-aged, sad guy in brown, leather jacket and fed up wife joined the queue at the bus stop. I watched him secretly eye up Yolanda when he thought his wife wasn't looking. Yolanda must have been giving off a special signal because the pull of the old guy's attraction was hard to miss. When he caught my eye, I sneered at him like he was a pervert. He took no notice until I folded my arms and stood right in front of Yolanda to protect her and he immediately started talking to his wife. A bus, backed up by two more screeched to a halt and it was over.

'Did you see that old guy staring at Yolanda?' I asked Evan when we were safely out of the way on the front seats.

'What old guy?'

'Never mind.' I don't get Evan at all sometimes and turned to see Yolanda several rows back chatting to a bearded guy in gym garb, flexing his arm muscles while hugging a black tub of protein powder.

There's no way Yolanda could possibly tell what I was thinking which was, is she man-crazy? She stopped grinning at Muscle Job for a second, gave me an *'Isn't he cute?'* look and gently, coyly, sweetly tapped his shoulder to point me out as if we're great friends, when today is the first time we've spoken.

Acting is what she was doing for the benefit of the guy she just met and the whole thing passed right over Evan's head.

Perception is everything and I have to admit, I quite like Yolanda now. She was having fun while I watched the lights change from red to amber to green, wildly excited about nothing, wondering exactly how Dad and Shell got together on the number 43 bus and if she gave off the same secret flirty signals as Yolanda.

Must say, I seriously think if Dad hadn't gone off with her after Mum found out, which she won't talk about, then he would have fallen for someone else and the result would have been the same; no father living in our house anymore.

SEVEN

Watty, whose real name is Walt Trotter (I know), is the guy I fancy like crazy. He's in the year above and a complete brain box when it comes to French and Spanish.

With deep-set, blue eyes and a naughty smile on his pointy face, I don't know why, but he triggers a strange knowing in me. A kind of heavenly, familiar feeling, like I met him in a past life or something, and it's been like that for almost six months.

Crush isn't the word for it. There's Watty in this world and then there's everyone else.

'You're not with it when he's around,' is what my friends say. There's nothing I can do about how I feel because his face is forever flashing through my mind and when I see him, it's like, *Ah, there you are,* even though I hardly know him.

Take last week for example when I was pushing past all the slows down the High St. on Saturday morning, excited by the possibility of seeing him when heading to the menders with Mum's old, black, work shoes under my arm. Something that happens often due to the amount of running around she does.

Watty waved from the doorway of his uncle's cafe. 'Hey, Marya.'

Don't rush, I told myself and he smiled at the road. Or it might have been at himself. It was hard to tell.

Hair gelled back, hands in the pockets of his tight black jeans, he looked so gorgeous I nearly stopped breathing but gave him a big, practised for ages in the mirror, type of smile, 'Oh, hi, Watty,' as if I couldn't care less.

Pretending to be surprised, I was desperate to get an answer to the question I'd been wanting to ask all week which finally shot out. 'You going to work here for the summer holidays?'

My big fantasy is to run into him every single day.

'Not sure.' He glanced at a man smoking a cigarette, fumbling for change to feed the parking meter and then his eyes met mine. That grin again, and the street, sky, the world went wide before he said, 'It's been pretty quiet here the last few weeks.'

'Yeah?' was all I could come up with. A nearby car alarm began screeching and my eyes drifted to the bus coming along the road. I mumbled something about going to the shoe menders which I'm not sure he heard and then we just stood there. Staring conversations are pretty annoying but I just couldn't think of anything to say.

Finally, he looked me over like a towel just fell from my naked body and said, 'Fancy a free coffee? My uncle's gone home early for his birthday.'

'D'accord.' That was me being cool and heart thumping like crazy, trying to forget the look and appear sane, I followed him inside the almost empty little cafe where I spotted a couple I vaguely recognised sitting by the wall, gaping at their phones.

Dumping Mum's shoes on the chair closest to the counter, I nearly worked the whole thing out in French but said, instead, 'Did your uncle make his own birthday cake?'

Watty shook his head, poured two coffees from the hissing machine, sat down opposite, leaned forward and the ground opened up in every language. I honestly freaked out when his blue eyes started burning into me like he wanted to dissect my soul. 'You OK?'

So tense, I nearly burst out laughing but managed to nod. 'Yeah, as always. Hehe,' and took a few sips of milky coffee.

'I hear you fancy me?' he said at last. Eyes on the wall.

'Who told you that?'

'Not saying. Well?'

'What if I do?' was the cagiest reply I could think of when *oh-my-god, he knows I like him* thoughts were beating my brain to pulp and I was just sitting there, staring out like I'm hypnotised or something while manically scanning my brain for the face of the suspect who betrayed me.

Finally, he laughed and I'm not sure if he was laughing at me or not. 'Look, I know you want me.'

He actually said that.

'Oh, yeah?' I froze and a whole bunch of feelings fell on top of each other. I mean, who does he think he is? Skinny, pointy face, isn't even good looking.

'Give me your number,' he said.

Without thinking, I handed over my phone, trying to act calm when shaking with confusion. Thank heaven two women came in and began salivating over the croissants, powdery buns and frosted cupcakes behind the glass which floated past my eyes in a dream. Watty jumped up to take their order while I wondered how long I could sit there going in and out of myself – good for nothing but picking at the leather of Mum's shoes.

The combination of clinking spoons, the couple in the corner bent over their phones and the slow-moving traffic outside, teleported the moment into infinity, hell, or both.

Watty kept glancing at me and I had to force myself to remember I'm not gorgeous and he wasn't patiently waiting for me to come down the street. I'm not even sure he likes me.

Sitting there got too much and when I stood up, he turned round briefly with that hint of a smile on his face which clearly said, *Run away if you want but we both know the truth of how much you like me, little girl.*

Watty spread his arms either side of the door to stop me from going and I was almost breathing normally with the shoes held tight, when I said, 'I bet you're into hardcore porn.'

Weirdly, it felt like that was meant to pop out of my mouth and somehow rescue me because his deep-set eyes flared for a second then flickered with embarrassment before he sighed and hugged himself.

'If you want to go down that road, I'm happy to chat,' he said and back came the crushing smile.

I sniffed in a sort of smug way and turned round to see the nearby couple were watching us and suddenly realised where I'd seen them before. They used to come into Wolf's Winery and lounge around for ages on the window seat with a single beer between them. I gave them a brief wave and the woman called me over.

'Hi, Marya. Isn't it?' I nodded. Racking my brain for her name wasn't getting me anywhere so I gave her one of my stupid grins instead.

'We were looking at the vid our daughter made. Want to see?' The proud father beamed. The sweet mother fidgeted. Watty came and stood behind me and I'm like, so aware of him breathtakingly close, I could hardly stay still as she held out her phone to show us.

As much as I wanted to get away, even though I had nowhere more important than the shoe menders to go, for some reason I couldn't move. Watty leaned over me and blew all tingly warm breaths on my neck. Too attentive in the wrong kind of way as we watched three minutes of a made-up, cute, blonde kid of about eight in silver hot pants and gold crop top, writhing around in a weird, adult way to a horrible pop song, and all I could think was, *What kind of mad parents are you?*

'Isn't she sweet?' The dad smiled with seriously wonky teeth.

'I've never seen anything quite like it.' Watty nodded and stepped back.

I quickly checked my phone, 'Yeah. Wow. Yeah. Sorry,' and pointed at the door. Without looking at Watty, I blinked like a confused nut, gave the mad parents a quick grin and left.

Not until I was in the menders where the sound of tapping and clopping reminded me of all the ways I could have smacked Watty down, did I get my breath back.

I've got too much pride to be another one of his conquests but I'm thrilled he gave me a free coffee. I mean, that was nice. He didn't offer me a cake though. Not that I would have taken one.

Why didn't I admit to liking him? Was it because I was afraid he might then expect me to give it up without us having the tiniest thing going on?

As for the video of that kid flashing her childhood like it was for sale, what seemed innocent because of her age, sweet giggle and mad dancing, had the opposite effect when she started grinding her hips and pouting. At one stage she even poked her tongue out. If her parents are going to boast about their daughter by showing her off in that way, aren't they seasoning her to become some kind of sex object?

By the time I'd worked out the French for did your uncle make his own birthday cake: Est-ce que votre oncle faire son gâteau d'anniversaire? I was halfway down the High St. and my phone pinged with a message from Watty.

'You're hot and if you want to get down to it any time soon we can arrange something?'

I blushed. He called me hot. WOW. I read it again and then got annoyed. Flattered and insulted at the same time, I texted back to even things out, 'When I'm desperate I'll let you know.' And could almost hear Shula cheering.

It wasn't long before he replied. 'No, you won't. Feminists don't like sex.'

'Really?' I messaged. 'You know millions of feminists? I'm impressed.'

Suddenly I'd gone from being hot, to a sex-hating feminist because I didn't jump at the chance to 'get down to it' with him.

Why did I think we could maybe go out and have fun together? Share our thoughts and dreams, kisses and everything? Like a real boyfriend. Something I'd never had. Perhaps I should have said what I want but then he'd have evidence of uncool, 'feminist' me on his phone, being drippy, like the rest of his conquests, and would probably show it to everyone for a laugh. It wasn't worth the risk and as he didn't reply there was nothing I could do.

I thought back to the way he reacted when I said, 'I bet you're into hardcore porn,' and yeah, his deep-set eyes flared for a second then flickered with embarrassment… like he'd been caught out.

EIGHT

You could say Mum's a bit different. I mean she doesn't gush when random babies start gurgling at nothing in the street or ooh-and-ah at puppies in the park. She never jumps for joy like my mates' mothers do when asked to go clothes shopping. Not that I like going clothes shopping. I prefer hanging out in book shops. A little nod and smile is all I ever get when I bring her a surprise mug of tea because her face doesn't change that much no matter what's going on. Mum never laughs really loudly and it's hard to know what would make her go ballistic but I'm used to all that and I love her. She's kind and gentle and just herself but when she gets a bee in her bonnet she really does not let go.

'The pop industry is totally male oriented when it comes to this stuff,' Mum said when I told her about the video of the writhing girl. 'It's big business. All of it and that girl's sexuality is being hijacked for profit.'

Ever since Evan made that awful comment, Mum has become totally aware of the porn industry and what it's doing to young people.

'Sexy singers are empowering girls, not harming them.' I read that in a magazine but I'm not sure it's true.

'Celebrities have enough status and money to perform their edgy sex acts and get away with it. Many young girls don't have enough knowledge of the world to understand what they're mimicking and who they are attracting. Their freedom of choice is actually choice-less.'

'Maybe Evan should see a shrink?' I said in a clumsy attempt to divert the conversation.

'Far too expensive. I haven't paid the water bill yet. It's bad enough trying to hang on to the house. Without Jeremy we'd be well and truly stuffed.' Looking good in a yellow shirt and black jeans, Mum plumped up the red cushions on the brown, fake velvet sofa and folded her arms.

'Take Evan's iPad and phone away,' I said, filled with dread for the ensuing fight that would break out between them. 'That will get him offline and save money. My laptop's clean, by the way.'

It's strange how much she trusts me and never doubts what I say.

'More drastic action than removing electronics is needed right now and your grandpa bought them for him and insists on paying for the internet so I can't really. Well, not without explaining why – which would finish him off. He's already got a wonky heart.'

Mum put on her determined, managerial-type face which I ignored by pulling the straggly ends of my hair together under my chin to see it had hardly grown at all since the last time I checked.

'It's not as if Evan meant it,' I moaned and then Jeremy showed up. 'Hi Jeremy.'

'Hi. Um, just wanted to let you know my holidays aren't until the beginning of September so I'm happy to look after the cat while you're away.'

'Thanks,' Mum said. 'What would we do without you, Jeremy?'

While he grinned and Mum blinked, I gave it to her from all sides. 'What? Where? What have you gone and booked?'

Mum held up her hand to shut me up and Jeremy became concerned. 'How's Evan doing?'

'That's something we really don't know. Anyway, his last exam's today,' Mum said. 'School breaks up soon and then we'll see.'

'See what?' I asked but Mum didn't answer.

Jeremy swung a tatty backpack on his shoulder and said, soothingly, 'He'll be OK. Evan's a nice kid. Better run. I'm on post-operative care this shift.'

The minute he was gone, I demanded, 'Where are we going?'

It was clear Mum had a plan. She shrugged. A big idea was written all over her face, and knowing her – it was something no one else had thought of. 'You'll find out soon enough.'

'But Jeremy knows.'

'Not really. Just the dates.'

'What are the dates? I might have plans?' Bumping into Watty every day was the main one. Followed by reading all George Elliot's novels.

The front door banged and Evan came in from babysitting Faruk next door and thumped up the stairs without saying hello.

'We're in here, Evan. Evan?' Mum called but his footsteps quickly disappeared into his room and the door slammed shut.

'Maybe Faruk's the one who got him into porn,' I said. 'Or Evan's destroying his childhood by getting him into it?'

'Faruk's only eight.' Mum shook her head.

'But you said that's when it starts.'

'No way would Faruk's father let him near that rubbish. I've had enough of this.' Mum jumped up and called, 'Come down, Evan. You need to hear what dreadful thing I've got planned for the summer holidays.'

Through the open door I watched her fold her arms. Bend one knee. Lean back and puff for a bit before charging up the stairs two at a time, elbows akimbo like a cartoon, land-locked eagle.

Not much was said or at least I couldn't hear anything because Mum always goes super calm when she's angry and Evan was soon in the living room, in a mood, on the sofa next to me while Mum pulled up the red armchair that matches the cushions.

'Remember when you were talking to my friend, Chris, at Wolf's Winery a few weeks ago? Yes, you do,' Mum said.

Evan and me looked at each other. Both thinking, *What the hell is this about?* Mum can take ages getting to the point when she has something important to say and Evan was trying to block her by staring out of the window where there was nothing to see but the houses opposite, a few cars and a parked up, yellow ice cream van.

'Now, this might not be the way you want to spend a month this summer but I've got four weeks' holiday owing and have found a way of working somewhere at the same time which will pay for the trip.' She nodded. I blinked. Evan sighed.

'If you think back,' Mum said, 'you'll remember Chris talking about when he worked at Arcadia, the self-sustaining eco-community where they grow their own food and use solar power for most of their energy needs.'

'I ain't going to no hippy place,' Evan piped up.

'Just because they live in a community doesn't mean they're hippies,' Mum said.

'They use solar power for wifi? No way.' I frowned. 'How does that work?'

'I'm not staying in a tent,' Evan said. 'Don't care how big it is. Creepy crawlies get in the sleeping bags, climb in your ears, lay eggs and...'

'Stop it,' Mum said. 'I don't know how the wifi works but they definitely have it otherwise I wouldn't have been able to make the booking. There are dorms for teenagers who come from all over the world to do all kinds of things apart from sitting on their iPads and phones all day.'

'Weirdos,' Evan said.

'You can pretend you don't know me if you like,' Mum said and Evan nearly smiled.

'Where is it then?' I was intrigued.

'Well, actually, it's in Andalucia.'

'Andalucia?'

'Spain,' she said. 'In the cork farming district.'

Evan's eyes nearly popped out of his head and Tickle wandered in, purred, jumped on Mum's lap and settled down while I pined for the missed opportunity of seeing Pointy Face every day this summer. Then I began stressing about what Evan might do when confronted with numerous girls in floaty dresses and skimpy shorts in a hot country and was like, *How am I going to protect them all, knowing what's on his mind the whole time?*

Mum found last-minute, no-frills flights from Gatwick and it wasn't until we arrived in boiling hot Malaga that I discovered why Evan was so shocked.

'The age of consent in Spain is sixteen, the same as us,' he said as we jumped in the taxi at the airport to get to the station.

'So?' I was mystified.

'It used to be thirteen. Yeah, it did. In Portugal it's still fourteen.'

A taxi at the airport whizzed us to the station where we boarded the train for the cork farming district and I was more worried than ever.

NINE

From the train window, Mum pointed out lovely villages, vineyards and olive groves which almost did my head in. I mean, how many polite, 'Yeah, nice,' comments can you make when trying to get lost in *The Mill on the Floss* which Shula's also reading and insists on messaging thoughts like:

'I must get a handkerchief to sob into like Mrs Tulliver. There's no drama in tissues is there?'

Trying to concentrate on the perfect reply was difficult what with Mum going on about the scenery and Evan moaning, 'Why can't we go to the Costa del Sol? I hate holidays.' Like he's in nursery school, about to have a tantrum because he's spilt his orange juice, but it was a beautiful day. The train was clean and new-looking and when he finally shut up, the time passed quickly.

When the doors closed and the train chugged away, leaving us on an empty station with nothing but two pale, crumbling buildings and the glaring sun, the hopeful feeling this would be OK completely died.

What do people do out here in the middle of nowhere?

'Arcadia is shaped like a tree,' Mum said for no reason. 'The land is bigger at the trunk and thin strips branch out to the neighbouring cork farms.'

'Interesting.' At least I was making an effort. Evan wasn't.

There was nothing for miles around the empty station except parched earth and a few trees and in the sudden silence a weird feeling spread over me as I squinted at the blue sky, wondering… how exactly do you farm cork?

It seems certain kinds of oak trees are the answer.

A wild, grey-haired man called Serge arrived like a long-lost relative in a beat-up, dusty blue car. After an insane grin, harsh handshakes and loud hellos, he loaded up Mum's case, our backpacks with new, rolled sleeping bags and pointed to the five evergreen trees beyond the scrubby road.

'Foresters strip the outer layers of bark and leave the oaks bare with those painted red trunks. They look as if they're bleeding, yes?' he said with a relaxed German-sounding accent.

'Does it hurt them?' I asked.

Serge's tanned elbow landed on the open window as the car pulled away and he laughed. 'No. No. Not at all but it takes ten years for the bark to grow back. Newly planted trees take twenty-five years or more before harvesting. Farms are suffering now badly from the increased use of screw caps and plastic stoppers for wine bottles which is causing a slump in prices. There's a need to diversify. Farmers have to rent their cottages for tourists and such.'

'How do you know stripping the bark doesn't hurt the trees?' I said.

'Ah, we know,' he laughed and I looked at the huge, still trunks as we passed, wondering if bark is sort of dead like fingernails.

'We only have corked wine bottles at the restaurant where I work,' Mum said and Serge gave her a long, appreciative nod.

'That's good. Very good.'

'Cork's made from oak trees.' I nodded, unused to trees. Any kind of tree. There isn't a single tree on our street in Lewisham and Evan mimicked my satisfied knowing with a sneer. I was too hot to react, pulled wispy hair from my sweaty neck and leaned as far away from him as I could on the sticky seat which, for some reason, smelt of corn on the cob.

'What happens to the bark after the trees are stripped?' Mum said, almost beaming.

I think she likes Serge, who never stops taking his eyes off the bumpy road to look at her. 'First the planks are stored to avoid insects and contamination. Then boiled to clean and soften the bark before they are punctured with holes to make corks. It's a very

31

thorough process.'

Evan pulled a face. 'How far is it?'

Turning right round to look at him, Serge said, 'The community? Not long. Half an hour. No more. Oh and there's no smoking anywhere in Arcadia. There's a high risk of forest fires in the summer months.'

'Nobody in our family smokes,' Mum said and Evan smirked.

I gave him a filthy look. *Is he smoking now? No, he can't be,* I reassured myself. *He hasn't got any money.*

Eventually the road turned into a narrow, scorched earth track as we listened to Serge tell Mum about when he left Munich to come and live here and help with the building projects and provide the taxi service.

'This is going to be horrible,' Evan whispered as the car stopped outside the guest house; a long white building with several rooms next door to each other beyond an old caravan with nappies on a line between two trees. 'Hippy hell,' he added.

TEN

There wasn't a single person around as Serge pulled Mum's case from the boot of the car and led us to the other side of the guest house past a paved area with benches and tables.

Through the shady trees was a view of distant, isolated white buildings, higgledy paths, smooth fields and hills, rough grasses and woods, all owned by the Arcadia community. Sadly, this perfect place to loll around for hours with a book wasn't where me and Evan were staying.

The door opened to number eight, Mum's home for the next four weeks. Two massive yellow and red paintings of bright shovels, or maybe they were angels, it was hard to say, hit me in the face. A double bed with plain blue cover and spare single bed were pushed against the walls next to small chests and chairs.

Serge pointed to the basic shower and flushing loo shared with the next room. 'The rule is; if your door is left open then the next guest won't try to use it.'

'That's fine,' Mum said as she thumped the hard bed with her knuckles. 'Do you have the key?'

'Ah, I can get you one but we don't like keys,' Serge said. Mum was surprised and he went on, 'You start work tomorrow, yes?' Mum nodded. 'For dinner at six tonight follow the path on your right. Go round to the left. Down to the fork and you'll see the steps up to the refectory on the other side. Unless you want to come and see the dorms?'

Mum shook her head. 'I need to unpack and have a shower.'

I was hoping for a sandwich or something and wasn't sure I could last until six. Evan was angry as we climbed back in the car and drove along a proper tarmac road for a bit then up another pebbly track where I spotted a few scruffy tents pitched between some trees.

An older woman in a flowery dress, carrying a baby, waved to Serge as we passed and a young couple in shorts and worn T-shirts were busy filling glass bottles from a tap coming straight out of the wall of a large, yellow, two-storey building where we came to a stop.

It took a minute to unstick myself from the cobby car seat and first off, Serge showed us the bathrooms – if you can call them that. Up the narrow rocky path we went to the far side of the yellow building where sheds of compost toilets with creaking doors mean you have to put paper in the bins. Ergh. Gross.

'The toilets are waterless,' Serge said. 'They don't smell, are low maintenance and the use of chemicals is therefore unnecessary.' Which made me suddenly jealous of Mum's inside flushable loo in the guest house. So that was why she made us pack torches. I wanted to help change the world but it was all a bit sudden.

Behind the toilets, the basic showers were nothing more than concrete cubicles decorated with hand-made, painted ceramic tiles of birds, trees, clouds and, of course, rainbows. There was no sign of any buckets and the practical issue of where the water comes from without a mains supply shifted to the back of my mind.

Neither of us said a word as Serge led us back down the rocky path with our eyes everywhere, half expecting something weird to happen. There must have been deadly spiders and snakes in the long grass but we didn't see any. So quiet, I could hear my own footsteps and when I spotted a guy with long, curly hair sitting Indian style under a tree, meditating, I thought, *Well, this is different.* Evan, on the other hand, pulled a monster face and stared at the guy like he was a psychopath.

Inside the yellow building, Serge showed us the large, airy downstairs meeting room before pointing to wooden stairs on either side of the entrance hall.

'The dorms. Girls on the left. Boys on the right,' he said. 'The refectory is the way we came, then turn left. Keep going to the bend in the road. Stay right and follow the others if you get lost.'

'OK,' I said, despite not understanding the directions at all. We collected our backpacks and sleeping bags from the boot of the car, said thank you – well, I did, and went to climb the stairs, freaked out by the thought of needing the loo up that lonely path in the middle of the night with only a small torch to light the way.

'You think I'm going out in the dark?' Evan said the moment Serge's dusty blue car disappeared. 'I'm not painting rainbows on tiles either.'

'How about boobies?' I wanted to make him laugh but he didn't, and a beautiful girl with thick, auburn hair, big brown eyes and the longest body you've ever seen, came tripping into the hall in navy shorts and white shirt. Already I wished I'd packed fewer books and paid more attention to what clothes to bring and we watched her swan up to us with real awe.

Considering I'm such a mix, I'm quite disappointed to have narrow, non-almond-shaped, hazel eyes and a froth of wispy brown hair when I should have been born with huge green twinklers and reams of swirly, black hair like Shula, whose family are from Palestine, but that's just the way it is.

'Hi, I'm Sharrow. You must be Marya and Evan. Welcome.'

Taken aback by the sight of so much sudden, other worldly beauty, complete with dots of silver glitter on her honey-coloured face and bare shoulders that sparkled in the sunshine, we both froze. Not sure Sharrow was real as she explained the routine in a cute, sing-song, North of England accent.

'Breakfast's at eight, lunch at one and dinner at six. We help with the food sometimes and there's art, swimming in the lake, hiking. After lunch we rest and then it's the group meeting. Activities vary in the evenings but there's star gazing, table tennis, pizza making, dancing and please make suggestions if you want to do anything else. We're up for most things. If you need help, just ask.'

Evan swaggered in a way I've never seen before. 'What about wifi?'

'Intermittent,' Sharrow smiled. 'The best place is up at the refectory. It doesn't work here. Think you'll manage?'

Everything went quiet for a moment until Evan burped. 'No.'

ELEVEN

The stuffy dorms were something else. Huge, dark, dingy, messy attic rooms with wooden beams. No windows. One skylight. A ceiling fan that clicks. Thin pallets laid out in rows like coffin lids on the wooden floor with sleeping bags thrown on top, opposite a wall of lockers with no keys.

It was hard to imagine sleeping in that miserable cave for one night let alone a whole month and I've never felt more out of place. Just looking at the dirty sandals and sneakers dumped on the lockers, balls of clothes everywhere, made me want to run home to my neat and tidy bedroom and close the door tight.

I changed out of my jeans into the baggy, beige, knee-length horrors I wear in the garden at home and without a mirror it was hard to see how bad they looked with my favourite orange T-shirt so I took a pic with my phone instead. Wrong face. I looked mad as well as scruffy but never mind, I was desperate for the loo and dropped the rolled sleeping bag on an empty pallet, stuffed the backpack in a locker and made a run for it.

By the time I found the wooden sheds, used the compost loo and washed my hands in an ordinary sink with taps, I was even more fearful of coming up the path in the middle of the night on my own.

Finding Evan sitting on a homemade, wooden bench outside the hall talking to a hot guy in surfer shorts with shockingly blond hair and an ugly scar down one side of his face, made me feel even worse.

I did my best to smile when Evan said, 'That's my sister.'

'Hey, Marya. I'm Blake,' he said in the poshest voice I've heard in real life. 'I work with Sharrow to lead the youth group.'

'Hi, Blake,' I said like the new girl at school and turned to Evan. 'The good thing is Mum's miles away.'

He nearly smiled but the gloomy look on Evan's face made it obvious he only cared about having wifi on demand. Unable to go overboard about anything else, I broke into a sweat, it was so hot, and Blake was staring at me. Like, why?

'Don't worry, you're going to love it here,' he said.

My brain closes down when I meet a strange guy or when I'm starving. Now it was both and it just shot out, 'Did you go to Eton?' (In case you don't know, Eton is the poshest boy's school in England and costs a fortune.)

'Haha. No, a cheaper one you won't have heard of. After dinner we will get together and introduce ourselves properly.'

Never before have I met a guy who glows like a sandy white beach, and then I thought, if you take away the ugly scar on his cheek, it wouldn't make any difference. His bright blue eyes and welcoming smile are still not enough to make him gorgeous because of the weird, posh voice.

'See you at dinner.' Blake high fived us and flip-flopped off towards the loos. 'Don't forget your napkins.'

Napkins? Was that a joke?

'Bet he was a druggie,' Evan said.

'He could have been born with that scar.'

'Bet he wasn't though.' We were both a bit bewildered by Blake as we followed an earth mother with fleshy arms in a loose grey dress down the hot, rocky path, past silvery lavender bushes and wild roses.

'It's not the kind of scar you can hide,' I said. 'I wonder what he thinks about when he looks in the mirror.'

'Probably the awesome fight to the death when he was stabbed seven times in the heart and his face was slit in two.' Evan punched the air. 'And stitched back together by a blind doctor.'

'It's probably just a birthmark,' I said to calm him down.

Sweating like crazy, we came to a desert-like, cleared open space and started boiling half to death. In the distance, four narrow tracks wound in different direction towards green and blue hills. In one corner of the scrubby open land there were tall trees with a few old tents underneath. A huge, shimmering lake ringed the whole area.

We wondered which path to take and covering our faces from the sun with our hands, squinted at the tents and when we looked back, the earth mother had disappeared and a small, white car skidded past with an old guy with long grey hair of about ninety bent over the wheel.

'We should have stopped him,' I said.

'For pumpkin seeds or a lift?' Evan said. 'Muesli then?'

'Stop being sarcastic, Evan. He was just an old man.'

'An evil, old maniac you mean.' With flaring eyes and stretched lips, Evan mimed a dangerous killer as we turned down the path through the bushes that led to the silver lake which went on down the valley as far as the eye could see.

'Wow. I wasn't expecting that,' I said. The green sloping banks, distant hills with patchwork crops and winding silver water made my London eyes ache.

Evan was quiet until he said, 'The hippies built the lake and the complicated water retention system is AMAZING according to Scarface.' And laughed with a posh accent. 'Har. Har.'

'His name's Blake, Evan. How does the water retention system work?' I was seriously interested.

'Can't remember.' Evan turned away from the lake and we went through the bushes back to the cleared, open space where the relentless sun battered my head.

We followed the sound of low voices going in the opposite direction and it wasn't long before we heard laughing and talking. Wooden steps up a small incline brought us to the refectory where people were standing around. To one side were two spacious eating areas under bamboo roofs. Several community members waited in line for huge metal containers of food to be uncovered and it felt like they were all friends and bought their bright, unfashionable clothes from the same shop. Just what I imagined Arcadians to be. Not quite Lewisham. More New Cross.

Evan and me didn't know where to go or what to do and hung back until we spotted Mum talking to Serge which was a huge relief.

'Isn't it beautiful?' Mum hurried over. 'Dorms OK?'

'Mine smells of feet,' Evan sniffed.

We grabbed trays, joined the queue and a lady with heavy, blue eye make-up served us roast vegetables, pasta and something called mushroom bake that resembled mashed spiderwebs. It tasted all right though and we listened to five-minute sentences about real world problems: the wars in Afghanistan, Iraq, Libya, Syria, the trouble in Israel, North Korea and Yemen, the millions of refugees, Brexit, climate change, the extraordinary Greta Thunberg and the necessity for the world to go vegan.

We had nothing to say. Like ghosts at the table, we were invisible to everyone and felt totally out of place. I tried to blend in after a while by smiling but Evan didn't bother. He just looked at me and frowned. Mum, though, looked happier than ever and Serge appeared to be her new best friend. With her hair tied up and wearing an old, cream, work dress, she was nodding and nodding away.

Where were Blake and Sharrow?

I go crazy if I have to spend every day surrounded by people instead of being able to escape with a book and all of a sudden felt totally trapped. It got so embarrassing just sitting there, I made the effort to speak to a nearby old lady with grey dreadlocks. 'Do you live here?'

'Me, honey?'

'Er, yeah.'

'When I can. The rest of the time I work for a small press in Lagos. I'm a poet. My name's Bolanile.'

Wow. A real poet. I wanted to hear more but the long-haired guy with a huge silver earring sitting opposite nodded me to pass the salad bowl and she started talking to someone else.

The good thing was, there were several attractive guys around and that was something worth hanging on to.

TWELVE

After dinner, Blake found us and shepherded us back down the steps on a trek through an unmapped frontier – well, that's what it felt like. There were no cars, no people, nothing but dusty, scrubby desert, scraggly bushes and tall trees to look at until we came to another cleared area with a huge, open-sided auditorium and stage with metal roof in the distance.

Blake waved us down a side path and pointed to a unit selling discarded clothes from previous visitors, book shop – yeah, round clay pizza oven, eating area and sheltered ping-pong table in the far corner. The sight of normality cheered me up even though everything was closed.

I looked at my phone. The battery was almost dead and no signal. I could have kicked myself for not checking earlier.

'We have two hundred acres of land and we're always creating something new,' Blake said as he sat down on a bench, facing out from the table, tapping his fingers. 'The others arrived a few days ago so they know where to come. They won't be long.' And he got up and rushed off to talk to a guy up at the auditorium, leaving Evan and me waiting for who knows what.

'He seems nice.' I tried talking.

'You're not a good judge of character,' Evan said. 'He's gross.'

'Why do you say that?' But he ignored me and I started worrying about what to do without a working phone if I couldn't find him. 'Don't go wandering off on your own. It'll be easy to get lost at night round here. We don't know any of these people.'

'What am I, five?'

'You know what I mean.'

'Think I'm going to get attacked by a beast in the lake?' Evan glared. 'We're on an island in the Coral Sea. Piggy's been killed and the conch is shattered. What can I do? Oh, no.'

'Arcadia's the opposite of *Lord of the Flies* but be careful,' I said.

Ever since Evan was born I've felt responsible for him. It's like if anything happened to him I would never forgive myself which is why Mum's happy to leave us to our own devices. She knows we're well and truly stuck and the thought started to piss me off. Maybe she was the one who wanted her freedom, not Dad.

'When we change ourselves we change the world,' a high-pitched voice screeched and we both turned to see a pretty girl in grey, Aladdin-type trousers, backless purple T-shirt and thin rows of delicate beads jangling from her long neck. Opening her arms wide, she turned to Sharrow behind her and gave her a swinging hug.

'Hey,' Sharon grinned. 'Where's Coco?'

'She's coming. Hi you two. I'm Sanvi,' and a second later we were surrounded by a group of teenagers talking about their lives.

'If I wanted to be a painter, you know I'd be a painter, man,' a skinny, pale boy said.

'Only took three hours to bring me round,' said the forlorn girl in a little tie-dyed dress with a strong American accent.

'We don't follow politics but then I got into animal welfare and everything changed,' an unbelievably gorgeous Sun God, said.

Mouth open and staring, I nearly gave myself away but rummaged in my black tote bag to look for something I knew wasn't there, pulled out the phone and yes, it was still dead. What a surprise.

'It's wonderful to have you all here,' said Blake, plonking himself down cross-legged and crossways in the middle of our table. Brown knee practically in my face. One glance at his grubby toenails and, thankfully, my heart remained beating normally even though he had an exceptional smile.

'Good. We've pretty much got everyone now,' Blake said. 'This is Marya and Evan from London. We'll take a moment's quiet and then introduce ourselves. Remember we are in a protected space, another reality here, where we respect and honour ourselves, each other, the land and all living things at all times. Nothing is beyond knowing or understanding in Arcadia when we open up through trust because healing comes from truth.'

I avoided looking at Evan. I knew what he was thinking. *A protected space? Another reality? Healing comes from truth? You what? This is never going to work.*

Sharrow threw her head back and closed her eyes and a hush spread through the eager to get going teenagers. It was hard to keep a straight face and my eyes settled on a bulky guy with a lion's worth of brown furry hair on his head and cheeks with only a few patches of bare tawny skin in between. He positioned himself on the bench opposite as if on a horse about to charge across a field and it felt like I'd already been trampled to death.

'OK, who wants to start?' Blake said.

'I'm Lilla from Barcelona. Sixteen only. English not so good, but try.' The strong-featured girl in white cut-offs and lemon T-shirt looked moody and when she crossed her brown legs, Evan shifted awkwardly and stared at the ground.

'Good to have you here, Lilla.' Blake smiled and I pretended to be unfazed and looked away when brown, furry face caught my eye and stamped all over me again, leaving me metaphorically bruised and gasping.

A bold girl with impressive purple hair in a slip of a silk dress that revealed most of her slim body, lowered her head. 'Constanza. Italiano via Romania. Seventeen.'

'Welcome, Constanza,' Blake said.

I didn't want to go next and by the look of him, Evan, didn't either, so it was good when the serious guy with ghostly white, bony shoulders in torn green vest and mouldy jeans, half raised his hand.

'I'm sixteen and from Birmingham. My name's Tomas and I'm going to say this now because I can't hold it in any longer. I've watched so much porn, I'm desperate for sex. It's all I think about.'

I nearly peed my pants I was so shocked. Who introduces themselves like that? He needs help.

Lilla blinked. I'm not sure she understood but Constanza certainly did and her eyes blazed. Evan just about kept his face from exploding but the muscles in his jaw popped and I swear I could hear his heart bursting out of his chest. It's the hardest thing on earth to stop your emotions from showing when you've been struck by lightning but I think I managed it by staring at Blake's wiggling toes.

'Your desire is coming through strong and clear,' Sharrow sparkled. 'Thank you for being truthful, Tomas. That took courage. We're glad to have you in the group. Does anyone want to add anything?'

We're glad to have Tomas in the group? Is Sharrow crazy? He's a complete nut. What's he doing here?

'Hey, I so get how you feel, Tomas.' The guy with the lion's mane of hair swished his fur from side to side. 'My name's Guthrie. I'm seventeen and live in Archway, North London.'

His name's Guthrie? It so goes with the fur. Oh-my-god, that smoky voice. There was danger in his brown eyes as they travelled round the group. Beware was the word that sprang to mind when they reached me and I smiled. Then patted the bench for no reason like I was the lunatic, not Tomas.

It was heroic of Guthrie to support desperate, crazy Tomas but maybe not a good idea because everyone will think he's demented, too. Blake's toes stopped wiggling. Everyone was quiet for a moment then Sharrow grinned.

'Thank you so much, Guthrie. That was helpful as well as honest. Do any of the girls have anything to say to Tomas?'

Blake uncrossed his legs. Flipped both flops on the bench and as much as I forced myself to look at the ground instead of Guthrie's face, every cell in my body was battling to attach themselves to him or run away and destroy themselves.

'Well, yeah.' Sanvi glanced at each of us in turn with penetrating, black eyes. 'I'm just an observer here but I want to say this: With me, it's not sex on my mind so much as the intimacy it provides. Kissing. Holding. Physical closeness that makes me feel dizzy just thinking about so if you want a long, slow hug, Tomas, I'm up for that.'

I gulped. *What's going on? Have I landed on Mars?*

Awkward Tomas widened his eyes. He wasn't impressed by the offer, gave a brief nod and turned to the sad-looking guy on the floor with limp, dark hair in a pony tail, hugging his knees for dear life, who I hadn't noticed.

'I'm Carl. I was born in Leeds but live in France where my parents grow their own weed and have a bed and breakfast.'

I couldn't wait to tell Mum about him.

'Our culture is having us on,' Carl said. 'It says boys are desperate for sex and girls want kisses, cuddles and all the meaningful stuff. Yeah, it might sound true after what Tomas and Sanvi just said but I'm telling you, I know for a fact it's all illusion and delusion. Yeah. Like lots of boys really hunger for the kind of connection she mentioned and tons of girls have nothing but sex on their brains.'

I didn't dare look at Evan. These kids were obsessed. What were they going to be like after a whole week? Maybe I wouldn't tell Mum about Carl.

'That's a wonderful thing to say. Thank you, Carl.' Sharrow grinned her head off.

'Good. Thank you. Good.' Blake glanced sideways at the ping-pong table. 'We'll get into this subject in more depth during one of the meetings but for now let's relax. Anyone for a game?'

Thank heaven Blake didn't ask us to join in the sex chat.

Sharrow jumped up eagerly to search for the bats, leaving me wondering what Mum had got us into. Evan nudged my arm and it was clear he was as shocked and baffled as me.

Was this place offering teenagers some kind of sex education? Are Blake and Sharrow trained counsellors? Or maybe psychologists? Why did Blake shut down the conversation before everyone had the chance to introduce themselves? Was it because he's the kind of guy who needs to be the centre of attention all the time and the others were taking up too much space? This *was* another reality. An extreme version of a way of life that felt began to feel threatening not fun.

Furry Guthrie and desperate-for-sex Tomas got into a whispering huddle while Evan pretended to be interested in the ping-pong game. The compulsion to disappear was palpable in him.

Pop. Pop. Smash. All eyes and arms, Blake socked the ball to Sharrow and threw himself about like his life depended on it while she tapped and hopped around the table like an exotic bird. It was fascinating to watch how desperate Blake was to win and even though it was difficult I forced myself to look happy.

Sanvi, Lilla and Constanza sat back chatting and I wanted to join them but couldn't leave Evan on his own being miserable.

One fair-haired girl in big round glasses linked tattooed arms with a tall guy and wandered off. Then the bronze Sun God who was too good looking to even think about, leaned over the pizza counter to talk to a grey-haired lady kneading dough.

'There's no way of getting a fix because the internet doesn't work,' Guthrie said loudly, lifting his head. 'Let's walk.'

'That's what I'm worried about,' Tomas growled and jumped up. 'Wanna come, Carl?'

'Where you going?'

'Grab some exercise.' Guthrie smiled and I felt about ten years old when he glanced at me as they left.

THIRTEEN

When the sun died, it was chilly and the sky changed from navy blue to a black carpet of glittering stars. Millions of them. It was incredible and I could feel the skinny moon float through me whenever I looked up. Crickets were thrumming (I heard Sanvi say that's what the racket was) and Sun God, Lilla and Constanza disappeared to fetch warmer clothes.

Blake and Sharrow left soon after and Sanvi came to join us on the bench outside the closed shops. 'Bit different from London isn't it?' she said, revealing a tiny diamond in a front tooth.

'You could say that.' I was relieved the guys were out of sight and it was just us left behind. There was space to breathe at last.

'The community where my family live in India is much bigger than Arcadia. We have a thousand people with ordinary jobs in local businesses and schools as well as working with each other so this is a real change,' she said. 'There are less than two hundred people living full-time in Arcadia and another sixty are on the Healing the World course my dad's helping with.'

'Healing the World course?' It was the first I'd heard of it.

'Yeah, but first we have to heal ourselves. That's the really hard part. I'm going to put up some blogs when I get home. Meanwhile, I'm just a fly on the wall who's already been here for three months. Is it OK to talk to you?'

'Sorry?' *We were talking, weren't we?*

'Just to see how you're feeling about it all.'

'Fine. I'm fine,' I lied.

Sanvi nodded. 'Oh, OK. How about you, Evan?'

'What?' he said.

'Want to tell me what you think of Arcadia?' Sanvi said. 'You know it was started by a Spanish couple, Paulo and Odell whose parents fought for the Republicans against the fascists in the Spanish Civil War?'

Evan shook his head, making it clear he'd prefer to fly to the moon rather than chat. Plus what he knew about the Spanish Civil War was less than nothing and I didn't know that much more.

'They wanted to continue the revolution by setting up a non-hierarchical, sustainable community where sharing is of prime importance,' Sanvi said.

'Are they still alive?' I asked. Evan wasn't the least bit interested and didn't even blink.

'Oh, yeah,' San said. 'Paulo and Odell are always around.'

'Does he drive an old white car?' I said and Sanvi nodded. So the guy we saw earlier that Evan thought was an evil maniac was the amazing cofounder of Arcadia.

'Paulo and Odell were only twenty when they got here,' Sanvi said. 'They bought the first plot of land for next to nothing, started growing vegetables and lived in a tent for the first few years before upgrading to a caravan.'

It was impressive to think it took only two people to start this whole other way of life. To my surprise, I began imagining trying the same thing but not with Watty. It would have to be with a guy who knew about growing potatoes because I didn't want to be left doing all the digging which would probably happen with him.

A breeze came up in the trees and shivering slightly, we sat there in the dark, listening to Sanvi tell us about her Maylasian mum who met her Indian dad at the community in Gujarat where they live, while I stared at the distant, open-sided auditorium where adults were gathering at the lit-up bar.

It seems all the different communities of the world know about Paulo, Odell and each other. They work on the same principles of close contact with the land and live without unnecessary things. It's easy to imagine being that free but I have an irrational fear of not fitting in so it wouldn't really work for me, or would it? Good exam results, university, a proper job that squeezed you into acquiring social status and endless stuff, they were the things we were told that mattered but what did they lead to but stress and panic? Without a sense of belonging what was the point in any of it?

'We do everything we can to make our hearts sing,' Sanvi said and with twinkling lights hanging from the metal roof of the auditorium and figures in bright clothes dancing softly to humming music, the scene had a fairy-tale vibe that added to her words.

The family-type people were enjoying themselves, free from the threat of loud explosions, knifings, vans crashing into pedestrians on purpose, acid attacks, sad drunks and all the horrible *Hunger Games* incidents I'm ready for when waiting at the bus stop with exhaust fumes in my face.

The hugeness of the universe struck home. Other ways of living suddenly felt possible. As for all the talk about sex perhaps the group were encouraged to share things like that during the introductory talk that we missed. No way would I get pulled in and I'm sure Evan wouldn't either.

I started to relax. It might be all right and Sanvi gave me a huge smile as if she understood.

'People also come on meditation and yoga retreats,' she said. 'Arcadians believe every stone, tree, plant, grain of sand and cell in the universe has consciousness and feels curiosity, love, annoyance and betrayal just as we do in our community in Gujarat which is why it's important to love everything and everyone.'

Her impressive English and mind-expanding words whited out my brain and for a minute I couldn't think. At school they would laugh at me if I said the same thing. A stone wants to know what's going on? A cupboard feels love? Street lights get annoyed? Yeah. Right. But I didn't say anything, just nodded, because Sanvi is gentle, different, easy to be around and I liked the idea the world is more alive than I thought.

This bench likes me. I knew it. That tree knows what I'm thinking. Great. Isn't that what fairy stories and loads of books are about? Hmm. Shakespeare does magical forests really well. Perhaps he believed the same thing?

Rubbing her tingling arms didn't do much to distract Sanvi from telling us how they cultivate the land according to the cycles of the moon and how the centre of the universe is inside, not outside us. And all the while Evan made circles on the table with his index finger from the cork water bottle someone knocked over and I tried to spot Mum up at the auditorium but everyone was too far away to make out.

The door of the clothes shop swung open and the old dresses and worn sandals were full of character like the woman in blue jeans who smiled. I wasn't tempted to move though because the book shop remained closed.

'We've got bikinis, belts and cotton bags as well. Lots for young people at the back,' the woman said, reading my mind, but I shook my head. Shopping for anything but books has never been my thing and Evan didn't even look up.

'Did you miss me?' Guthrie appeared from nowhere, plonked a wet kiss on Sanvi's neck and they started a non-stop, swinging back and forth, close and giggly hug on the bench.

I tried not to notice her dainty, coloured beads getting tangled in his hair. Not wanting to stare, I looked around shyly but their affection was hypnotic and swept through me like a half-remembered dream I didn't understand.

The nuzzling and pressing into each other began to feel intimidating and then humiliating when Guthrie's big brown eyes caught mine as if the hug was meant for me.

The intensity felt part of the night, the blackened clay pizza oven and table itself. Sanvi's explanation of consciousness got to me like the distant figures dancing to soft music under the fairy lights. I desperately wanted to belong and Evan's sulky silence made it hard to pretend we ever could.

Aware of Guthrie every second that passed, I sat soldier straight, staring at the woman arranging belts on a wooden hanger in the clothes shop until it became an ordeal that almost made me faint and I leaned on the table with chin in my hands and eyed Evan's watery mess.

Everything about Arcadia was a challenge and when I looked at Evan it was clear he was finding it just as hard to be himself.

FOURTEEN

'I'm going back to the dorm,' Evan said at last and we got up, lost Londoners that we were and walked away as if nothing had happened and there was somewhere important to go, when really I wished I knew what the hell was going on, especially with that Guthrie guy.

All the voices and music faded into the silent night as we hit the dark rocky path where the world felt suddenly empty without him. Everything was still. Nothing moved. We crunched along side by side and, of course, soon got lost.

Neither of us had a torch in our pockets.

'I knew it was going to be weird here,' Evan said. 'Nothing's normal.'

The strange thing was, his voice shrank the darkness and the ordinary clatter of our feet on the track blocked, for a moment, the fear of never finding the dorms.

'Like you're normal?' I couldn't help being honest. 'Sanvi's nice. She made an effort to talk to us. You didn't say a word.'

'Yeah, well.' Evan bowed his head. 'I'm crazy in another way.'

It was clear I'd touched a nerve.

Soon it was darker than ever and impossible to see more than the overhanging trees in the light of the skinny moon. There could be maniacs behind every bush and walking close, we bumped into each other every few steps. Frightened and excited at the same time, it felt like the power cut from ages ago when we opened the kitchen door, stepped out, screamed at the thick black where there should have been a brick wall and ran back inside.

'This is well creepy,' Evan said. 'I wonder what's on the other side of those trees?'

I shivered. We bumped up and grabbed arms with our eyes on the approaching bend, totally terrified. The thin moon and thousands of stars above were no help. They just made me feel dizzy. When we came across the forlorn girl from earlier in a tie-dyed dress, leaning on a tree beside the silvery lake looking as lost as us, I was too relieved to realise I didn't have to shout so loudly through the pitch black.

'Excuse me,' I yelled. 'Can you tell us where the dorms are?' Startled, she raised her head, pushed messy bundles of dark hair behind her ears and burst into tears.

'What's wrong?' I rushed to put my arm around her sharp shoulder. 'It's OK. It's OK,' I said and she scraped the earth with wedge sandals, sank to the rocky ground, rubbing her eyes and I ended up, feet out next to her, all gritty and concerned with a sore bum from landing on a stone while Evan stood there gaping.

'I don't know,' she said with a strong American accent and an awkward silence broke out that added to the feeling helping her might take some time. Not having the heart to move while she sobbed, I pulled rough stones from under her legs with my free hand.

'You must know.' I squeezed her shoulder but she didn't answer. Slightly foreign looking, I wondered where she was from originally but didn't ask because I know how irritated Shula gets when that happens.

It felt like we were going to sit there the whole chilly night but completely out of the blue she turned to me and said, 'Someone I like doesn't like me.'

'Oh.' I nodded, not daring to ask who it was in case it turned out to be Guthrie. 'That's awkward. Sorry, but I can't remember your...'

'Coco,' she said. 'You?'

'Marya and that's Evan. It's quiet here,' I said to distract her from his grumpy face.

'Not so quiet,' Coco sniffed. 'Want to go skinny dipping?'

'I'll come,' Evan said and she laughed, got up, sniffed a few times, dusted off her tie-dyed dress and looked at him through watery eyes.

'You're the best,' she said. 'Maybe next time. Follow the lake until you get to the path on the right which leads to the dorms. It's quite safe.'

'What are you going to do?' It was good Evan had come back to life and I was relieved Coco had stopped crying.

'Probably drown myself,' she said and I didn't know whether she was joking or not but the prospect of schlepping all the way back while worrying about her just wasn't possible.

'Don't be silly. Come with us. It's getting cold,' I said.

'Why?' She started crying again. 'Don't you know the world would be better off without me?'

I'd blown it but didn't give up. 'I'm not going to leave you here on your own feeling bad.'

'No one will know.'

'We know,' I said.

'You'd care if I died?'

'Yeah, it would piss me off because we're the last people to see you. We'd be blamed for not stopping you from jumping in. Your dead body would be there until morning, floating face down in the black water and...'

'Woah, calm down, babe,' she said. 'You're going all goose bumpy on me.' But I couldn't.

'Getting upset about a boy is crazy because there are millions of them and your mum and dad would never recover from you ruining their life. What stupid boy is worth that?'

Coco smiled. 'I guess you're right, English girl, but how did you know it was a boy?'

She got me there. Truth is, I didn't know. 'It was just a guess. Sorry, if that's like, wrong.'

'You're funny,' she said. 'The someone is a combination of two guys. I like them both.'

'I think she should do what she wants,' Evan said and I glared at him. 'Maybe if she had a good night's sleep and something to eat she might feel better in the morning?'

He wasn't the least bit worried by my angry, threatening look when he said she and not Coco but he took no notice, sighed, looked up at the starry sky and shoved two fingers in his mouth to whistle squeakily at the glassy lake.

'My brother,' I said.

'Right.' Coco nodded. 'That sound didn't change the world, did it?' And she bent her head, stretched back her lips and let out a high-pitched, atmosphere charging, searing warble that sliced the night in two. Before, when the path was jagged hard and the shadowy air was still and heavy, and after, when the trees, bushes and water shivered with metallic whispers that drifted into the black beyond.

The sound broke me. Unrolled me. Rooted me to the spot and the magnetic ambush lasted long after she stopped.

'I'll walk back with you nut jobs,' she said and Evan grinned as if he believed his hopeless attempt at whistling had distracted her from killing herself. The idiot. Still, maybe it had, and the thought sent a shiver down my spine.

Coco kicked a pebble on the path and turned to me. 'Do you like any of the boys here?'

'No,' I said.

'Liar.' Evan laughed. 'Marya was blushing when Guthrie kissed Sanvi just now.'

Was I? Oh, no. Save me.

Coco stopped. Horrified. 'He was kissing Sanvi?'

'Not much.' Evan back tracked. 'They were mucking around and I was joking. Marya never blushes, do you?'

'Guthrie's not my type.' I snarled, shook my head several times to convince Coco it was true and she relaxed, uncrossed her arms and continued kicking stray pebbles into the bushes all the way back to the dorms with me thinking, *I can't do this. My real life is like a billion universes away and if Coco does end up dead in the lake it would partly be my fault for not saying the right thing.*

Reading is so much safer than getting to know these odd people but without enough light in the dorm to curl up with *The Mill on the Floss*, when we got back, I just charged my phone and stood there motionless in the dark, wondering who the other bodies were.

At the end of the row, Coco flopped down and fell asleep in her dress. I pulled a T-shirt from the bag in the locker, got changed, stuffed the baggy horrors inside and crammed the small, metal door, shut.

'Peace, Sis.' Sanvi arrived, patted me on the shoulder, ripped off her beads, threw them on the floor and fell on the sleeping bag in a heap.

FIFTEEN

I got up early, heart clicking in tune with the wooden fan that started on its own from electricity produced by solar panels on the roof. I remembered learning how the direct current is generated from the sun's energy and fed into a solar inverter that converts it to electricity. What I didn't understand was why we don't use it for everything.

Solar energy is cheap once it's been set up but we're still burning fossils and wrecking the planet. There aren't any solar panels on our street. If it was down to me all the old-fashioned cables would be ripped up and destroyed. For a moment I knew I was stupid for remaining part of the problem in London while these people lived their beliefs without fear of ever being thought selfish or dumb like me.

Daylight drifted through the skylight and desperate for the loo, having held out all night, I grabbed a long, green T-shirt from the locker and threw it over my shoulder, hoping it would work as a dress.

I decided not to care what I looked like and rushed off with blue towel wrapped round me, waving the approved, hard, brown, vegan tablet under my nose that Mum assured me was soap and insisted I pack to avoid contaminating the water system with nasty chemicals.

'If everyone did the same thing, the world would change overnight,' Mum said. It was a big statement to justify such a little bar of soap but this was the kind of thing you have to take into account when washing in Arcadia with polluted seas and dead fish on your shoulders.

The water was hot. The showers were clean and a tiny, white butterfly kept me company as I pulled the green T-shirt dress over my head and threw the damp towel on the line to dry. I felt better and everyone I passed gave me a brief smile that proved their minds were on something else.

I guess healing the world is a difficult task but soap was a good start. I crammed everything in the locker except the non-organic deodorant, glanced at the sleeping bodies, decided I was OK and headed off with a cheap black tote swinging from my arm.

Pausing at the bottom of the steps to the male dorms, I was tempted to knock for Evan but decided there were enough people around for him to get directions, and set off into the bright day.

Silvery purple, lavender bushes lined the path and I picked a stem, rolled the leaves between my fingers and breathed in the powerful, warm scent like grandma used to do in her garden in Inverness.

'Lavender is part of the mint family and bees love it for making honey,' she said and her face used to light up when she sniffed the flowers. I couldn't imagine what life was like for women like her before porn was invented. It's not something I'd ever say out loud. For a start she's not alive and then, who would dare ask an old lady a thing like that? I can't even talk to my mum. Still, I wished I knew what Grandma thought about boys when she was growing up.

Guthrie was on my mind the rest of the way down the empty rocky path to the refectory and I wondered how to play it. Cool and uninterested? Smiley and friendly? Unbothered in every way? None of which comes naturally. Intense is who I am with a touch of bubbly now and then.

The silence of the surroundings added to the idea that it might be best to forget him and just find a quiet place to read. Ignoring reality by getting lost in a good book is my favourite thing to do. It's the purest of escapes. The easiest calm to achieve and the best way of understanding the world.

When I got to the refectory the first person I saw was Mum. She waved, patted a space on the bench beside her but pointed to the food table before I could sit down. Quickly loading a tray with water, tea, grey/brown porridge, an orange, chunk of melon, two slices of rye bread and houmous, I couldn't wait to eat as much as I could and get online.

'Where's Evan?' Mum said as I plonked the tray down beside her plate.

'Probably still asleep.' Eyes on my fully charged phone, I snapped a full-on breakfast pic. Then added the words, 'Note the bowl of gruel.' Sent it to Shula, looked up at Mum and smiled.

Breakfast with my phone. Ah, great. No need to stress. Life was back to normal.

For a moment Mum stared and I flashed her another smile before getting a familiar pinging sound. 'I always liked poor Oliver Twist,' Shula said. 'What does the gruel taste like?'

I swallowed a spoonful of the cold, gritty porridge, almost gagged, pushed the bowl away and replied, 'Punishment. This stuff isn't even a distant cousin to the oats my grandpa makes in Inverness.'

'Can we have breakfast together?' Mum interrupted.

'Just a sec.' I pressed send and in between shoving bread and houmous in my mouth, said, 'We never have breakfast together at home and like — we are.' My thumbs had to work overtime to reply to Dad who was on his way to work and wanted to know if we'd settled in.

'Put that phone away,' Mum insisted. 'Tell me how it's going.'

Forget doing what I want, I had to talk to her and dropped it on the table.

'It's OK, I suppose.' I could hardly tell her. 'Look, there's Evan.' Bloodshot eyes peering out of his floppy hair, he looked half dead in the crumpled grey T-shirt and jeans he was wearing yesterday.

'Why didn't he get changed?' Mum said, as if I'd know.

'We're over here,' I yelled. The place was almost full and Evan looked shocked to see us, grabbed some food and sat down.

'Everyone's crazy here,' he said, lunging at his phone, spoon in the other hand.

'Who exactly?' I was willing to argue but he wasn't game.

'Evan, why aren't you wearing clean clothes?' Mum said.

He didn't look up. 'I will later.'

'Put that down while we're eating.' Mum took a sip of strong, dark tea. 'I want to know how you are? Well?'

'Dunno.' Clearly Evan wasn't awake enough to say much and after a couple of seconds dropped the phone on the table but kept his eyes on it. Family breakfasts are a dead loss but he should know Mum doesn't give up.

'Evan look at me.' He did and widened his eyes.

'Have Blake and Sharrow explained the course?' she said.

'Yeah, ping-pong, talks, star gazing,' I said. 'Oh and art. Are they counsellors or what?'

I spotted Guthrie at the food counter and made an effort not to look at him again. Then noticed our group were sitting all together at another table in the far corner and we were in the wrong place.

'Something's not right with any of them,' Evan said.

'There's more to it here than you realise,' Mum said. 'You'll see.'

'Like what?' I really wanted to know but she just shrugged. Evan finished off a large helping of gruel which made me feel sick just watching. I attacked an unbelievably sweet, juicy orange, licked my fingers and saw Serge heading our way with a glint in his eye. A pink rose in his big hand.

No. Please. Don't. Please. Get back in your dusty blue car and get lost.

'Good morning everyone. Smell this,' he told Mum, standing over her. She turned, smiled, took the rose, buried her face in the pink petals and gave him a searching look.

'We need to join the others. Come on, Evan,' I said.

Pocketing his phone, he grabbed a chunk of melon to take with him, slugged a noisy gulp of water, wiped his mouth with the back of his hand and we escaped. But not before I messaged Shula, 'By the way, what's a three line script?' I've been meaning to ask her that for ages.

SIXTEEN

The group were chatting, giggling, laughing among themselves and we finally managed to catch Blake's attention by standing back for a few minutes and staring like newly arrived aliens from Mars.

'Push up, everyone.' Blake swept blond hair from his scar and made room. Coco, in another tie-dyed dress, turned and smiled with big brown eyes. The sadness had gone and I was like, what? She looked so happy it was hard to picture the same girl crying and whistling mournfully at the lake last night.

'I'm still here, guys,' she laughed. 'But need the washroom.' Brown legs clambered out from the bench and she waved us to take her place next to Guthrie.

'We were just talking about love.' Guthrie grinned at Evan who made for the gap beside Blake instead, clearly not in the mood for him.

I glanced at Carl who lives in France with the weed-growing parents and he'd ditched the pony tail and the limp, dark hair was hanging in rags down his back. There was a space next to him but he was too busy chatting to the girl with round glasses to notice, leaving me with no choice but to take the seat next to Guthrie and awkwardly twist, kick and knee my way over the bench while pulling down the green T-shirt, now dress.

Halfway in and waggling my phone, it suddenly pinged with a message from Shula. 'Hey, glad you asked. A three line script is when a guy makes it clear: You got it. I want it. Let's do it.'

'Interesting,' Guthrie smirked.

How dare he read my messages? I gave him a patronising smile which was part of a massive trembling sensation trying to take over my body. I got it to stop by asking, 'Is the porridge always so unforgivable?'

'What?' Guthrie was mystified by the stupid question. So was I. What was I thinking? It was the kind of line you read in a Victorian novel. Books can affect your personality, you know, and my brain was barely afloat with all these new people to deal with.

'Hi Marya.' Warm, golden arms wrapped round my neck and I turned to see twinkly Sharrow in a white, sleeveless tunic, long body arched behind her and no shoes. Thankful to be greeted so warmly, I smiled, she let go and stepped aside on the hot, crumbly earth to fall on Guthrie in the same restful way. Her face touched his furry cheek for a second before moving on when he closed his eyes. The big hug thing is a form of greeting in Arcadia and I'm not sure I like it. Evan certainly didn't.

Guthrie glanced at me briefly and I froze when he said, 'I'm not that into grains.' I wanted to ask if he was gluten intolerant but didn't dare and politely looked away to admire the nearby tree. If there was a mirror on that tree it would reflect stupid, out of her depth, me. I must stop judging myself being myself was my next thought and only when Guthrie turned to talk to Carl, who for some weird reason kept plaiting his limp brown hair, did the world go back to normal and I could breathe again.

With her arms out, Sharrow reached Evan for another warm hello. 'Not now.' He jerked forward, nudged her off and went back to his phone.

Sharrow didn't care. 'Oh, OK.'

'Hey. My turn.' Sanvi twisted round and did the same long, swinging, side-to-side hug with her that she'd done with Guthrie yesterday. This time though, Sanvi, went into a deep, dreamy state that was more like a trance, and even when Sharrow let go and straightened up, she carried on swaying and hugging herself and no one took a blind bit of notice. Weird or what?

At school, girls hug each other all the time, faces squashed together while boys punch each other and pretend it doesn't hurt. For me, nothing is ever left behind when a hug ends as quickly as it starts but touch seems to unbuckle Sanvi. She's chatting away one minute and the next – open to a bunch of feelings I can only imagine.

'There's nothing wiser than your own body,' Dad always says and I thought he meant trust your instincts but instead wondered if he was trying to tell me something more important. Something about surrendering when you feel good. About to message Dad and ask what he meant, an empty glass clunked down on the wooden table and brought me back to earth.

'From now on,' Sharrow paused, glass in hand, 'we meet at the place where we're going and we'll eat there, too.'

Blake nodded, 'And don't forget to bring your sleeping bags tonight.'

Guthrie smiled at me and I smiled back, wallowing in the electricity long after he turned to Sanvi with the same lingering grin.

*

We set off up the winding, hillside path and Sharrow didn't seem to mind walking barefoot on the burning rocky earth as much as Evan cared about losing the wifi connection to his phone.

'It's bloody gone.'

'What are you doing on there all the time, anyway?' I said. 'Watching more porn?'

'None of your stupid business,' he said. 'Shut up.'

'Nice.' I was shocked. He's rarely rude to me but it was too hot to argue and there were people around who don't know Evan and I didn't want them to find out by hearing us fight.

The steep path went on forever and we soon fell behind. The sun beat down like an out of control fire and the trees, sparse bushes, dusty earth and sound of Constanza teaching Italian to Guthrie, Sanvi, Coco and Tomas up ahead, blurred everything else out.

Sun God hurried to catch up with steps far shorter than they should have been and then Blake dropped back. Suddenly beside me, the dark, crescent scar on his cheek was up close.

'You two OK?' he said.

'Yeah. Yeah.' The knot in my throat got tighter. I tried not to look at the puffy scar but it was hard. We walked side by side in a kind of daze until Blake turned and smiled.

'It takes a couple of days to settle in and you were the last to arrive so it might be longer. How are you finding things so far?'

'Vile,' Evan piped up.

'He means we don't really know what we're meant to be doing.' I looked at Blake's kind, glowing face and nearly told him everything but managed to stop myself.

'Oh, I see. Your mother didn't explain?'

'She never tells us anything,' Evan said.

'That's unusual but not uncommon.' Blake nodded. 'Sharrow and I are leading the group because we've suffered from the same...'

Evan took off, running back down the hill like a maniac. Everyone turned at the sound of thudding steps as the crumpled figure skidded round the bend and disappeared.

SEVENTEEN

I stood there embarrassed, staring after Evan.

Blake touched my elbow. 'Let him go. He hardly slept.'

Grateful for the concern but really worried now, I asked, 'Was he snoring? Did someone wake him up?'

'Ha. I don't know about that.'

I broke out in a cold sweat. 'What then?'

'It's better to say nothing to Evan but I saw him on his own up at the refectory, glued to his iPad at 2am and Sharrow said he was still there at 5.30am when she passed by.'

'Oh, God. I better tell Mum.'

'No, really. Please don't. We've been here before.'

'Before?'

'On another RFP course.' Blake's eyes wandered from me to the rest of the group who'd carried on and were almost half way up the hill.

I looked at him, mystified. 'What's an RFP course?'

'Respite From Porn.'

'What the hell?' I was stunned. 'This course is about porn?'

'The worst ones grab whatever chance they can to get a fix when they can't access the internet any place but the refectory. They feel deprived. Act out. It's how we know how badly along they are. Arcadia started the RFP courses. This is the second one. You didn't know at all? OK, well it happens. No problem. You're here that's all that matters.'

'I don't watch porn. I'm just Evan's sister.'

'OK.'

'Porn's not me,' I said and by the look on his face he didn't believe me which wasn't surprising because I wasn't making sense.

'This summer's porn.' I was so shocked my brain short circuited, forcing me to repeat myself. 'About porn?' and I had to make an effort to change tack. 'No wonder everyone's disturbed.'

There was no need to answer and we stood there for a while.

'There's a fine line between attraction and obsession,' Blake said at last. 'And we provide a much needed rest.'

Annoyed with him, Mum, Evan and myself, I turned and tripped backwards over something. Blake caught my elbow to stop me from falling and it was obvious when his sympathetic eyes met mine that he thought me and Evan had the same problem.

'I'm not into porn. I love books.' I looked at him defiantly and he smiled in such a patronising way it took my breath away.

'I'm not on trial.' I held up my phone. 'Look at my messages. They're about *The Mill on the Floss*. Do you know what that is?'

Crossing one arm across his chest, Blake sighed, took the phone and I wondered if the words *Mill – on the – Floss* could be misinterpreted in any way. Then I remembered the chat with Shula about the three line script and grabbed it back.

'This is stupid. I don't have to prove anything.'

'No, you don't and I'm sorry if I made you think otherwise.' Blake nodded like an old man. 'Let's join the others, Marya, and allow Evan the space to get some rest. I expect that's what he's doing.'

A huge bird flapped its wings and took off from a nearby tree. I watched it soar and fly away in the shimmering heat. So that's why all the talk was about sex. Everyone knew why they were here except for us and I suddenly understood why Mum had been so secretive. She wanted to make sure I would look out for Evan while he received help. How unfair is that? I get that she was desperate after what he said, but I refuse to be his minder.

'I'm going.'

'OK,' Blake said and I picked up two marbled stones and rattled them in my hand as I turned to walk away.

'Come back when you're ready, Marya,' he called.

I looked at the parched, gravelly earth beneath my feet. At the stain on the chest of my green T-shirt dress where the first tear fell and cried for my brother who used to be normal, brave and confident and now is nothing but a porn addict who needs help. Then I felt afraid. The black cloud came back and this time I couldn't shut it off.

EIGHTEEN

Through the fog in my brain I saw Mum leaning back, half asleep on a wicker chair outside the door to the kitchen of the refectory. If there's one thing she likes it's a ten-minute nap and I almost felt bad disturbing her even though I was spitting venom.

Standing there for a second, I noticed her face was going red despite being mostly in the shade of the wall. 'Mum, you should put some sunscreen on.'

'Hi, sweetie.' She bolted upright, covering her eyes with both hands. 'Where did you spring from?'

Unable to think straight I pointed in the direction of the lake. 'I left them up the hill.'

'Why?'

'To look for Evan.'

This time Mum was out of her seat in a shot. Up close and worried, she whispered, 'What happened?'

'Why didn't you tell us the course is for porn addicts?'

'It isn't for porn addicts. It's an RFP course which is respite from porn. For kids who've been affected by it.'

'Kids are only affected when they're addicted,' I said and folded my arms.

'That's not true. It's there in the background of all our lives whether we admit it or not. Where's Evan?'

'Huh. He was seen on his iPad, sitting around here all night and ran off before we even got started. He's probably asleep. It's not fair. I'm not going to mind him like he's five and hang around with porn addicts all summer. I'm not, Mum.'

'That's the whole point of this place. You don't have to mind him and you might learn a lot. They're not all porn addicts.' The wicker chair squeaked when she plumped back down.

'You don't know that. Blake thinks I'm addicted to porn. Me?'

'Why would he think that?'

'MUM. You just said the course is a respite from porn. Why else would I be here?'

'You're his sister. That's how it affects you and both of you could do with a break from it, anyway. Tell Blake.'

'I did but he didn't believe me.'

'Look, I couldn't leave you behind, could I?' Mum said. 'It was a chance for all of us to have a holiday.'

'Holiday? This place is horrible. I'd have been quite happy to be left behind. You know I would. It's not fair. I need respite from Evan and now I'm stuck with him and the rest of them. *You* tell Blake.'

I walked off in a temper. Furious I'd been landed with the problem, and as for Guthrie, I immediately went off him. He could be the worst of the lot. Tomas, Carl, Sun God, they all were horrible porn addicts and I felt physically sick. Why should I have to deal with them because Mum didn't have the guts to tell me the real reason for the trip? Just then my phone pinged with all the messages I'd missed since breakfast and I read them in a temper with the sun frying the back of my head.

'It says there's a heatwave in Spain. Are you OK?' from Dad.

'"A sense of stairs descending as if in a dream." God, I love *Mill on the Floss*. It's hard to believe *Silas Marner* is by the same writer. Not sure about that one. What page are you up to? I'm almost finished,' from Shula.

And… a pic from Watty of an iced bun bursting with cream and the words, 'Want one?'

Huh. He likes me. He likes me a lot and I enlarged the pic and didn't feel so all over the place as I studied it from every angle but it was hard to see the bun clearly with the sun glazing the screen. I almost flaked out completely, trudging back up the hill with my eyes glued to the cryptic message, wondering if Watty wanted to buy me a bun or if the meaning was more obvious. Have to say, I hated him then.

The wide sky grated on me. The sight of the harsh, dried out, still landscape dragged up horrible memories and it felt like Vernon Wood stalked the tractor marks on the path with every step I took.

Unable to send messages until I got back to the refectory, I composed replies to send later.

I told Shula, 'Agreed. *Silas Marner* is strange.' It was the book that started the George Elliot Summer Reading Challenge and I explained how there was no time to read because I was stuck looking after Evan.

I didn't mention the respite course because it would take too long, she'd want to know every detail and anyway I was out of patience. I stopped to pick up a round stone and fling it at the sky. Blinded by the blue neon squinting from the fields and distant hills, I collapsed in the shade of a tree for a moment.

The landscape was too empty. I wanted the world to hurry up. Move on. Cut to the bits where I was in charge of my own life instead of worrying about Evan. All the space and stillness, slowness, silence, hills that go on forever, kept forcing me into the past. A place I didn't want to go.

I picked up another stone. A flat grey stone. The smoothness was reassuring and playing with it for a while somehow got me back together enough to struggle up and carry on.

In two minds whether to answer Watty, I tried a few not so witty one-liners, deleted them, gave up and left the iced bun flashing in the sunshine, unclaimed.

I figured the hot dorm, the gruel, how weirdly isolating Arcadia was after London was enough information for Dad and purposely didn't mention porn or Evan. He can find out for himself.

Almost finished, I remembered to ask, '"There's nothing wiser than your own body," means what exactly, Dad?' And for a second just glancing at the word Dad made me feel safe.

Totally cross there was no signal, I looked up and saw Carl, the serious guy who lives mostly in France with the weed-growing parents, and looked at him suspiciously.

NINETEEN

Gazing at the sky, Carl looked out of place in smart jeans, short-sleeved, blue shirt with buttoned-down pockets and patches of stubble on his pink face. He was neat and clean except for the stubble and the limp brown hair combed into a pony tail.

I took in the ramshackle wooden building with covered terrace and oily tables crammed with paint-caked jam jars, brushes, old branches and dried lumps of colour and the sight detonated a memory. A memory of the art block in school before it was converted into classrooms.

'You have go deep to calculate where you're going next. The longer you stay with a picture, the further inside you have to go to find the next move,' Mrs Astley, the art teacher used to say. I hadn't thought of her in years and the memory felt strangely near and at the same time far away.

The scene in front of me was of a group of porn addicts or victims struggling to recover and only by an act of will could I force myself to stop drifting into the past and watch Constanza and Lilli bent over sheets of white paper, painting carefully arranged gold leaves. They didn't move and were in deep, working out the next stroke, while I wondered if they were porn addicts. Heads down, Blake and Sharrow were also locked into their drawings. The rest were nowhere to be seen.

'Hey.' Carl lifted the limp pony tail from his neck. 'Marya, yeah?'

Dropping the phone in the tote, I swung up to him. 'Yeah.' My voice was all shaky. 'Hi. Where are the others?' I don't think he noticed how disconnected I felt.

'Scattered around.' Carl turned and waved at the sky. 'Getting into the rhythm of nature. Trees. Those cactus. Anything that wants painting.'

The rhythm of nature? I swear I almost forgot where I was. Carl must be crazy or he wouldn't be there, yet he talks like a poet?

'Anything that wants painting,' rang in my ear as I looked at him.

'It wasn't going right this morning so we're having the chat later on.' His grey eyes strained to see me better in the bright sunshine. 'Where's your brother?'

'Sleeping,' I said. 'I think.'

'Your mind's doing acrobats. Yeah?'

'Sorry?'

'In the heat. You know. Want some water?' Carl said. 'I don't have a spliff.'

He thought that was funny. I didn't. He walked off and I was expected to follow the porn-addicted druggie round the shadowy side of the ramshackle building to who knows where.

It was daylight.

There were people around.

I had nothing else to do so I did. I don't know why. Maybe because it was too hot to think and I was glad because when I looked up a magical oasis opened out.

For a second it felt as if the world was playing games with me but the delicate purple flowers, clusters of tall, white blossoms and sunlit branches dipping into a small silvery pool, were real. I floated over them. Over the curly, see-through emerald jug and glasses on a rickety table and for a split second it felt as if they were conscious just like Sanvi said, and were happy to see me. Was I losing my mind or suffering from sun stroke?

'It's a fight trying to be true to yourself, isn't it?' Carl said.

'Is it?' I wondered what he was getting at and frowned. Why did he keep touching that thin pony tail? Maybe he thought I was one of them? An addict in need of respite?

He rescued two folded chairs from the long grass, clacked them into place and steadied them on the shady, uneven ground of a tall tree then looked at me, confused. I suddenly came round, picked up the jug, poured two glasses of jewelled water and gave him one.

'I guess some feelings are hard to label,' he said.

Heart racing, nervously tucking one leg under the other, I perched on the chair and sipped the warm water. I'd never been in the countryside, not even to Hilly Fields with a guy before, let alone a porn addict so it was weird to be alone with him.

The hat-like lilies in the pond, willowy tree and tickly grass on my ankles, made me feel I'd landed in a luscious picture book illustration except the gold grass and folding flowers were real and their reflection glittered in the emerald water I thrust at the sun and then my lips.

Carl looked at me. 'You don't say much. Prefer to first weigh up every word?'

I coughed. 'It's just so beautiful.'

'Not easy are you? OK then. Yeah. So, last year we all ended up naked in the pool when it got this hot.'

'You were here last year?' No way was I going to ask how they ended up naked in the pool. Or why he came back. Didn't he learn enough last time?

'Yeah. It was great. But I think Blake's fed up with me.'

Scared to death the naked in the pool thing might be an end-of-course event or worse, a frequent impulse, I managed to ask, 'Why's Blake fed up with you?'

'Well, I can kinda see how this year's going to pan out. Know what I mean?'

'Not really,' I said and he noisily gulped the water, jumped up, clunked the glass back on the table upside down, undid the buttons on his shirt, opened it and turned round to reveal a slice of skinny white chest.

'I better not tell you then,' he said. When he started to unzip his jeans, he saw the look on my face and laughed the sort of laugh

74

Watty usually makes. Deep and throaty – dirty even.

'Do you mind?' he said and looked past me, surprised. I half turned and Blake came through the long grass from the shadowy building where the midday sun tipped him into the glistening light.

'Hey, you guys,' he said. 'Can you help do lunch? Everyone else is busy.'

'Sure.' Carl did up his shirt and marched off. Jeans left half unzipped.

'We talked about this, Carl.' Blake called after him. 'Remember?'

'Yeah. Yeah.' Carl waved as he disappeared. 'It's just, like you know – so hot.'

'You OK, Marya?' Blake said.

'Yeah.' Uncurling my leg, I got up. The chair tipped over and collapsed with a clack as if in a hurry to return to the safety of the long grass.

'Anything I can help you with?' Blake said and I stopped gazing at the flat chair and turned to him.

'Just because my brother's a porn addict and Mum expects me to look out for him why should I play along? I don't watch porn but you don't believe me, do you?'

'Can we have a proper talk about this?' Blake said.

'What about helping with lunch?'

'Never mind that.' After several attempts, he unfolded the chair in the grass, batted it down hard on the uneven earth, held it there and said. 'Please, sit down, Marya.'

This time I kept both feet firmly on the ground and perched on my hands, ready to be talked to like a little kid at school and then argue and fight every step of the way.

Blake took the chair Carl vacated and leaned dangerously back.

Arms behind his head, he looked at the sky with me wondering why the collapsible chair belonged to me and not the solid one he bagged.

TWENTY

'I'm twenty-eight and in a good, healthy place. I had everything growing up but wanted something more, needed an outlet, you know, and at twelve started watching porn.' Blake was stunningly direct.

I thought he was older.

'Guys hate themselves for wanting what they want,' he said. 'Doing what they want. Feeling how they do. Thinking things others don't like. That no one likes. Things that aren't real but they can't stop thinking about. By the time I got to college I was angry. Confused. Ashamed. Desperate for sex and a virgin.'

It must have been obvious I'd rather crawl naked over broken glass than sit here for a second longer because he paused.

'I can stop if you want,' he said, 'but conversations like this are always easier if you know where I'm coming from and Arcadia is about truth and transparency, however hard.'

Conversations? He was doing all the talking.

'No. I'm fine. Honest,' I lied with a twinge in my gut that told me I was under attack. His desperation wasn't something I wanted to spend time thinking about. No guy, especially a porn addict his age, has ever talked about sex without boasting his head off. Shocked, not just by what he said, but by his posh, ever so clipped, out there accent, I wished I was strong enough to avoid the story that was about to swallow me up.

'At college, the guys on my silent corridor were all slaves to porn and stayed behind closed doors every evening,' he said. 'We were free. So free we chose bondage to our screens and one day the chap in the room next door who I'd hardly spoken to – he was nineteen – said, "I've had enough," and the next day they dragged his body from

76

the river.'

I didn't know what to say and hunched over. That poor guy. I felt sick and stared at my ridiculous gold flip-flops half buried in the soft grass. At the tiny yellow fronds twisted round a stick. My pale knees poked from the green T-shirt dress, and nothing – nothing but a pale body being dragged from a river, felt real.

'I hardly knew him. Wasn't aware of him,' Blake said. 'They investigated the reasons. Emptied his laptop. You can guess the rest. It was then I realised I needed help. I went online and found thousands of pages.'

'Thousands?' I was shocked.

'Yes. I talked to everyone and discovered a secret epidemic was taking place. An epidemic that few people talk about because watching porn is mainstream. Our culture has sanitised it to the extent that it's as normal as brushing your teeth but most porn is hardcore, showing men getting satisfaction from violating and dominating women who are continually abused.'

His pause grew longer and filled up the awkward space between us until I shifted slightly, the chair creaked and I half smiled to lighten the tense atmosphere.

'I told a friend I'd known all my life and do you know what he said? Nothing in daily life compared to the stuff he watched online and he wished it did.'

Blake stopped and looked at me.

'Boys claim it's harmless fun. Some girls do, too.' My stomach rumbled. I had to say something. It worked and he was off again.

'That's where the danger lies unless you believe humiliating, life-threatening, racist violence is harmless. Before these kids know what they want to do with their bodies, how they feel about sex or what they imagine it to be, they're fed male adult fantasies which are rarely about loving or satisfying a woman. Many girls think porn doesn't affect them when the most visible identity offered them is sexual beings strutting their attractive body parts. What happened to the goddess who nurtures love? The earth angel whose beauty lies within? They've become invisible.'

'It's big business,' I said, echoing Mum and we sat in silence for a while gazing at the pool.

'Huge business and we've grown up digital where it's impossible to miss,' Blake said. 'Instead of trying on different identities, creating and acting on their own desires, kids have come to believe that what they see on these sites is true to life. Boys' brains are programmed to believe all females like being hurt, tied up and drugged, and we wonder why we have continual war.'

'Most watch it then?' I said.

'Studies show sixty per cent of eleven- to sixteen-year-olds have. It's probably more by now.'

I shook my head, thinking back.

'And how do kids react when friends take the piss and bully them for not visiting the cool porn sites?' he said. 'They're forced to agree it's harmless and take a look even though it feels wrong inside.'

'It's bad,' I said and shivered despite the heat.

'Listen, the destroyed feel better when you join them. They carefully coerce you into going against your own instincts then compromise you into doing something you hadn't considered because it energises them but the energy is vampiric. A one-way road.'

'Vampiric? Really?' My mind zoomed to the Twilight poster on my bedroom wall. It was a poster for the vampiric energy I'd been living with. This was interesting.

'Yes.'

'I don't watch it,' I said.

'Now or never?'

'Pardon?' My mind was still on the poster.

'You made a decision not to watch it. Something led you to making that wise decision, Marya. It would be helpful to know what that was.'

'Not everyone's been damaged by porn,' I said.

'It's a major part of our culture so that's hard to judge, Marya, but I don't know, somehow I suspect there's more to it with you than concern for your much loved brother. In a place like this everything is up for grabs. We have that most precious of things, time to think. Time to reflect on the past. Eliminating shame is important and we have the opportunity here to share the things that matter without worrying what's said will be spread around.'

Who is this guy? I wanted to argue, get away and talk to him, all at the same time.

'Hey, everyone, lunch is ready,' a voice called. Other voices started up. Footsteps sounded at the front of the building. Chairs scraped on the wooden terrace. I smiled. Relieved but troubled. We got up to join them and with so many thoughts bashing my brain, it was easy not to focus on the secret I'd been dragging around for years. Aware Blake had seen into my soul and knew more than he was letting on.

TWENTY-ONE

It was easy to forget about Evan over the next few days because he didn't once make it to the art building. I saw him with the iPad under his arm coming from the compost loos at the back of the dorms when I'd just woken up and he was on his way to bed.

When it came to crashing out at night most people stayed there while I scurried back to the dorm to enjoy the peace of an almost empty attic. Blake said not to worry, Evan would come round but I doubted it was true, alert to the possibility of him vanishing into thin air at any moment.

'He won't disappear,' Blake said.

'I know him,' I said twice but he just smiled.

Trying to stay cool while working on hopeless drawings of trees, chairs and the magical pool behind the building was fun at first and the quiet interlude was, I guess, a way of winding down from real life.

The internet signal at the refectory disappeared for a few hours every now and then and I wasn't prepared to make the effort to hike there and back during the day for nothing so stayed put. If Evan wanted to wait around to get online, that was up to him.

Less big and muscular somehow, Sun God had changed into an ordinary, good-looking guy with short legs, and unable to stop working on her painting, Sanvi mostly sat apart while he tried to interrupt. She ignored him. There wasn't much talk.

Sharrow dabbed at a spotty abstract and desperate-for-sex Tomas peered at the drawing of a tree that Guthrie ripped up when he leaned over his shoulder. Everyone was lost in their own little world while I sat at the edge of the group and read, aware that no one would know if they looked at us ordinary teenagers that anyone had a problem with porn.

With my legs in the sunshine, food and water on my lap, book on the ground, still feeling a bit like an outsider, I looked at myself through the rest of the group's eyes. Sensible, self-conscious Marya, who says she's here with her problem brother and probably needs more help than him.

Why do I need more help than Evan? Why did I think that? No one's thinking that. Shut up and eat the quinoa.

'Just be yourself,' Mum says but who the hell am I?

Blake appeared from the direction of the toilets, nodded, smiled and passed by as if we hadn't talked about his porn addiction and the student on his corridor who killed himself. Once something is said in Arcadia it's left to settle which is good in one way but hard in another because every day feels like the first and starting over each sunny morning leads to the same thoughts about where you fit in and what being on this earth at this time in history surrounded by these people actually means.

Twiddling his limp pony tail, Carl stood over a bent sunflower in a jam jar that wasn't a million miles from the old painting in front of Guthrie's furry head, and neither noticed me.

I looked at my phone. The battery was full but, of course, there was no signal. I reread the messages I still hadn't sent and finished the cold quinoa that tasted of peppery cardboard. Still unsure what to say to Watty about the pic of the iced bun, I wondered why I thought I could eat three whole slices of hard, grainy bread for lunch when it was two more than I'd swallowed for breakfast.

*

Shula would delete the picture of the stupid bun. I'd been worrying about it for too long but finally settled on, 'Did you steal it? Looks too big to belong to you, Watty?' Then deleted his nickname and felt an urgent need to get away. What did people do to hide their emotions before they had phones?

I looked around. Everyone was eager to finish eating and get back to their creations. Satisfied with the way the day was going while I sat there staring at a stupid photo of an iced bun, thinking about *The Mill on the Floss* and a rural way of life that was hard to understand even while living in Arcadia. Then I realised I needn't stay. It wasn't school and I took my plate and the uneaten bread back to the food table.

'Do you need help with the washing up?' I asked the girl with big sunglasses, pierced nose and tattooed arms busy filling a plastic bowl with soapy water.

'Nah.' She wiped her hands on a scruffy apron and grinned. 'We've got two helpers today. Thanks, Marya isn't it? Hi, I'm Mo. It's about time we met,' she said with a musical Welsh accent.

'Hi Mo.'

'Better get on.' She threw a pile of cutlery in the bowl. 'Take the bread for later if you want.'

I emptied the bread in the bin and trudged to the compost loos which were even more basic than the ones at the dorms then did a detour down a wiggly path that led to a lopsided hut with a tiny porch. There was a yellow bike outside so it was clearly someone's home and I scooted round the side of a decrepit caravan to another narrow track leading down the sunlit hill.

The sudden wide-open view of olive groves and the path itself was fresh and alive after the claustrophobia of being stuck all morning fidgeting and blushing while everyone was engrossed in their work.

Soon the path gave way to the track beside the lake and I stopped to look at the water twinkling with haloes. If I was brave and wild and everything I'd like to be, I'd kick off the gold flip-flops and T-shirt dress and leap any old way into the cool water. I'd splash and shout, fall back, laugh, bury my head in the lake and all the dark rooms over there would disappear.

TWENTY-TWO

In the distance an orange tractor rumbled along the track. There was no one around. It was just me, a craggy rock and the magic of the moving lake. The sweet smell of blossom drifted from the bushes and the patch of flat, stony ground in between was the perfect place to throw off my bag and T-shirt dress.

I took in the silence and the lake pulled me to do something I wouldn't normally do but the churning feeling inside left me with no choice. Then I worried someone might come along and see me in my old navy bra and knickers with baby pink bows on the straps and sides.

I could take them off? No. The thought of jumping in was brave enough.

A breeze came up and specks of dust blew into the water as I ripped the grubby tote from my shoulder, tugged the T-shirt dress inside out over my head, bundled them together and stuffed them in a bush with white flowers.

The grubby gold flip-flops looked better on the twiggy branches than on my feet and I waded through the shallows and slapped into the lake like a fish falling on a plate.

Wet and cool. No longer cramped by anything and treading water, I looked down at my favourite navy bra and my breasts were bouncing. They even looked big while I kicked my way to freedom.

Floating on my back with my eyes closed, the sun's kisses grew stronger. I twisted round, splashed and swam until I heard scuffling on the path and stopped. Through the dazzling light on the water, wiping wet hair from my eyes, heart thumping, I squinted at the wavy patch of land between the wavy bushes and a caveman came in and out of focus. Sunbeams bouncing, a half-naked guy covered in curly brown hair, stepped out of his jeans. T-shirt already on the ground.

'Guthrie.' I choked. He saw me — must have. Into the lake he vanished then reappeared, swimming towards me like an invading horde, arms pounding the water. Furry head bobbing up and down like someone intent on murder but when he rolled up opposite and stopped, bathed in a film of amber light with sparkles flying from his hair, he looked at me like a warm, loving friend and we fell into a deep, heavenly sleep with each other. Eye to eye. Non-stop smiling and smiling. It was easy to believe we were the same person with our arms spread wide, feet dancing under the water.

How it happened I don't know but nothing interfered with my heart in the lake even though I'd decided that morning not to like him.

TWENTY-THREE

Guthrie headed back to the art block after a final wave that took up the whole sky and I walked down the hill to the refectory in a daze, plucking bits of T-shirt dress from my wet body. A good reminder I wasn't walking on air but firm ground while my favourite bra was probably at the bottom of the lake fraying its way to dishrags.

It was fine. Yes, it was, even though Guthrie was in Arcadia for a reason I didn't want to think about. All good. It absolutely was. Every cell in my body told me so. Elated, excited, I was flying somehow on one level while on another I was sinking fast because I was totally overwhelmed and it wasn't because the coins of sunshine on the path glittered like fairy gold. No, it was because of him. Because of the kisses in the water – kisses like soft water, like nothing I can describe.

At the bottom of the hill my phone began vibrating in the shabby black tote. Yay, a signal. Dad probably thought I was dead it had been so long since he asked how I was but my happiness set the mood for confronting Evan and when I sent the replies to Shula, Dad and Watty, I found him sitting on his own at a shady table in the almost empty refectory.

Everyone was probably having a siesta to escape the sticky afternoon heat while Evan hunched over his iPad with three melon crusts at his feet.

'You had lunch?' I picked them up and dropped them in the grey plastic bin by the entrance to the kitchens.

He yawned long and hard. 'They're not mine. Mum gave me some rice and tofu. There wasn't any melon left when I got here.'

'You still could have picked them up.'

He didn't answer.

'Are you going to spend every night down here?' I hovered over him to get a glimpse of the screen. Evan pulled a face and hugged it to him.

'Might do.'

'What did Mum say?'

'Nothing. She doesn't care.'

'Evan, we're in Spain.'

'So?'

'There's attractive girls everywhere and you're stuck here on your own.'

'You look wrecked,' he said. 'Worse than me. Why you so worried?'

'They're all painting and drawing. Having a good time at the art building. I went for a swim in the lake. It was amazing and you're doing nothing.'

'Not the lake?' He grinned insanely, eyes spinning like he'd taken a sudden knock on the head. 'That's where couples do it.'

'Don't be stupid.' Appalled, I was too weak to remain standing and flopped down beside him. 'How do you know?'

'A woman with blue hair told me.'

'What woman?' There wasn't a soul around.

'One of the hippies. She's lived here all her life with two kids by two different guys and they're all friends. She was normal weird, unlike the rest of the nuts here. Said we're having a session soon about the power of real hooman connex-shun and the lake is often blessed with lurve, man. There's huts where they go to as well.' He glanced at the iPad, turned it over on the table and scratched his knee. 'You can do what you want here.'

'Huts? What huts? Shut up, Evan. You can't do what you want. You're here because you've been affected by porn like all the kids and Blake and Sharrow.'

'Porn?' he was shocked. 'It's not a love and relationship, old people sex education, we are all one, thing?'

'No, and Mum expects me to look after you which I'm not going to do.'

'You've got it wrong,' Evan frowned.

'You're the one who's got it wrong,' I said. 'Blake was addicted to porn and a student on his corridor at college jumped off a massive bridge and killed himself because he had nothing but evil videos to live for.'

'He told you that?'

'More or less.' I fidgeted. 'It might not have been a bridge. Blake said he'd never had sex when he went to uni.'

'Blake?' Evan gasped. 'You're lying.'

'Porn stopped him from living. The same as you.'

'Where is Blake? I'm going to ask him.' Evan shoved the iPad under his arm.

'You won't ask him.'

'Where is he?'

'Up at the art building,' I said.

'Not that hill. I ain't going up there. You can if you want.' Evan pushed the table away and climbed out from the bench.

'Evan, this course is for you.'

'I'm not talking to no one about porn. Why should I when I don't watch it?'

He trudged away while back and forth went the memory of the chat with Blake.

'Evan, come back.'

'No,' he said and carried on walking. I couldn't shout. People might hear me and I was too dazed to run after him. Evan wasn't ever going to admit he had a problem and whatever was between Guthrie and me no longer felt special after what he said about the lake and the huts 'where they go as well.' *Who goes? The people who live here?*

I sat there and an attractive man with dark hair positioned his laptop on the far table and two screeching, mischievous flower children with black, felt ears on their heads charged out from inside the refectory and ran off down the track.

A chubby woman with spiky, blue hair hurried out and called them back. They took no notice and speeded up. She put her hands on her hips, shouted again, waited a few seconds, kissed the guy on the head and went back to the indoor eating area. The kids were nowhere to be seen.

I hadn't seen anyone else with blue hair. She was the woman Evan talked about.

Round the corner came Mum. She broke into a huge smile when she saw me. 'I just ran into Evan. He's having a rest.'

'I don't care what he's doing.'

'What's wrong with you?'

Gradually I turned right round. 'Guess?'

'For goodness' sake, Marya. Right now we're in a beautiful place with lovely people who go out of their way to help and I'm sorry not to have told you why we're here but I thought you'd understand. We both want Evan to learn the error of his ways, don't we?'

'Yes, but you should have said and he's not going to learn. He says he doesn't watch porn.'

'OK. Sorry. I am. Really. You're right, I should have said. Evan will come round. You'll see. It's hard to avoid the truth here. You OK now?'

'Fine,' I lied.

'You're all wet.'

'I went swimming in the lake.'

'On your own?'

I wasn't going to answer that one and quickly came up with something to distract her. 'I was wondering about the water retention system…'

'While swimming in it?' She knew I was lying but didn't press me. 'It's pretty much desert here in the summer.'

'I can see that.'

'Temperatures can go way past forty degrees.' Getting excited, she said, 'They started by digging out the lowest point in the valley to build a dam, tractor rollers impacted the base in layers a metre deep with natural materials like clay. The result of all that work is easy to see ten years later. Look at the fruit trees and wildlife everywhere. A natural spring formed to irrigate the surrounding land and it's really incredible how when we listen to nature, it will teach us what to do.'

'When we listen to nature...' I repeated. 'Are you turning into a hippy?'

'Me? For heaven's sake, Marya. You can see Arcadia's pretty impressive and it's not just about an alternative way of life,' Mum grinned. 'They believe the micro affects the macro. If you throw a pebble in the lake the ripples get bigger and bigger as they spread. That's how the universe works. It's the same with conflict in relationships. Lies and betrayals lead to constant war between couples, communities and then nations which is why honesty is at the heart of Arcadia.'

'Right. I get it.' It was the shortest, easiest answer. This was Arcadia after all and well worth agreeing to because Mum was ready to rant and I was eager to go. What with my damp hair drying to an unmanageable frizz itching my neck, Mum's support for Arcadia wasn't up for questioning and I hoped she wasn't planning on leaving London. We'd have to move in with Dad and Shell if she stayed and there's no room for us in that tiny flat.

My phone buzzed with a photo of Shula eating something called Rooz Ma Lahem (rice with meat). *The Mill on the Floss* clamped to her chest, fork in the other hand and Vaseline tears streaking from her twinkly eyes. I know they were Vaseline because the jar was open on the table.

TWENTY-FOUR

Fresh and clean and smelling of all natural, coconut shampoo, I felt more like myself after a quick shower. Abandoning the T-shirt dress, I gave up any attempt to look cool and put on the old skinny jeans I live in at home.

What happened in the lake hadn't lost its drama but instead of fear there was a deep anxiety that Mum might consider wrecking our lives by becoming a member of Arcadia. As for Dad, he was still in his own little world and had no idea how much I missed him.

A freckly woman in a red swimming costume, neat sarong tied at the waist and blue sneakers, made a sudden deep moaning sound. With shaved head and silver globe earrings, she lunged sideways at the earth to do a cartwheel. Her legs spun over her head like a folding compass and she landed perfectly. Dignity intact.

Towel under my arm, I crept past, smiled and stood back. Cartwheels are compulsive viewing and it felt like her spinning was a perfect reflection of the craziness going on in my head. There was intention. Hope. A kind of order then a mad upside down fling that threw the world into a blur.

With someone like her to scrutinise and a situation that allowed me to stare, the feeling, I guessed, was the same for both of us. Intense concentration linked in time for no other reason than we were the only people there.

'What comes to you always matches you.' Mum's friend, the cyclist, Rosanne, who is mad about spiritual YouTube vids, told me someone said that, but I can't remember who and I wondered if the woman doing cartwheels was trying to reveal a deeper meaning to the hot spinning feeling in my head and, if so, what was it? Perhaps Sanvi would know? This is what happens to your brain in Arcadia. When it's not frying alive it gets completely, absolutely, maniacally stumped.

The woman's silver earrings shook until she was ready and again raised both arms. Holding the pose, she stared at the ground, waited a few seconds, took a breath and sprang sideways like a viper. Over she went. Arced legs in the air rested for a moment with impressive control before falling elegantly to earth.

Wiping her red face with a hand, she smiled and headed for the tap. I coated a chair with my towel to dry, went inside and climbed the stairs to the dorm, wishing for an athletic body like that.

I must have fallen asleep because the sound of voices downstairs startled me.

It was almost six. I was hungry and leapt up. Where was Evan?

The memory of the lake was a bit out of reach as I brushed my hair, grabbed my bag and checked to see if my phone was fully charged. It was. As I wandered down the stairs, I finally got round to reading the deathly long scroll from Dad after asking him to explain, 'There's nothing wiser than your own body.'

'What I meant was as we move around in daily life we don't pay much attention to our bodies or our surroundings but when we focus on contact with the ground and air and tune into how we're breathing, standing etc. we slowly become aware of our habits and restrictions. What's happening changes when you start to listen to your body which is about more than things like, I feel sick, perhaps I shouldn't have another cake. Really deep work alters ways of moving, breathing, standing and gives the potential for greater ease, vitality and most importantly, different responses. If something disturbs the body, inquire why. Most often, something, a horror film maybe, scratches away at your stomach, at the side of your head, so stop. Switch it off. Knowing our bodies are wise gives us the information we crave. We do some of this work with offenders and it goes down well. I've got a couple of books you might find interesting. Now, don't get sunburnt. All love, Dad xxxx'

'Love you, Dad,' I said out loud and when I looked up Coco was standing in front of me.

'Hey Marya. We missed you.'

'I fell asleep,' I said.

'Guthrie was looking for you.' Coco narrowed her eyes. A bit suspicious. 'You sure you don't like him?' My face must have given me away because she frowned.

'It's OK,' she said.

'Was he the guy you were crying over?'

'Yes and no,' she said. 'Well, yeah but hey, it's OK 'cause I know he likes Sharrow and I like her too, but she's ten years older than him and I don't think she's interested but that might be way out, and anyway we're friends, Marya? I don't do that girl against girl thing.'

We're friends? 'Er... yeah.' *He likes Sharrow?* I nearly threw up. 'Have you seen Evan?'

'No.' She swung an arm round my waist. 'My belly's screaming for a burger so houmous again then, yeah?' And that was how we ended up marching off together even though Coco was much faster than me and it was hard to keep up.

'Where did you learn to whistle?' I puffed when we got to the steps leading to the refectory tables.

'A guy showed me. We shouldn't be here.' She stopped and stood still. 'Oh, yeah. We're supposed to eat at the pizza place tonight.'

'Oh, I expect that's where Evan is then. Will it matter if we don't go?' My stomach flipped at the thought of a long uphill walk and seeing Guthrie before I was ready. Not that I'd ever be ready after hearing he likes Sharrow.

'We're starving aren't we?' I said. 'Let's eat here.'

'I'm almost dead from lack of beef,' Coco said and we rushed to fill our plates with mountains of chickpea curry, her American accent bubbling in my ear. 'Don't touch that soup. It smells of urine.'

I wanted to tell her about Guthrie but didn't have the nerve and all the time I was wondering why she thought he doesn't like her. If he's into Sharrow and maybe me, why wouldn't he go for her, too?

With masses of fluffy-as-candyfloss dark hair, tiny nose, button mouth and big gestures, she was cute but there was far more to her than American good looks. One minute Coco took up all the space on the table and everyone glanced admiringly at her, and the next as if haunted by something, she plunged into sudden darkness and they quickly looked away.

I told myself it wasn't anything to worry about but I knew deep inside it was. Then it occurred to me she's a bit like Evan whose ordinary expression can also flip into a remote death stare. He has none of Coco's charisma or cuteness which makes it worse.

What with climate change, constant wars, starvation and poor, sad, homeless people and abandoned refugees, I figure we have to pull each other out of dark tunnels otherwise why are we here? I touched Coco's arm, afraid to ask what she was thinking about and she came back, smiled and carried on eating.

When we finished, we took our plates to the serving table. I pulled my blue sweatshirt over my head and wished there was some kind of emergency surgery available to remove people's dark thoughts.

'I used to be notorious,' Coco said as we hurried down the path towards the pizza area and shops.

'Wow.' I was intrigued. 'I've never been anything.'

'Yeah, you have, babe,' she said. 'In your past lives.'

'More like in my dreams,' I laughed. 'What did you do?'

'It started at a party with my best girl friends. We were dancing, wild music pumping blood so fast I couldn't breathe…' Her eyes sank into a secret den and her voice became almost a whisper. 'Hell in a way…'

'Do you need a hug?' I said.

'Ha. You're sweet. I'm cool.' She sat on a flat rock at the edge of the path and looked up at me. 'It was a blowout at a friend's weekender, one of those houses with a wraparound porch. On the beach. You know?'

I nodded. I'd seen those perfect white houses in American films. I couldn't imagine ever visiting one.

'Then a girl's brother started filming. He was unbelievable this guy and it was fun performing for him. Like it was safe to act out because we were in her house and this was her older brother – only he wasn't and we competed to bump it up for him. I fell back. Stood in the doorway, watching when the music got louder and he hit on Marlene. Camera up her arse. Take it off, he told her. Take it off. With a perfect body, she was really happy to obey.'

The smell of blossom from a nearby bush and the reality of the cool evening melted away with the familiar, awful warning something terrible was coming next. I looked at her sad, resigned face and took in the fear in her eyes. 'We kinda like followed to be cool,' she said. 'Dancing half naked. Crazy for him and his camera. I'm telling you it was exciting.' She paused to look at me and I froze.

'The film of us naked made it to the *Young Hotties* site and loads of others. Only he'd grained out our faces.' Coco sat there with hands in her lap and I stood over her, reluctant to hear another word.

The sudden silence made it feel as if giants were pushing through the gloom to get to us. Above, the sky was closing in and the dark path shifted from still leaf brown to a mass of panther shadows moving across the words that couldn't be stopped. Running, drumming. Unwilling to listen, part of me floated away.

'We laughed about it at first,' she whispered, 'when really we didn't know what to do. I was in the background. Marlene was the main event and I wanted to be her, kinda jealous to be honest and then the guy arranged another party.'

Party. The word jumped out.

'We guessed we could handle it,' she said. 'I was scared. I never went out much but my friends persuaded me.'

'Getting naked on camera isn't the worst thing,' I said and her face hardened.

Fluffy hair fell into her eyes. Small and distinctly fragile, she twisted sideways on the flat rock. 'We were only eleven, honey,' she said. 'Sucks? Yeah? That was the start of something really bad.'

'Eleven? I hope they arrested that bastard for filming you.'

'Yeah, if only we'd told someone but we didn't. We were too ashamed to even talk about it among ourselves. The worst thing is I kind of enjoyed dancing half naked for him until someone explained how easy it is to get caught up in something like that when a gorgeous, well-practised guy pays you an amazing amount of attention. No one wants to be the uncool one, do they?'

'I suppose so but you're OK now?'

'I decided I was a slut.'

'But you were just a kid.

'Not even five-year-olds are kids these days. Believe me, you don't want to know the rest of it.' Tears rushed down her cheeks and I leaned over and hugged her. Hugged her until she stopped crying and started smiling and I wished George Elliot was writing today. Writing about this stuff for our age because this is what's happening to us. She would make it complicated and multi-layered unlike the simple, unsatisfying, easy books you give to the charity shop when you've turned the last page.

'We better go. Thanks for listening.' Coco wiped her eyes and we walked arm in arm the rest of the way with me telling her about Evan and how messed up he is because he's never had sex.

'But he's special,' Coco said. 'He got it when I threatened to drown myself.'

'Evan?'

'He said I should do what I want. Remember?'

'That was a terrible thing to say.'

'It's maybe not always a good thing but then it brought me back, you know? It made me realise I was the only one who could save myself.'

It was my turn to feel grateful and I liked the feeling. It meant everything when she said that. By the time we reached the path to the pizza area we'd told each other a lot about our lives though for me the important stuff remained as hidden as the chickpeas in my stomach.

'You must come to New York,' she said as we turned the corner. 'I have my own studio apartment with two pull-out beds.'

'Really?'

She nodded. *Who has their own apartment at seventeen?* I was impressed but didn't dare ask how she got it. We turned the corner and saw everyone, except Evan, playing a group game of table tennis, running around in turn to slam the next ball and compared to the things we'd been talking about, the softly spreading glow from the light over the ping-pong table, the chilly evening and eager voices were the perfect remedy for our lost hours and sad chat.

'Anyone seen Evan?' I asked and Carl shrugged. Tomas shook his head.

Faces were pinned to the table when Blake missed a ball. 'He's around here somewhere,' he said and a huge laugh went up when he took his turn. At first Guthrie was too busy darting round to look up. Then he turned and the bright look in his eyes as he looked at me then Coco and grinned, sealed my fate.

'There you are.' Sharrow waved a blue bat with cream rubbers. 'Where have you been?'

'Talking to Marya's mum,' Coco said.

Why did she say that? But then where had she been? I bumped into her when I'd woken up but had no idea why she was at the bottom of the dorm stairs. The thought finally led me to ask the question on my mind, 'Why was Guthrie looking for me earlier?'

'Dunno,' Coco shrugged.

I glanced at the closed shops, the clay pizza oven and darkness behind the empty tables. Where was Evan?

'Come on,' Sharrow shouted. In fresh white jeans and silky orange top she was sparklier than ever and Coco and I looked at each other, grabbed bats from the basket and dived in.

TWENTY-FIVE

'I'm feeling it.' Coco pushed through and whacked the ball over the net. Blake batted it to Tomas behind her. *Pop. Pop.* His flip-flops slapped as he slammed it back. Carl crashed into the table, leaning over to reach the ball before it rolled to the floor, missed and cracked up laughing.

It was fun. It was hot. It was crazy and I threw off my sweatshirt.

Leaping sideways to take a corner ball, I full-on patted it back and Guthrie was opposite for a second. He glanced at me before crunching up for a low ball. Breathless and smiling, eyes on fire, the game got faster, tackier and madder. The table vibrated. We were practically airborne. Crushing topspins until one hit the net.

Coco paused but the game didn't flag. We carried on, racing to catch a backhanded smash.

Carl, Tomas and Guthrie kept on when Lilla, Constanza, Sanvi and Mo who were dressed for the night in flowery dresses, waved their bats in breathless defeat and dropped out along with Blake.

It's Sharrow, Coco and me now. *Guthrie's girls,* I thought.

'My Stiga Evolution bat could blow this old thing away,' Tomas spat.

Reaching for a high one which pinged the net, Carl groaned. 'What the hell's that?'

'A super-fast paddle unlike this old thing.' Tomas picked a fleck of blue rubber from the rim of his bat, swayed from side to side, took Guthrie's ball flat, spun it over the net, twisted round in a flash and gave another perfect forehand push, while we waited, mouths open.

I managed to keep going without shaming myself and lovely Coco clapped whenever me or Sharrow made contact with the ball. There didn't seem to be any special awareness between Guthrie and

Sharrow. She wasn't in his eyes more than Coco or me. A quick smile was the most evidence there was anything going on.

Guthrie's sidespin swerves were almost as good as Tomas and Carl was better than Coco who looked right at home with the boys: digging Guthrie's arm when he missed, patting Tomas's bony shoulder when he slammed the ball high and hugging Carl when he blocked a speedy return. She was fully alive now unlike before when she told her story. It was good to see. I hoped the telling had helped but what did I know?

The game was harder with less people playing and further to run; we dived to pick up the rolling balls more and more. Soon I was out of energy, grabbed my sweatshirt from the floor, stepped into the shadowy night with the bat in my hand, gasping to get my breath back.

The darkness smelt sweet as I headed to one of the empty tables in the pizza area, fairy lights twinkling in the distant auditorium. Soft music drifted from the stage in competition with the grunts from the game behind me as I sat on my own with the bat in my hand. I should have dropped it in the basket but didn't care. It was just me, the lovely night and the massive urge to lie on the bench and stare at the millions of stars.

I pulled on the sweatshirt. Guthrie had behaved as if there was nothing between us and it felt like the kisses in the lake were a made-up dream. Our secret. A secret imprinted on every star up there while the dark trees, pizza oven and voices sliding from the game were insignificant static photos in comparison with the huge, startling image of Guthrie in the silvery lake flashing through my mind.

Without the nerve to find the path and walk back to the dorm on my own – on my own without a torch – I put my feet up and lay still on the bench. Blake said to bring my sleeping bag to the art building but I didn't want to. There was no way I could crash with Guthrie nearby and lay there determined to stay attached to the stars in that romantic in-between place where waiting is exciting, enticing even, and where laughter from the game included me even though I wasn't there.

The moment I started worrying how long it would be until the game ended, the stars lost their magic and I sat up, trying hard to push away the things that wanted to pull me in. The thought of not being special to Guthrie returned. I could hear Coco whistling and turned round but the beautiful, eerie sound wasn't coming from the table tennis area way behind, but from the lake. I dropped the bat, about to get up when Guthrie, Carl and Tomas flew out of the darkness like a pack of wolves and charged right past me. Leaving me in the great nowhere, alone and embarrassed.

Why didn't they notice me? Care where I'd gone?

No, not they. Him.

I walked the opposite way towards the twinkling lights and soft music of the auditorium with a cold, pulsing heart. No way was I going down to the lake where I'm sure Guthrie had gone but then if I couldn't find Mum what would I do? I'd be even more on my own than I was before.

At the edge of the dance floor I found an empty table. Trying not to look out of place I crouched on a bench in the semi-darkness.

People were drinking at the bar, chatting at tables in large groups or dancing, dressed for the night in smart shirts, bright dresses, jeans or leggings.

Closest to me was the poet from Lagos, swinging her stunning, embroidered, turquoise dress with both hands until she stopped to speak to the man she was dancing with and said: 'You see honey there are two types of truth; one is loaded with up-swimming facts for the head while the other swoops with gossamer wings straight to the heart.' She patted her heaving chest and laughed. 'Right here is the kind of truth your soul can't deny.'

I knew exactly what she meant and wished she would sit next to me.

The attractive, dark-haired man I saw in front of his laptop at the refectory leaned in to whisper something in the poet's ear. The same man the woman with blue hair had kissed on the top of his head.

Someone clapped and I twisted round. Hand in hand, Serge in old blue jeans and checked shirt brought Mum onto the dance floor. She pinged the straps of her navy dress and trembled weirdly for a second. I'd never seen her dance before. By her awkward moves it was clear she wasn't sure how to start and moved far too slowly to the music.

Crisp packets cracked open at the next table and when I glanced back, Mum was wildly waggling her arms, Serge hanging over her with a broad grin, arms out as if ready to pounce. A sudden ache broke out in the pit of my stomach. It was a shock to see how much she liked him. I wanted Dad to be Serge and them back together. Wanted Dad to dance with Mum, not him.

When the music got louder and a woman with grey smoky skin told me to squash up so her laughing friends could grab my table, there was no point staying. I stumbled from the bench. For some reason not one of them begged me to stay.

Away from the music, spiralling lights and Mum's eager dancing playing out in my mind, the approaching quiet made it feel as if the darkness began with them. I didn't want them to see me and pitching into it, jumped back at the sight of a smiling man coming from the lake path.

'Excuse me, where are the dorms?'

He looked as if he knew something was up with me, didn't react and pointed to the left. 'Just follow the lake.'

'Thanks,' I said and three huddled-together kids ran ahead down the pitch-black path. A part of me was proud to be on my own, crunching along in my best white sneakers while another part was hyper alert.

Don't worry, I told myself. *No need to be afraid. Everyone's nice here. It's not far.* The kids' voices faded and they disappeared into the forest. I looked around, focusing on the still bushes and moon-splashed water and the smell of earth and leaves flooded through me. There was a white house in the distance through the trees and I guessed that was where the children lived.

The further I got from the auditorium the more every cell ticked with fear. A sudden breeze shook the branches and when the moon slipped behind a distant hill I started running.

'Evan, don't be stupid,' I shouted, in case there was anyone awful close by and they thought I was alone. 'It's just over there,' I said to the silence then thought I heard a moan. Heart pounding like crazy, I stopped to listen, not daring to breathe.

There wasn't a sound. I must have imagined it and with a quick scan of the bushes decided it was safe to follow the path around the bend and screamed.

It was one of those pivotal moments when every thought stops and a thousand point presence takes over and a strange calm descends. In a dream-like trance, I looked at the girl lying bleeding on the bank and screamed.

TWENTY-SIX

The familiar tie-dyed dress was dirty, stained, stuck to her body. Her candyfloss hair and face were greased with blood and her lovely brown arms and legs were limp and folded in. I knelt down and touched her cold arm. She was chilled to the bone. I pulled off my sweatshirt to wrap around her shoulders and saw one foot was in the lake. She looked dead but was breathing faintly. I yelled but she didn't open her eyes. Crunching boots sounded in the wood and Spanish voices grew louder as they drew closer.

Afraid, I got up and stood back, ready to run. Two men in workers overalls came out of the trees, took one look at distraught me then Coco on the banks of the lake, one foot in the water and a hush spread as one of the men with black curly hair and a beard ran to lean tenderly over her. He picked up her wrist to take her pulse while the other smaller man with a mystified expression, stuffed his hands down the pockets of his dungarees to fish out his phone then said something to me that I couldn't understand.

I shook my head, 'English,' and he nodded. The breeze came up. I rubbed my frozen arms. He put the phone away. There was no signal and he shouted to someone behind him. Soon there were three men in overalls talking loudly among themselves. The first gestured to one side of the lake then the other.

The smaller man raced back through the trees and I stood there while the sound of a rumbling engine started up. A tractor and trailer loaded with thick branches appeared from nowhere, mowed down bushes, flattened the grass and came to a stop.

The bearded man beckoned his friend and between them they gently lifted Coco with the sweatshirt wrapped around her, carried her to the tractor and laid her on the seat beside the driver. I followed, nervously wondering where they were going. Wanting to go with her, I tried to get up but the driver waved his hand.

'No room. Is OK.' He nodded. 'Hospital go.' The men stood back to watch the tractor roar carefully down the narrow path, crushing twigs and bushes as it passed.

The first man spoke to me again in Spanish and I shook my head, somehow holding myself together. I don't know how and he held his arms out, gesturing to show the path was safe to walk.

I stood there looking at him. He smiled. Nodded again and watched over me as I stumbled away. As soon as I was out of sight I heard the men plod back through the trees, talking all the time and ran as fast as my legs would carry me.

Evan, where was he? What did he do? Heart thumping, I almost collapsed when I reached the yellow, lit-up building.

The doors were wide open.

A radio was playing a tinny tune and a woman with a torch, clutching a towel, glanced at me for a moment, unconcerned and hurried to the showers.

I raced up the stairs. The door flew open and I crashed into Carl coming out with a sleeping bag round his shoulders.

'Hey, Marya. These are the men's dorms.'

'I know. Where's Evan?'

'No idea. What's up?'

I could hardly breathe.

'Hey. Hey.' He pulled me down beside him on the top stair. Leaned into me and covered us both in a warm, sleeping bag hug. His skin smelt of soap and the comfort of being folded and wrapped like a baby made me cry like one.

'The world looks bad sometimes but it's worth remembering we exist on another level at the same time where everything is just fine,' he said.

I didn't know what he meant but the little tent, sudden pressure of his arm and soft nylon on my cold neck and arms, made me cry even harder. He sat there patiently waiting for me to stop. Sleeping bag on my head, he peered in now and then and the pearly button on the pocket of his smart blue shirt twinkled. After a while, I don't know how long, I rubbed the tears away, wiped my face, tugged the sleeping bag from my head and looked up at his patient, smiling face.

'I found Coco by the lake,' I stuttered and his smile faded.

Breathing hard, I tried to say it all in one go. 'She was half dead. Some Spanish tree workers came and they took her to hospital in a tractor. There was no room for me.'

His eyes widened. 'Wow. What happened to her?'

'I don't know. She was unconscious, covered in blood. One foot was in the lake but she wasn't wet. At first I thought she was dead. Have you seen my brother?'

'Evan was with her, yeah?' Carl said.

'I don't know.'

'Come on.' Carl jumped up, folded and shoved the sleeping bag under his arm and held my hand to make sure I wouldn't trip as we hurried down the stairs.

Leaving the light and safety of the building for the dark shadowy night was impossible. There was a huge rock in my stomach. A hard and heavy enemy dragging me down with its weight and pausing at the door to lean on the bench by the yellow wall, I crumpled. 'Sorry. I'll have to stay here.'

'There's no signal,' Carl said. 'I can't call anyone.'

My eyes filled with fresh tears while several emotions crossed his face: sympathy, concern, affection, fear. I was grateful for all of them, wiped them away again with the back of my hand and sniffed so loudly he laughed, but he saw I had nothing left, no energy to do anything but sit and wait.

'OK, I won't be long. Here.' He wrapped the warm sleeping bag around my shoulder and took off, scooting into the darkness like a mad thing. I listened to the sound of him gravelling the empty night, and the silky cloth sank into my cold skin like warm water the closer I hugged it tight.

Evan had to come back at some point unless he'd run away or drowned himself after attacking Coco. It was him. I was sure it was him. Hardly any wonder after what he'd said in the car that day on the way to school.

I looked up at the sound of joined-at-the-hip lovers in cut-off jeans and baggy shirts walking past chatting, probably on their way to one of the tents under the trees. With sunny days in her smile, the blonde woman glanced at me. She was too happy to see through my quick grin and I was soon left behind in the wilderness, angry with myself for not looking for Evan instead of playing table tennis. Where was he? Where could he have gone?

TWENTY-SEVEN

I sat there for ages and nobody came.

Where was everyone? I stood up with the sleeping bag on my shoulder and looked around. I dug the phone from my jeans' pocket. It was 21.45 but felt more like 2am.

I walked a little way down the path towards the auditorium and as soon as the light from the yellow building faded and I was alone in the darkness with only the trees for company, I looked at the stars through the network of branches, thinking life is nothing but a scramble from one crisis to the next.

Desperate for my mum, I suddenly wanted Grandpa, too, but couldn't get hold of either without the vaguest hint of a black bar on my phone.

Grandpa, Mum's dad, is Polish. I hardly ever see him because he's always busy at his vehicle, accident and repair shop in Inverness where he lives with Tanya. They've been together for years and say they're going get married one day but probably won't. We call him Dziadzio, which is pronounced djah-djoh. Sadly, my Indian grandma died ten years ago. She was headmistress of a London primary school and very cuddly. It was Ofsted that did her in, Mum says. At least I had her until I was seven. I'm grateful for that.

Dad's family is a bit more complicated. His mother, the grandma we never met, divorced his dad early on, learned Spanish and went to live with a fruit farmer in Bolivia. No one's heard from her since and Dad and his brother were brought up by his father and step-mum in Tottenham. They emigrated to New Zealand when he was twenty-one.

Explaining my heritage is a waste of time because no one can remember a thing about it the moment I stop talking. Sleeping bag on my shoulder, terrified by what might happen next, I stood there picturing a fruit farm with apples, cherries and figs in Bolivia wishing that grandma would come back.

In the moonlight the lake was smooth molten silver, faded in places by shadows from the trees and slowed my thinking for a while. The blackness inside lifted. Perhaps Coco tripped or fainted and hit her head on a rock? Maybe Evan wasn't to blame?

I went back to the bench hugging the sleeping bag and saw the freckly woman I'd seen doing cartwheels striding out from the door in embroidered Aladdin trousers, old sandals and quilted travel bag on her arm.

She glanced at me and stopped. 'Hey, honey, you OK?'

I shook my head, fell on the bench and pulled my knees up under the sleeping bag until I looked the way I felt; a heartbroken, crumpled mess.

She stood over me. 'Lambikins, I wanna help yuuuu. I do. Only I have a free lift leaving for a flight to Gatwick soon, so tell me quickly, is it drastic?'

'No. Just a stupid boy.' I fake grinned.

She squashed her kind face into one of those 'great, I'm off the hook' looks and touched my sleeping bag arm briefly. 'We've all been there.' She winked and ran off, quilted bag bouncing from her Indian print trousers as she disappeared down the path. The same cool, Aladdin-type trousers as the ones Sanvi had on. Maybe they were the best things to wear here. Cool in daytime with only a change of belt and jewellery needed to dress them up for the evening. Perhaps I should get some but I don't have any money and they might look weird but then, nothing could be worse than the multi-pocketed horrors I live in and jeans are boring. Hardly any of the girls wear them here.

Dad would probably say it's fascinating how the healthy mind refuses to stick to worrying about horrible things for long. How the natural repair mechanism can flip from pain in the heart back to mundane obsessions and when that stops happening we must talk about it and seek help. It's something, he says, we should all be aware of and I am but there are things I still can't tell anyone.

A long corridor with closed doors started flashing through my mind. Blake's old college, empty of life with everyone inside their rooms locked in their own little bodies. With a quick shuffle I unwound myself from the sleeping bag. Someone laughed. I stood up. Trembled. Walked a few steps and listened.

TWENTY-EIGHT

The voices died away and it was back to the cool empty night. Standing there in the halo of the yellow building with sleeping bag cape round my shoulder, I must have looked like a lost camper until footsteps pounded the earth in the dark recesses behind the building and Carl broke through the light.

Resigned by now to Coco's fate, 'She died,' I said.

'She didn't?' He was shocked.

'You don't KNOW?' I said like a mad person. Eyes blazing with fury.

'Marya, calm down.' He placed firm hands on my shoulder and shook me until I started breathing normally. Only then did he let go.

'Coco's going to be all right. She's only a few miles away. I went up to the refectory and Janice phoned the hospital and talked to the doctor in Spanish for ages. Coco was covered in bruises but nothing's broken, just a bit concussed so they'll keep her in overnight.'

'Her face was covered in blood. One foot was in the lake,' I gasped.

'Yeah, it was boar's blood.' Carl raised his eyebrows. 'Janice was really surprised about that. There aren't many wild boar in this part of Spain but apparently a neighbour is trying to shoot them all. You should have seen Janice's face.'

I was mystified. 'Boar's blood?'

'Yeah,' Carl said. 'I guess they know they won't be hunted or harmed here but it sounds like one was wounded and wandered on to the path at night where Coco tried to help it. The boar panicked, knocked her sideways and she cut her head but the blood on her face was mostly from the wound on its leg.'

'One foot was in the lake?'

'Maybe she just fell that way.'

'A crime writer would describe the foot in the lake as a red herring, if it really was?' I said and he laughed.

'You are so weird, Marya.' And he gave me one of those long swinging hugs that Sanvi does so well. It went on for a long time, longer than I was comfortable with until I decided to surrender and then it was nice.

'Is Janice the woman with blue hair?' I said at last.

'Yeah, she's thirty-five. Lived here all her life.'

'Evan said she has two kids.' I stepped back.

'Little demons.' Carl laughed. 'Evan was playing computer games with them all evening and the youngest one was cheating like mad.'

'He loves kids.' I almost choked and Carl squeezed my arm.

'Now get your own sleeping bag,' he said. 'Yeah?'

TWENTY-NINE

We took our time silently walking up the hill in the cool night with sleeping bags on our shoulders until Carl said, 'How many boyfriends have you had, Marya?'

'Boyfriends?'

'Yep,' Carl said.

'Yep. OK. Well, one, sort of though not really, but then there was another one who kind of was, but I don't really count him so…'

'Colour it true, Marya,' he said. 'Otherwise how will anyone know who you are? You can say what you want here without being judged.'

'Colour it true?'

'Your life. Put the right colours in the right places for once. Is it so hard?'

'Oh. None then. Not really. I didn't once with him and then yeah, nearly with another boy but it didn't happen and you know here it's… I don't know. Here it's… Really different.'

'Hang on. You sort of had sex once and then no but have never had a boyfriend? Yeah?'

'Never, no.'

'Well, so what?' he said. 'You've got your whole life to find out who you are.'

'Suppose so.'

'I had a girlfriend when I was fourteen, yeah? But she wouldn't sleep with me, so yeah, I dumped her, got into porn – into extreme porn and became traumatised, then a neighbour saved me.'

'A neighbour?'

'Yeah. She said I needed to grow my feathers, gave me a few spliffs and what I wanted.'

'What you wanted? You mean?'

'Sex, yeah, but I was fifteen then, so shut your mouth.'

There wasn't much I could say but managed to ask, 'Why are you here a second time?'

'Huh. So like, I realised how warped my instincts were when I had that first real, loving relationship but I still push girls to give me what I want from them and I have no right to do that.'

'Is that why you undid your shirt and half unzipped your jeans?'

'Yeah. Yeah. Like I can never forget I'm male when I'm with a girl. I have to learn control and respect.'

'You could just stop being an arsehole around them.' I hoped that was the end of it and regretted agreeing to sleep under the stars with everyone tonight with even more things on my mind that I didn't want to think about.

'But I'm going crazy like we all are,' he said. 'There's no distraction from sex here.'

'Isn't that the point?'

'Yeah,' he said.

'Evan escaped,' I said.

'Nah, he'll be brought into line tomorrow. You'll see. The first week is about Blake and Sharrow figuring us out and then before you know it Arcadia's hall of mirrors opens to reflect your deepest, darkest secrets and all will be revealed.'

I laughed at that. As if...

THIRTY

There was a strong whiff of paint and the long quilted shapes of Lilla, Constanza, Tomas and Sun God were on the grass under a huge tree. Their whispers and giggles were softer than the voices coming from behind the building where Sanvi and Guthrie seemed to be enjoying themselves.

Guthrie's deep throaty laugh hit me in the gut. A reminder of what happened in the lake but if he can act like nothing took place between us, like it's so easy for him, then so can I.

Sharrow appeared from the direction of the compost loos and smiled. 'Hey, you missed loads of shooting stars.'

'Aw!' Carl was miffed.

'Have to go back for my sleeping bag,' Sharrow laughed and I wondered where she lived. Someone said the community had their own bunch of houses but where were they? What were they like? No one seemed to know.

'You heard about Coco?' she said and we nodded. 'We mustn't treat wild boars like pets. Don't worry, something like that rarely happens. The poor animal was wounded. Luckily, Coco's fine.' She hurried into the darkness without a torch and I looked up at the millions of reasons to believe there is more to life than Guthrie and the sight magnified my growing envy at the sound of him and Sanvi having fun. It was probably innocent fun but I coloured it true and when the stars told me, *Why grapple with it, Marya? Understanding guys is beyond you*, I felt free but only for a second or two.

Under the tiny light coming from inside the art building, Blake was painting the view across scrubland to the surrounding hills and waggled the tip of the brush to acknowledge us without looking over. He was painting sunlight while sitting in darkness. Painting the scene in his head, not the one in front of him and Mo, the girl with big round glasses, was meditating beside him in the lotus position. Lost in another time-space.

Only Evan was missing.

There was no room in the circle of star gazers near the tree. We could take one of the rocky humps a little way off but wouldn't be able to see many stars through the thick branches and wouldn't be part of the group.

'Here's good,' Carl said and threw his bag on the rough ground a little way behind the covered area. Dropping my bag, not too close, I kicked off the gold flip-flops and the ground was hard and cold. I glanced at the stars as if I was leaving them behind, climbed inside and felt small stones cutting into the back of my head.

I sat up, wriggled the bag further away from Carl and listened to the silence behind the building. Guthrie and Sanvi had gone quiet and I wanted the loo.

'I could do with some chocolate,' Carl said.

'Vegan chocolate?'

'Any kind.'

'There's an apple on the table.' I pointed to the bowl in the corner. 'I'll get it on the way back from the loo,' and crawled out of the warm bag, flipped on the flops and made a dash for it.

The moment I stepped into the darkness behind the building I couldn't remember where the loos were and the crackly twigs and thought of ants, snakes and spiders made me stop. The pitch-black, heavy night and glittering stars made it feel as if the rest of the group weren't a few feet away but on the other side of the earth. I was on my own and the gap between two cactus bushes that I sort of remembered from earlier looked eerie.

Tempted to shout for help, I almost ran back, yelling like a feeble idiot and my heart started pumping at the scuttling sounds coming from behind a tree. Half expecting a wild boar to appear, I came face-to-face with Guthrie.

He grabbed his neck. 'Marya, you gave me a shock.'

'Sorry, I was trying to remember where the loos are.'

'I'll show you,' he said and the second he touched my arm, I went under. Every move he made was part of me as we made for the gap between the cactus bushes, breathing in tune up the narrow track until we reached the sheds.

'I'll wait,' he smiled and I didn't know what was worse; going to the loo with him listening or walking back on my own.

Finding the loo seat in the pitch black was difficult enough with my heart half out of my body but patting the wooden walls feeling for the paper was impossible. Luckily, I had tissues stuffed in my jeans and did the slowest, quietest wee in the history of womankind. Kicked around to find the bin which wasn't there and then did the evil thing of dropping paper down the loo without a second's regret because I figured that was better than leaving it on the floor. When I pushed open the squeaking door, Guthrie was sitting on the bank a polite distance away and watched while I dipped my hands in the grey bucket of water instead of the outdoor sink that was full of grime.

I shook my hands at the night and looked at him.

'I didn't hear a thing,' he said, which made me blush even harder. 'It was you who found Coco, wasn't it?'

'Yeah, I thought she was dead but she's doing OK, Carl said,' and he wanted to know every detail. There wasn't much to tell and it took every ounce of energy to concentrate on the words instead of the fact that we were on our own again and anything could happen.

Arms folded, I gazed at the stars. Anything but him. And he sat there with his eyes on me the whole time, taking in every pause and hesitation.

Trying to avoid the microscopic attention, I looked at my feet. Was he going to unload his story? There was no chance I would. My brain was flapping around until he scrambled from the bank, wiped his hands on the side of his jeans as if he'd just washed them and smiled in a detached way like he just paid for a packet of crisps.

'We better get back or Blake will think I've kidnapped you,' he said.

The idea felt good, even better than gazing at the millions of stars up there but clearly kidnap wasn't on his mind as he marched off with me running behind, thinking I'd dreamt up our encounter in the lake. I'd blown it but how and why I didn't know. I'm possessed around him; fated, doomed and exhausted when all I want to do is lie down and kiss him.

I turned the corner and was confronted by the yellow light coming from inside the building. The wooden terrace was quiet apart from Blake, who was packing up and dropping brushes in a glass jar and he glanced at Guthrie.

'You called me a high-class English jerk the first day we met,' Blake laughed.

'You're still a jerk,' Guthrie said and walked off.

'Unlike you,' Blake said. 'You have a place to sleep?'

'Yeah, over there near Carl.' Guthrie turned to look at him.

'OK, goodnight and night, Marya,' Blake said. 'Tomorrow will be less of a free-for-all. At some point we'll hear from the community and set out some operating methods. Don't forget there's a meeting after breakfast. Hopefully, Coco will be back soon and Evan will join us.'

I wasn't really listening. I only cared about where Guthrie had gone.

'Night.' I looked at the quilted shapes under the tree who were still staring at the stars and through the open door to the kitchen I could see Sanvi, Sharrow and Mo were arranging themselves on the floor with a spare bag beside them. Was it Guthrie's?

'You were ages.' Carl turned and sat up on his elbow when I sneaked inside my bag. 'Where's my apple?'

'Oh, I forgot.'

Carl did a big extravagant wave at Guthrie over by the trees. He ignored him. I wouldn't look twice at Carl. Surely Guthrie knew that? Was that why he marched off and was a bit cross with Blake? Did he think I was playing games with him?

Already half zipped up, I was ready to climb out and get the apple until Carl said, 'Sharrow ate it. Goodnight.'

All night long the smell of roses became the perfumed shadows shuffling to the loos. Whispered conversations drifted through the lace nets of trees. The moon vanished and Guthrie's soft footsteps pattered across my heart.

THIRTY-ONE

At the beginning it was fine. The sound of cutlery crashing on wood made me glance through the open door of the ramshackle kitchen where pale hands were dropping oranges in a turquoise bowl. Blake was wiping smudges from clean plates with a damp cloth before laying them on the table. Water whooshed from the single tap and what with everyone bustling around Arcadia almost felt like a holiday for the first time.

The trouble was, I couldn't see Guthrie anywhere. Maybe he slept somewhere else?

'We need to collect the fresh bread.' Sharrow grinned and ran on down the hill with Sanvi. I wanted to help but didn't know what to do. The single shower behind the loos with only half a door wasn't an appealing way to start the day so I wandered over to Constanza, Lilla and Mo, who were clearly thinking the same thing as they rolled up their bags under the trees.

'Wash here no good,' Constanza said. 'We go?'

Still half asleep, Sun God twisted away from the girls and his bronze arm landed on the ground. Tomas opened his eyes. Looked up and closed them.

'Long. Too long way,' Lilla said. 'OK. I go.'

Adjusting her cool sunglasses, Mo took one look at her phone. 'No signal. What a surprise. Come on.'

'Wait for me.' I ran back, looked at Carl who was still fast asleep, rolled the bag and dumped it under the tree.

Halfway down the track, a red tractor disappeared into a misty hill. The distant yellow building shone like a reflection of the sun and the path smelt of manure. Despite the smell and holiday feeling I should have felt free. Instead, bits of me had been torn off by all the worry about Evan, Coco and Guthrie. The new little world was proving difficult to manage and I needed rain to fall on the dry slopes and open the earth. Charge the deep roots that were crawling around inside, searching for a place to settle and I could act good, look fine, make it seem easy – so easy it was scary. Would I? Could I really tell?

We were smiling.

I was smiling harder and eyed Constanza's blue-painted toenails when she turned to me. 'You was with Guthrie last day? You like him, I think?'

Lilla nodded and Mo hid her face by gazing at her dead phone.

I shrank back, mortified. *Am I so easy to read? Had I been staring at him? No. Where the hell did this come from?*

'It's gooood. You can sayyy,' Lilla shook her head. 'We know.'

'Sorry?' I blurted.

'They saw you in the lake,' Mo said. 'They just happened to be walking down but don't worry, nothing like that matters here. We like you. You're shy and sweet and we think you're great.'

'Thanks.' I almost choked.

'I was porn girl. Online. You don't worry nothing with me,' Lilla laughed.

'I live Italy with mother traffic sex, Romania,' Constanza said.

'Your mother was a sex trafficker?' I gasped.

'No. She was traffic.'

'Trafficked?'

'Yes, trafficked. Gang father me. But she do escape. Now is good.'

'There's an international fund to help kids affected by porn and they've paid for some of us to be here. Me included,' Mo said. 'I've tried everything to get Mum off watching porn night and day. Dad left home a long time ago and men come round the house all the time when I'm at school. I've got a sister who's always wasted and a brother who's the nicest one in the family but he moved to Swansea last year so I hardly ever see him. Thing is, I feel responsible for Mum.'

'God, that's awful,' I said.

'What's your story?' Mo said. 'Woah, wait a sec. You're thinking we look pretty normal? Listen, everyone's struggling with something. Don't bite your nails over it, Marya.'

'I wasn't,' I said and she grinned.

'Go on, we're listening.

'Evan, my brother, is addicted to porn. Mum's working in the kitchen to pay for us being here. I've always looked out for him and I guess she thinks it will help. I don't watch porn. My friend Shula says it's the same as swallowing other people's vomit so I don't really...'

Lilla was confused and Mo opened her mouth wide and did a dry retch to explain the unfamiliar word. 'Vomit,' she said. 'It's the same as chucking up.'

Constanza translated with a 'here you are' hand, and wide open mouth. 'Bleugh up.'

'Ah, vomit.' Lilla started gagging and when Constanza threw her legs around and wobbled into the hedge to bark at the ants, we laughed until our throats hurt and carried on all the way to the dorms then play-puked to death in the showers.

THIRTY-TWO

I arrived at the meeting hall rolling an orange that was breakfast in my hands, surprised to find Evan already on a chair nearest the sunlit door, staring at his phone.

There was nothing much to look at apart from a few kids and an old brown piano by the stage. The walls were empty and painted an earthy ochre that matched the views of the surrounding scrub from the windows. After worrying about where Evan had got to the previous evening, I felt resentful when I saw him.

'Where you been?' Evan said.

'Shouldn't I be asking you that?'

'I've been waiting for ages,' he moaned.

'You heard about Coco?'

'No one told me until Blake did just now.'

I couldn't help being abrupt. 'Hardly surprising, is it Evan?' He hadn't attacked Coco or been anywhere near the lake and I should have been pleased to see him but some of the hopeless feeling he was guilty, remained. 'Why you still in that old T-shirt?'

'You're the worst sister of anyone,' Evan snarled. 'I bet you think I hurt her.'

'No, I didn't.' I felt guilty for snapping at him. It wasn't the place to remind him what he said in the car on the way to school. Chairs were scraping at the front of the hall and it was getting busy so I just moved aside to let in a few older, look-alike people who had the same calm, sweet ways as the younger community members. They only had to look at Evan's angry face to see there was a problem between us.

I sat down next to him and watched a tall, plain girl with suntanned skin and highlighted blonde hair, flip open the brown piano lid, stand over the keys and play. The dazzling burst of sound was a soulful surprise that lifted the room; saturating it with memories of the same bolt to the senses I had in the lake with Guthrie.

I forgot about Evan and a dream took over of wet skin touching wet skin as the hall filled with people. Then she stopped, clunked the piano lid shut, walked away and the dream turned suddenly dull and sticky even though the door was wide open.

The room flattened without the music and I fluffed out the grey T-shirt to cool myself and spotted Guthrie with Sanvi near the stage. When he touched the side of her pretty face with the back of his hand, I died and went all-out clammy. At the far side, Mo caught my eye and smiled. She'd seen them too. Constanza and Lilla were beside her, on phones that now had signals. They hadn't noticed.

'I hate it here.' With a nasty look, Evan scrambled from the chair. It was the worst feeling when he charged off out of the door and several surprised eyes were on me when I jumped up and ran after him. I'd clean forgotten about him but soon I was right behind him, trying to grab the blue T-shirt as if he was a wild toddler. Lunging as he dodged out of the way. Stumbling when I almost got hold. All the time sweating like crazy and angry as hell.

'Evan.' I shouted loud enough for only him to hear but he took no notice. I wanted to be back with the others, listening to the talk but mainly watching Guthrie. I couldn't let Evan escape though and wasn't going to give up this time until we'd had it out.

He looked back once as I speeded up, sweat dripping but he was fast and scooted off down the dusty path, past the refectory where he almost bumped into a man with a basket of green bananas and ran on through the bushes towards the open land of the auditorium and down to the lake.

'EVAN.' Out of breath, I stopped and held onto my hips then thighs to gasp for air. My dry throat begged for oxygen. 'Please, Evan.' I swallowed and stared at the barren earth and when I looked up there he was.

'I hate you,' he said.

'What did I do?' I gasped.

'You and Mum set all this up.'

'No, we didn't.' I reached out to touch him but he jerked back. 'I wouldn't have come if I knew what was going on here. Don't be crazy, Evan, and if you think you're the one with the worst problem let me tell you, Coco was persuaded to be captured on film half naked when she was little. Yes, and it was online and that was just the beginning.'

Evan's eyes travelled over the nearby lavender bush as if expecting to find a nasty video of Coco hidden there and after squinting at the sun, his pale, spotty face kept moving over everything but me. He wouldn't meet my eyes.

'You thought I hurt her. Yeah, you did.' Then he lost it. 'You're the worst sister. You act like you know everything but you're stupid. You're nothing,' he yelled. 'You think you're someone because you read books all the time. It doesn't make you better than me. You try to fit in but you don't. You think you're special but no one likes you.'

When people yell they go all blurry. The world speeds up. I can hardly take anything in.

'You don't care,' he screamed.

'Shut the fuck up.' I was stone cold furious. 'I never said I was going to rape a girl, kill her and then kill myself.'

'No, 'cause you're perfect. Ooh, isn't Blake nice? Sanvi's so great. Isn't it lovely here? No, it sucks full of psycho fucking assholes and you're one of them.'

He stopped yelling and went back to stomping towards the lake, carrying the anger on his hunched shoulders. That was when I caught the silver light on the water shining like a billion joined up stars and a moment later I was standing next to him, calmly hypnotised.

'Constanza's mother was sex trafficked to Italy from Romania. Lilla was a porn girl. Don't know the details. I didn't like to ask. Carl had to come here for the second time because he was traumatised from watching extreme porn even after a neighbour gave him what he wanted. Everyone's a mess. If Mum knew the half of it she'd pass out and take us home.'

'You should have told me this holiday was about porn,' he said, pushing hair from his eyes.

'Mum knew. I didn't until Blake told me and you weren't around to tell, Evan.'

'Coco's OK, is she?' Evan finally squinted at me. I nodded. 'When's she coming back?'

'I don't know, Evan.' I lurched for a hug but he poked me with an elbow.

'Get off.'

I tried the patient routine. Stayed silent. Looked at him, the path, the dazzling water. 'The talk will be half over by now.'

'I don't care,' he said.

Eyes on the pale and shimmery water, it soon became hard to hold out. That kind of peace is irresistible and Evan's anger died a death when I said, 'I'm not going anywhere without you. You're my brother.'

He looked at me. I looked at him.

It worked and too hot to do anything but plod slowly, we walked over open land to the auditorium where a familiar dusty blue car came to a sudden stop. The window rolled down and a shock of thick grey hair flopped out.

'There you are. Get in. I'll take you back,' Serge said. We did as we were told and without any conversation apart from a thanks, he dropped us outside the yellow building a couple of minutes later.

Luckily the talk hadn't started and everyone was sitting around, chatting. The piano lid was still closed and the first person I noticed was Guthrie, sitting right at the front beside Sharrow with Carl and Sanvi behind. The rest of our group were scattered a few rows back.

For some reason, Tomas was sitting on his own, dressed in another worn, sleeveless T-shirt that exposed his white bony shoulders.

I grabbed two chairs nearby.

'Hi Tomas,' I said with a friendly smile.

'Hey,' Tomas nodded. 'Thought your brother went home.'

'No, Evan's here.' I nudged him to look up and Evan grunted. Wiping sweat from my face, I sighed to suggest the heat was getting to me instead of the fact that Evan was sadder than I realised. I was sad, too. My little life was a huge pretence. He was right. I wasn't any better than him just because I read books. I never thought I was and though it was obvious I wasn't perfect, I understood why he felt that way. I was never in trouble, *had* been trying to fit and was doing all right now. No one likes me? Huh. Evan's always saying that and it's something he comes out with when he hates the situation he's in and can't think of another way to attack me.

'This is going to be interesting,' Tomas said.

'What's it about?' I wondered and he laughed.

'Sex. What else?' he said and Evan's phone flew out of his hand and clacked across the wooden floor.

THIRTY-THREE

Ornate brass gong and wooden mallet held up like trophies, a tiny, blonde girl in a white sundress walked barefoot across the stage, took a deep breath and stared beyond the room as if waiting for the morning sun to rise.

The hall grew quiet.

She sighed, bowed and struck the gong.

Metal gong sounds reverberated from the stage, echoed round the walls, windows and wooden roof, filling the room until everyone was subservient to the hum.

With a slight tremor, she said, 'Thank you for being here this beautiful morning.' There was a long pause. She took a deep, satisfied breath after the important pause and bowed. 'Before we begin let's take a moment to gather ourselves in silence.'

Absorbed in the hushed atmosphere, Tomas dropped his chin. At the front, Guthrie bent his furry head so far forward I thought he was praying. Evan, like me, was wide awake in the sudden silence, watching.

Next on stage was Sharrow, smiling away in white jeans and pink T-shirt imprinted with the silver words, *Fun Forever*. She rubbed her hands together as if she couldn't wait to get going and said something to the girl with the gong who brightened then nodded.

'It's too hot,' Evan said.

He was right and I touched his warm elbow. My hand rested there for a second and he almost smiled. A kind of understanding began. The room was practically steaming. We were aliens together and I shifted around, locked into the intense expectation that something interesting was about to happen.

Sharrow raised her arms. The gong goddess smiled and left the stage to grab a chair in the front row not far from Guthrie, who glanced at her for a couple of seconds too long.

Tomas shouted. 'Yay, everyone.' I looked at him. *What was he doing?* A few embarrassed mumbles started up and Sharrow opened her arms wider.

'Hello Tomas. Good morning everyone and a big welcome to the young people who've grown up here, like Helen our gong mistress, who understands more than I do the importance of the work that's being done to heal the world. I'm sorry you won't be joining us for most of the activities but thank you for coming. It was a shame we couldn't have this talk yesterday.' Sharrow exchanged smiles with the residents and I looked at Evan who was eyeing the phone on his lap while pretending to listen.

'As you know, Arcadia is an experiment in another way of life. A way of life that respects all living things and the earth,' Sharrow said. 'We live in fast-moving times where extraordinary events are becoming normal and in between waking, dreaming, working, sleeping and internet distractions there's hardly any space left to wonder who we really are.'

Sharrow wasn't the least bit nervous. After pushing hair behind her ears she bent one knee, curled a dainty silver sandal in front of the other, walked a few steps and lifted her head with pride.

'Our summer programme for young people allows us to question ourselves, our relationships and the role culture plays in our developing sexuality, especially with regard to pornography. We'd like you to think about all these things and we'll talk more later, but for now – Tomas.'

To my surprise, the only Tomas I know jumped up, forcing me to twist out of his way. His jeans brushed mine as he shot past, ran down the aisle with everyone looking and took the steps two at a time.

Placing a protective arm on his shoulder, Sharrow escorted Tomas to a chair at the front of the stage and sat down opposite.

THIRTY-FOUR

'Before we hear from you, Tomas, it's only fair if I tell my story,' Sharrow said. A guy in the front row clapped. Guthrie turned to look at him and smiled. I wished he'd turn right round and look at me but he didn't. Instead he caught Sanvi's eye and winked. I felt on top of something until he did that. Like there was no down to this morning because I had Evan next to me and he'd said everything that was on his mind, but then I was lost again.

'I grew up on a large farm in Yorkshire where my dad works,' Sharrow said in her cute and easy Northern voice. 'The owners had horses. A massive house. Flash cars. Everything. My brother, me and my little sister lived in a small brick cottage down the lane. We had a nice life.' She smiled and Evan forgot his phone and sat up to listen.

That's what stories do; they draw you in. He was drawn and so was everyone in the hall.

'Then, when I was thirteen…' Sharrow leaned back and narrowed her eyes. 'I went for a sleepover at a friend's house and soon as the lights went out we started talking about boys, what we'd done, and all that. Only thing was, I hadn't done anything and made up a story about a cousin I hardly know.'

I caught Evan's eye. He started polishing his phone with a thumb. I was trying to hold my own, dreading what was to come.

'Desperate to catch up and belong,' Sharrow said, 'me and a friend joined a chat site. After ages talking – you know, without any weird stuff going on or anything. We knew how to play it safe. No meeting in real life and all that. Just fun. I couldn't wait to get home from school and get online and soon we were making plans we shouldn't have made. We thought it was OK by going together. We both had silly romantic ideas about a guy called Rob who biked around the countryside with his cat so then we went to meet him and a man turned up.'

Her voice dropped and I looked at Sharrow, the most beautiful woman in Arcadia, and thought this can't be right. Not her of all people.

'We knew it was wrong to get in the car but the man said he was Rob's dad and just wanted to make sure we were who we said we were, and his son was on his way home and he would take us to meet him,' Sharrow said.

A girl in front with spiky pink hair shook her head. Why would Sharrow do that when she knew how stupid it was?

'The dad seemed nice. Normal. Boring. He had a motoring magazine and bunch of supermarket tulips on the front seat. We believed him and got in the back of the car clutching our phones. There was two of us and he was just a worried dad. He looked like a worried dad. We told him we couldn't stay for more than an hour, absolutely certain we knew what we were doing.'

Evan glanced at me and I blinked, thinking Sharrow would tell us about undressing for a film like Coco, but what she said was far worse.

'The guy's wife was Susan. Big blonde hair. Pink plastic earrings. Nice cheery face. She made us tea. Her little house was in the next town to us. We didn't take any notice of the number or the name of the road. Had no idea but we weren't worried.'

Sharrow did a pretend cough for a second. It must have been hard to sit up there with only stiff Tomas beside her but she looked happy.

'The parents said the son was late. Would be back soon. Showed us photos of him when he was young. We heard the door bell a few times but took no notice. "Kids playing about," Susan said and we relaxed. There was a glass bowl of walnuts with a steel nut cracker on the shiny coffee table and really old fashioned, hand-made cushions on the sofa. You couldn't get a more ordinary front room if you tried and we were beside ourselves, so excited Rob would soon be there and we could share what happened at the next sleepover. I wanted to go to the loo but decided to wait.' Sharrow paused.

The atmosphere changed and the more Evan leaned forward to listen, the more I wanted to cover my ears from the grim consequence of her innocent desire to have something to talk about.

'We weren't expecting the door to crash open and three guys to burst in.' Sharrow's voice trembled. She leant back. Tomas reached out a hand. She took it for a second then let it drop.

We waited and my brain played out every vile situation I'd ever read about or seen in a movie. I glanced at the wide open door, the soothing sunshine on the cracked earth outside and told myself, *Sharrow's fine now.*

'Who I am is what I identify with, not what happened to me,' Sharrow said and a clap broke out, spread quickly then stopped as suddenly as it began when she raised a hand.

'They were caught when a neighbour who'd been watching the house saw everyone go in. When we didn't appear half an hour later, she phoned the police.' Sharrow paused and looked down.

'The police said they were all porn addicts. Victims of violent obsessions pushed down their throats by a billion-dollar industry. The news item forgot to mention that. At first, what got me, was the fact I peed my knickers. Then, well…'

Sometimes the world falls on your head and this was one of those times. Her words brought up the same, cold, nauseous feeling I had when I saw the picture on Evan's iPad and tipped me back into the hell of what Vernon Wood did. Ugly images pounced. How do you create a nice life knowing all this? These dangerous guys were everywhere and flickers of fear crossed Evan's face.

'We were given counselling and that set me off on a long journey.' Sharrow's sentences changed to the kind celebrities use after seeing a therapist.

'I'm in a good place now. My biggest fear was of being misled and I was helped to understand how easy it is to be duped when you're young. My ignorance at believing the guy online was the real thing, was down to my innocence. It's taken a long time to heal. I searched for information to explain why bad things like that happen and learnt violence and abuse stem from shame in perpetrators who lack self-knowledge and the inability to understand or communicate their feelings to friends or relations. Arcadia was built to create peace. Only love can destroy fear and I'm still learning how to be strong and move forward.'

I looked at lovely Sharrow, all calm and smiling on the stage and wanted to crawl out of the room and find a place to hide.

For a moment the scent of lemony perfume drifted from the woman in front who was searching her bag for tissues and I crossed my arms. Already I hated Watty and maybe Guthrie, too.

'We're talking about my past here.' Sharrow brought me round and I sat up.

'That was fourteen years ago and since then, I can honestly say, life has given me exactly what I was looking for. A loving community, fresh food, clean water, hope and plenty of love and those are the things we need to thrive. It isn't all *Lord of the Flies* on this planet. There are alternative worlds.'

She knows *Lord of the Flies?* Suddenly it occurred to me that kids have been abandoned to scavenge on a similar Coral Island in an online sea, where civilisation has broken down and evil characters play out sadistic tendencies, first in their minds and then real life.

'What stuck,' Sharrow smiled, 'was when someone told me, it's your choice to go back to that room. You don't have to. No one will make you. You're in charge of your brain.'

If Sharrow hadn't told us what happened, a brown coffee table with walnuts, embroidered cushions on a sofa and smiling wife with rosy cheeks in possibly a flowery dress with puffy sleeves, wouldn't be neon lit in my mind. Lit up before suddenly darkening with ugly men rushing through the door. Only it wasn't Sharrow sitting on that sofa, it was me. The scene was so real.

'We all have challenges. They won't end. We're here to learn,' Sharrow said. 'But when we are able to take charge of our emotions, not one minute of any day will be spent thinking about things we don't want in our lives. Tomas, are you ready to say a few words?'

'Yeah, hi. Er yeah. I was like — I said before that — yeah, so all I think about is sex. Told everyone, you know and that was it. What I thought, anyway. Then me and Blake and Carl went down by the lake. Right, and it was bad saying how porn makes me feel better when I'm worried about something and after what Sharrow said, I'm like, sad.' He looked at Sharrow and she smiled as if to say, *Go on. It's fine.*

'We like talked about all the ways we're pulled into this stuff, can't let go and... Blake, said it was like... I don't know how to... Sorry... Sharrow? Sorry. I can't.'

'There's no need to apologise, Tomas. No reason to stress. OK, I want you all to follow me.' Sharrow stood up and marched proudly from the stage with him shuffling behind.

The rows emptied one by one and soon everyone was outside, burning to know what would happen next.

THIRTY-FIVE

It was a relief to be outside. Birds chirped. The world felt clean and I almost had to cover my eyes from the glare of the bright yellow sun. The bushes smelt of flowers and before we went anywhere, Mo and Lilla ran to the compost loos behind the building. We waited and our flip-flops were covered in dust by the time they came back.

Mo touched my arm, prescription sunglasses bobbing and I looked back at Evan when she said, 'You're the mysterious brother then? What do you think is happening?'

'We're going for a sauna,' Evan said which confused her while I shuffled around, eager to get moving before he changed his mind and disappeared.

'He's joking,' I said and Mo lost interest and turned to ask Constanza the same question.

She didn't seem as troubled as I was by Sharrow's story and patted my shoulder. 'Don't be sad.'

Her sweet smile pulled me back to myself and I nodded. 'I'll try.'

Cliques broke out everywhere as we set off. Wearing backpacks, Blake and Carl were clutching glass bottles of water, weaving along together, deep in conversation.

Practically joined at the hip, Guthrie and Sanvi were side by side with Sun God not far behind.

Sharrow and Tomas were up ahead, and I was stuck with Evan who showed no interest in anything. Resigned to walking on a hot, barren, wifi-less track with his sister until something better came along.

It felt like the whole universe was involved with itself – except for me. I was outside of the world, avoiding the sun by keeping to the side of the path in the shade of the trees, desperate for more of the sudden breeze.

There was a lull when we turned off the unknown wiggly track and I looked for clues to where we were going. With nothing but trees, bushes and another path, it was hard to tell.

Eventually Sharrow glanced at Blake and he pointed to a far hill. We set off again in the same cliques and after a while came across the least likely building in Arcadia; a tiny, ancient, stone church half hidden by trees and grass with an old blue caravan on bricks to one side. It felt like a long time since anyone breathed life into the scene.

Blake signalled us to keep moving. I was disappointed. I wanted to open the wooden church door and peer through the stained glass windows but we kept trudging along. It was hard to make out why the blue caravan was parked there. It looked uninhabited. The side was dented and smeared with dirt. Who put it on bricks?

We followed Blake. Carl passed the water to him and he took a sip, handed it back, and that was that. Turns out there was once a small hamlet here, I heard Sharrow telling Tomas, but the dwellings are long gone.

'I remember reading seventeenth-century man had to recall in a lifetime what our brains hold fast in a single day what with passwords, pin codes, keys, bus routes etcetera,' I said to Evan.

'Well, life was simpler back then wasn't it?' he said and we both smiled. We were back to normal and it felt good. I wondered what it must have been like to already know someone's family rather than scroll through online existences for information that might not be true.

My life was wrapped up in school, exams, buses everywhere without ever walking across a field, glancing at a lake or coming across a crumbling church unless I was reading about them. A slow getting to know a guy who I was likely to come into contact with for the rest of my life was impossible to imagine. Knowing Watty forever? Now that would be weird.

Arcadia was a step back in time physically with no busy streets, crazy traffic, scary corners, neon signs, mad people, loud music, screeching sirens, the list was endless but the harshness of the porn industry was here too because Sharrow and Blake live among these quiet hills. Being forced to hear vile things made me want to escape to a more understandable age. But then, William Golding who wrote *Lord of the Flies* and was born more than a hundred years ago, admitted in his memoir that when he was an eighteen-year-old student at Oxford he tried to rape a girl of fifteen who fought him off. He misinterpreted what was written on her 'desirable mouth.' So maybe things haven't changed that much.

I remember Shula telling the class that Golding, who was in the Royal Navy during WWII, said he might have been a Nazi if he'd lived in Germany then.

'You won't find that in the SparkNotes,' she said. 'But I think he was saying we are all products of our culture.'

*

We came to a shady area smelling of freshly cut grass and a rambling, grey shack with neat pots beside a red door which wouldn't have been out of place in one of the posh gardens at a flower show. Nothing like the frail, shadowy church and caravan, the shack was pretty but had no long, lonely history and I wanted to go back and explore.

Blake dropped his back pack and sat down. We found spaces and gathered round him in a wide circle on the neat grass.

Aware that Guthrie was shuffling for a seat under the tree, I made sure he was out of my eye-line and positioned myself opposite Blake. Evan brightened for a moment when Sharrow plonked herself next to him and said, 'I've had enough walking for today. How about you?'

'Yeah,' he said and they started talking about sandals versus sneakers when your feet are boiling hot. Sanvi gave me a little wave. I waved back, leaned on my elbows, squinted at the pure blue sky and kept calm by taking a few, gong-mistress-type, slow breaths.

Everything kicked off when Blake said, 'As you know Tomas is desperate to have sex for the first time. That's normal. What's unusual is Arcadia acts on those kinds of desires. Remember, we're doing heart work here.'

Arcadia acts on those kinds of desires? We're doing heart work here? What the hell does that mean? A familiar panic started up. My throat went dry and I didn't dare wonder what was going through Evan's head.

'I've shocked you, haven't I?' Blake said and Sharrow smiled. Whatever it was, they were in it together.

'It's good sometimes to be shocked.' Sharrow knew exactly where this was heading and by their faces no one else did apart from Tomas.

'We believe that when one person is healed the whole world is also healed,' Blake said. 'Physics is catching up with the idea that the insights of sages, shamans, seers and prophets recorded in well-known works since the beginning of time, are correct. The reality of our everyday lives is a metaphysical experience and the micro affects the macro at every level. Our existence is just one realm of a multidimensional reality.'

Hang on. Hang on. My brain was spinning. We didn't study this in physics at school. We did electricity, atomic structure, forces and waves, magnetism and electromagnetism. There wasn't any mention of sages, shamans, prophets or multidimensional reality.

Time was ticking, thoughts flying. Blake paused, looked at each of us then turned back to Tomas.

'We're here today because Tomas is going to have his wish fulfilled.' Evan nearly fell off his chair.

THIRTY-SIX

T hin, pale Tomas doesn't have a happy-go-lucky bone in his body. When he tries to fake normal, it proves what a damaged soul he is and chewing his lip and staring at Blake, it was clear he was terrified.

The moment Blake said Tomas was going to have sex for the first time, the thought he was going to do it in front of everyone shot through my mind and when I glanced at Guthrie grinning his head off, it was doubly worrying.

Sanvi rested her head on his shoulder, closed her eyes and entered one of her dreamy trances. He touched her shiny black hair for a moment, all loved up, and my heart sank like a stone. Trying not to wind myself up, a squirming feeling told me Guthrie would never be together with Sanvi like that if there was actually something going on between them. All warm, easy and unconcerned, they were friends but the sight still hurt.

Tomas's new life had been arranged. We were shocked and fell silent. Everyone but Sanvi who turned away from Guthrie with a serene smile and started chanting long, delicate notes that echoed the movements of her fingers playing with the grass.

Tomas was about to have sex for the first time and the soft sounds Sanvi made were so far from the belting drunk songs in Lewisham on a Friday night, it was easy to believe that life here really was happening on another realm of a multidimensional reality.

Poor Evan twisted around. He didn't know what to do with himself and I ached all over for him. The thought that maybe sex was a rite of passage for teenage boys in Arcadia opened my blinkered eyes. Why do we get in such a state about sex? That's how we all got here. In ancient times sexuality was celebrated by certain tribes who shared the transition from child to adult. I'd seen a few of those documentaries but couldn't recall which tribes and what programmes. Would Blake have been obsessed with porn if his natural desire had found an outlet?

I found D.H. Lawrence's letters in the local library a couple of years ago and there was a whole thing about cruelty being a form of perverted sex and celibate priests going insane without women, hence the Spanish Inquisition. Lawrence said something about herded-together soldiers not getting satisfaction from sex and how frustration gets into their blood and makes them love cruelty. It made sense. In another bit he went on about women not being seen for who they are, only projections of what men imagine them to be. I read most of Lawrence's novels after that but didn't talk to anyone about them except Shula. We both agreed it was hard to find the sex passages in *Lady Chatterly's Lover* and they turned out to be so funny we couldn't stop laughing.

'I want to live my life so that my nights are not full of regrets.' Shula quoted Lawrence on the bus like she was hogging a stage. It was packed with kids eating crisps at the time. An old lady started coughing in my ear. We became obsessed with Lawrence and yearned for feelings we'd never had, desperate for experiences to fit into poems that needed no explanation. Our lives felt second hand. We knew we were missing out but it was good to know Lawrence was once a teacher in Croydon before he met Frieda and took off on his travels because of bad health.

With the sun pinging my head, I patted the prickly grass and waited for Blake to speak which he didn't for ages and then he got up and gestured to Tomas. 'Ready?'

The heart work was about to begin. Arcadia was acting on his desires and we were the witnesses. It was exciting. There was no way this would ever happen in Hilly Fields.

Mo slowly took off her sunglasses to polish in her T-shirt. Everything about her was the opposite of hectic and I wondered what it was like to have a mother who's into porn. It would be impossible to guess her home life by looking at her lumpy, creased, orange shirt and old-fashioned denims with the white pockets hanging out.

Holding her knees, Sharrow broke into a series of hums that blew under the breeze. The sinister, unspeakable crime of being assaulted at thirteen in a small town sent the gut-wrenching sound straight to my heart. Lost in her power, Constanza joined in, voice in perfect tune. Sanvi chanted as she swayed and their eyes became fixed on Blake and Tomas as they walked side-by-side towards the bright red door of the rambling shack.

When Tomas went inside – all I got then was massive relief.

Warmth poured from the group. 'Yay, we love you, Tomas,' someone yelled.

I leaned over to nudge Evan but he was flat out pretending to be asleep.

Blake soon came back, crossed his legs as he slid down on the grass and began chanting, too, adding a deep bass to the lightness of Sharrow, Sanvi and Constanza's voices. In a kind of love group, they wooed each other by trying out new sublime sounds.

Blake did something different with his voice and it was breathtaking. Beautiful. If only I could sing but my eyes caught the slow collapse of Sanvi and Guthrie backwards into the long grass and it killed the urge. Deadened the sound. Cut the connection.

I untangled a bunch of tiny, wild strawberries behind me and sat there, not daring to eat one. Not daring to wonder how it would feel to be able to let go like that.

THIRTY-SEVEN

I don't know how long we stayed there. It could have been an hour. Sanvi and Sharrow chanted and sang for most of the time. Intricate songs that Blake rowed along with in a deep bass voice while Constanza dipped in at will, patting brown knees to the beat.

The more their enthusiasm increased, the sooner they became experts at getting a better performance from each other. Everyone on the grass was soon sung into silence and we sat rocking, loving it all, glancing at the still red door of the rambling shack, thinking about Tomas inside. Doing it.

When the door opened, Janice, the woman with blue hair, appeared with a big grin. 'He's a bag of bones, that poor boy,' she said and we smiled. A bit shocked.

A squealing celebration broke out when Tomas showed his sheepish face. Mo and Lilla rushed to throw their arms around his skinny shoulders then Janice, each other and on and on until everyone got up and did the same.

Warm hands on my back, whiffs of moist perfume, softness everywhere, only Evan, on his stomach in the grass, remained untouched. Guthrie stayed where he was, arms locked around Tomas until Sanvi floated back from hugging Carl and slung a hand on Sharrow's shoulder. Cool as ever.

As the hug moved from person to person, I was all eyes and though I didn't have to look at Guthrie to know what he was doing, it was the hardest thing to pretend I didn't care.

Someone said something about swimming in the lake. Lilla and Constanza ran off to get their things followed by Mo, sunglasses on her head, Carl laughing alongside until he saw me watching.

'Hey, Marya. Up for it?'

Evan did a superb act of a kid just waking up and rolled over, all bleary eyed while me and Carl swung around in a crazy hug-cum-dance thing that made us both giggle.

'The lake, yeah?' Carl said.

'Have to get my stuff.' I pointed at the path. He let me go and ran backwards, looking at me the whole time. Arms out like he couldn't wait to hug me again.

'We're going,' I told Evan.

'Go on then.'

'Come on, Evan. Please.'

'No.' His jeans were splattered with grass and I grabbed his crumpled T-shirt and tried to drag him up.

Evan wriggled at every attempt I made to tickle his neck.

'Tell Blake you're desperate for sex like Tomas,' I whispered. 'Then he can sort it out.'

Evan spun round, shocked. 'So Tomas took his clothes off and did it with Janice. How amazing? No. See, I want more than that.'

Maybe it was my turn to be shocked because I was like, 'But, hey…' The idea of Evan opening his soul to a girl hadn't occurred to me. 'You said you wanted to…'

'That was before,' he said.

It was so hot, my flip-flops stuck to my feet. 'Before the stories?'

Evan wrinkled his eyes from the sun. 'What does it matter?' and loosened his T-shirt from the sweat patches on his back. 'I don't fancy swimming,' he said and walked off.

There was no choice but to watch him closely as I followed him along the track to the dorms, seriously doubting he was telling the truth. Was this his way of distracting attention from what he said in the car on the way to school? Does he really want a genuine relationship or was he just trying to fit in? Confused wasn't the word, I was utterly baffled and then I thought, maybe he's just plain scared.

THIRTY-EIGHT

The last person I expected to run into back at the lockers was Coco.

'Hi, English girl.' Apart from a few bruises on her right leg, she'd recovered quick as anything and threw her arms round my neck in a good, wild, hug. 'How's your brother doing?'

'Coco. Wow. You look great. Don't go wrestling boars again. We missed you. Evan's being moody.'

She threw a chintzy blue dress over the tiny, crocheted, apricot bikini she was almost wearing and laughed. 'I won't and I like moody boys.'

'Is Guthrie moody?' Untangling the high-neck, navy two-piece I'd pulled out of the locker was stressful with Coco standing there looking fantastic but it was easy to disguise how interested I was in the answer by attacking the knotted straps.

'Forget about Guthrie, English girl. One tussle with a wild boar is enough. Where did you get that thing from?' My costume was out of my hands in a flash and she held both pieces up to the skylight with utter contempt.

'Mum got it from the market.'

'Gross.' She flung it into the middle of the dark, muddled dorm, opened her locker and pulled out a strapless white bikini with acorns of covering too small for a five-year-old.

'God, no. I can't. No, really.'

'Suck on it,' she ordered.

There are people you can argue with and get them to change their minds but Coco wasn't one of them. She stood there in her skimpy, chintzy dress over stitched commas of a bikini until I gave in by squeezing into the tiny, white top. I insisted on foraging the dorm for the comfy bottoms of my two-piece which I wore instead of the embarrassing white string she swung at the room with one finger. We'd both given in and when I was ready she looked at me and nodded.

'That's better, English girl.'

*

Down at the lake, Guthrie was half submerged and waved. 'Hey, Coco. You're good now?'

She smiled. 'Was I ever bad?'

Like a bullet straight to the heart, he swam off without noticing me and I dragged my T-shirt over my head and bared my weird costume to the world with a pitiful look on my face. I know it was pitiful because Coco made a weird smile to demonstrate how easy it was to change my appearance just by moving my lips.

Swimmers were dotted about the silver-streaked lake and I squinted to pick Evan out. His familiar floppy hair caught my eye. He was treading water, talking to Blake, part of the group at last which made me feel slightly better. On tip-toes over the hot earth, Coco hugged my shy body to the water's edge and I fell into the safety of the lake, surrounded by sunbeams and bobbing heads. Then a whole Arcadian family swam past.

Coco splashed for a while before plunging to the middle where Carl and Tomas were upending each other. All bright and laughing, Tomas was going bright pink. Sex wasn't the only thing on his mind anymore and he looked happy instead of wounded and overwhelmed.

I couldn't see Sanvi. She must have been one of the swimmers on the far side. The combination of cool water, hot sunshine, smiling faces and Guthrie swimming in front of me made me feel anxious, as if he was mocking me by ignoring me.

When I finally roused myself to paddle to the edge and get out, it was easier to turn my back on the lake, slip into the sliding flip-flops and cross the hot track with the T-shirt stuck to my wet skin than it was to stay drowning in emotion in the water.

After spending the rest of the day reading *The Mill on the Floss* on the bench outside the dorms in my comfy jeans and fresh, white T-shirt, I saw Coco and Evan walking up the path hand in hand. His T-shirt was off and he looked manly for the first time in his life.

I made a dash for the loos. I don't think they saw me. Lurking at the sinks with the book under my arm, it was a while before I could take enough gigantic breaths to calm down and walk back. Were they together or just friends?

When I trudged back, the bench was empty and they were nowhere to be seen. I sat down and flipped open the book.

Glad to be alive at this time in history and not when *The Mill on the Floss* was written, I wondered how Maggie Tulliver, the girl in the story, would get on in Arcadia and realised I was like her in a way, always wishing I'd done something different.

I should have stayed in the lake and had fun. Should have sung my heart out with the others earlier. Should have brought the blue, floral dress Dad got for my birthday that I refused to wear because I guessed Shell had chosen it – and what about the new white leggings and navy cut-offs? They would have been perfect for this place.

Watching and waiting, book on my lap, Evan appeared, bare chested in denims, hurling a towel over his head on the way to the showers.

'Yoh.' He tried to high five me which he hasn't done for years.

'Yoh, you,' I said. 'Where's Coco?'

'Asleep on the grass. Why aren't you at the picnic by the lake?'

'I didn't know there was one,' I said.

'It was brilliant. Don't like that Carl guy though.'

'Why? What did he do?' I said.

'He's got a stupid pony tail for starters and acts special but he's nothing.'

'I like Carl a lot,' I said.

Evan shrugged, waved the towel in his hand like he was making music and it took a minute to realise it was me who was lost for words. He was happy. Really happy. Why?

THIRTY-NINE

Bare chested in his denims, Evan soon got tired of sweating around and slipped away for a shower.

People passed by. I checked my phone. It was 16.45 and I'd missed lunch. No wonder my stomach was rumbling, I only had an orange for breakfast. Tempted to go to the refectory, wait for food and collect my messages, I got up and realised how thirsty I was. Then something really wild happened: the gravelly ground and wall swayed and I knew I would fall before it happened.

Tiny brown stones wobbled as they reached up, shrouded faces bent over me, making noises and I was yanked into a sitting position. Weak head forced between my knees.

'She fainted,' someone said. A woman leaned perilously close, soft shoulder pressing in to suffocate me even more. 'Isn't it wonderful how the body falls naturally to protect itself?'

What?

Another person touched my back but I couldn't lift my head to see who it was. 'Any better?'

I shook my lolling head. It was impossible to breathe with hair in my face, hemmed in on all sides. Too dizzy to answer, they heaved me from the ground, sat me on the bench and someone held a glass of water to my lips while another flicked gravel from my arms and legs.

I didn't recognise any of them while moving my floating mouth to take a few sips.

'She's as white as a ghost,' a woman said and her words flashed my own pale face in front of my own half-closed eyes. Out in the world that face was, while I sat there behind it.

'Best let her recover in peace,' a voice said. Some of them walked off. Bits of me tingled as I took sips of water and the dusty cover of the book by my feet, shook. I wanted to rescue it but couldn't.

In my mind I was guilty of something. I wasn't sure what and said, 'Sorry,' and a woman laughed.

'Don't be silly. It's not your fault. Perhaps you should have a lie down?'

'Yeah,' I said. 'Thanks. I'm OK now.'

Just then Evan appeared on the way back from the shower with the damp towel around his neck and dropped the bombshell. 'You've gone all white.'

'She fainted,' the woman said. 'Did she have lunch?'

Evan had no idea. His bare, red back, fell down next to me on the bench. He actually looked concerned when I shook my head.

'I'll walk up there with her and get something. Our mum works in the kitchen,' he said.

The woman nodded. 'Right, well, look after her. Take care, love.' She picked up the book, brushed off the dust with veiny brown hands, placed it on the bench and walked off all matter-of-factly.

'Why did you go and faint?' Evan said.

'I wanted to create a scene and get some attention,' I whispered and he laughed.

'Finish the water. Have you gone anorexic or what?'

'Funneee.' I managed to smile. 'I was reading and lost track of time. You don't have to worry about me.'

'I wasn't.'

'Why the face then?' I wobbled, not up to arguing just yet.

Stretching his legs, he looked at his jeans. 'Since we came here you've been acting like someone weird. Instead of jumping around criticising everything and being in charge, you're all nervous and quiet like something's bugging you.'

'You better put a T-shirt on,' I said. 'You're getting burnt.' I got up then fell back down, still slightly dizzy.

'Tell me or I won't ever speak to you again,' Evan said.

'Yes, you will speak to me again.'

'No, I won't.'

Just say anything, I told myself and looked out at the melting into the horizon, blue hills that were filled with dreams from the book on my knee. Inconsequential passages packed with sentences worth examining had pushed me out of my bones and away from the world around me because I'd forgotten to eat or drink anything. The story was still swimming around my head, but he was right, there was a lot more going on than that.

'I'm figuring out where I am in all this,' I said. 'Don't know yet.'

'As long as you're all right.' Evan stood up. 'Won't be a minute.'

We smiled at each other. I didn't dare mention Coco.

He went, and I stared at nothing until he came back wearing a blue shirt and jeans I'd never seen before. His face was turning brown and with shiny hair flopping over his eyes, he looked good apart from one tiny spot on the side of his nose.

'You can leave that there.' He pointed at the book. 'No one will touch it.'

FORTY

Book under my arm, we arrived at the kitchen half an hour before dinner and the industrial room with shiny trolleys and sinks was empty apart from four, covered metal containers on hotplates ready to be taken outside.

Evan was brave enough to open the silver fridge and I lifted the steaming lids of the containers with an aching stomach. Quinoa and roasted vegetables again plus tofu stew and something that looked like sweet potatoes but could have been baked squash.

'Hey, you two,' Mum came through the door. 'Nicking food now, are we?'

'Marya fainted because she missed lunch,' Evan said.

'No, it was because it was hot and I forgot to have water,' I sneered.

'You look OK, Marya. Are you?' Mum said and I reassured her, helped dish up food and we all sat together on the bench nearest the kitchen door which was nice until Serge turned up and Mum blushed. Right in front of us he lifted her chin and gave her a quick fleshy kiss on the lips, hovered while we peered at our plates and no one said a word, not even Mum.

Chewing on roasted sweet potato which is dry at the best of times with Serge standing over us was close to impossible, especially when he said, 'By the way, I'm in charge of taking care of your electronics for a while. If you want to hand them over now, I can take them?'

No 'hello' or 'how's it going?' Only, 'I like your mum. I hope you noticed. Give me your stuff.'

'How am I going to know what time it is?' I said and thought by his weird behaviour he might be joking, but he was deadly serious and so was I. Who owns a watch these days? No one I know. 'You can't have it yet.'

Evan shook his head. 'There's no way I'm giving up my phone.'

'He also has an iPad with him,' Mum said and we gave her disbelieving looks that were shot through with deadly warnings of hysterical yelling which she ignored.

'It's only for a few days,' Serge said. 'Part of the course is to limit access for a little while. Most don't mind.'

'We'll do it later,' I said and fished out my phone to see five messages. Three from Dad about work and the lack of contact with Evan. One from Shula and another from Watty whose words I read first.

'When you back?' he said. How did he know I was away? Maybe Shula told him.

A minute later I'd told Dad all was well, it wasn't too hot and I'd ask Evan to talk to him then stared at the screen for the same amount of time to read Shula's long message which I replied to by saying, 'Yeah, I'm going to read Daniel Deronda next, too.'

Just thinking about Watty was enough to divert my attention from Shula's praise of the novel and in the end I told him, 'Not for a while. Why?'

'You see how connected they are to their phones,' Mum said.

'Ah, but they will hand them over. Everyone does,' Serge smiled.

'I'm not,' Evan said. Serge didn't believe him and stood there waiting while Mum fiddled in her bumbag, got out a purse, clicked it open, rattled a few coins and shoved it back. She didn't know how to handle the four of us being together. None of us did, hence the awkwardness.

'To get the best from Arcadia, it is good to go along with the things Blake and Sharrow have planned,' Serge said. 'But no one will force you.'

My intention was to give him the phone after Watty replied but that could take ages and I couldn't think of anything worse than not knowing what he said. I mean, why does Watty want to know when

I'm back? Was he missing me? Is he just playing games? I had to find out.

'OK, we can leave the phones until later. I must go and pick someone up from the station. Do you want to come, Tessa?' Serge said.

'I said I would.' Mum collected up our plates. 'Take them back to the kitchen, will you, Marya? I'm off this evening.'

I nodded. 'No problem. See you later,' and they left.

'Give it him? That's never going to happen,' Evan said. 'Grandpa paid for my phone and he ain't getting it.'

I felt suddenly guilty for standing by Evan. Perhaps it was best if we handed them over? Soon the eating area filled up and the man with long hair and huge silver earring and an old lady in baggy black trousers carried the metal containers to the wooden table and began serving food to the patient queue.

We sat there, staring at our phones until finally I gave up waiting for Watty to reply, dumped the plates in the kitchen and Evan followed me down the steps to the track and along the path to the lake with the phone pressed to his cheek.

When we got there the scene was straight out of a French painting of a picnic. Sun God and Tomas in blue swimmers were on their knees packing water bottles into a cooler. Carl was folding a red, checked, cotton cloth. Mo was busy stacking empty containers in a huge basket and all that was missing was the cheese and red wine.

By the sounds coming from behind the bushes, Lilla and Constanza were changing and I wanted to give the idyllic scene a little pat. It was so perfect.

'Hey guys, you missed a great lunch,' Mo said.

'Evan told me.' I nodded and Guthrie caught my eye and quickly turned away. With his back to me, he gazed at the water, arms around Sanvi and Sharrow and there was something secret about the way they were talking. I looked at them as if through a sheet of glass. They were out there like the hint of a perfect moon and I was a long,

long way away. Part of a distant, cloudy world.

In the mood for fun, Carl darted for Evan. 'You missed the tickling game.' And ran his fingers up and down Evan's neck. Elbowing him off, Evan stood his ground for a few seconds until Carl pounced, grabbed his phone and ran for the hills like an Olympic sprinter.

FORTY-ONE

It was quite funny watching Carl bolt. He kept turning back to see if Evan was going to run after him and from where we were standing the ridiculous figure racing down the hill and disappearing round the bend clearly had something to prove.

Disbelief tore across Evan's face but he stayed cool, sighed, looked at me and said, 'He doesn't know where my iPad is.'

For the first time since I'd been anywhere near the lake, my phone pinged and I almost missed the sound because it was barely audible.

'Who's that?' Evan said and I read out the message from Mum.

'Tell Evan I found his iPad and have given it to Serge. Sorry, but something had to be done about his unwillingness to take part in the course. Carl said he'd get his phone and give it to Serge which is why I'm messaging you instead of Evan. I know you'll give yours in. Tell Evan his hasn't been stolen.'

Evan clenched his teeth, eyes blazing with fury but with Blake looking, was too humiliated to react and turned to gaze at a clump of bushes beside the lake. After a rabbity twitch, he stuffed his hands down his pockets in a complete temper.

'Have a go at Mum if you want?' I said and held out my phone but Evan carried on stewing.

In yellow surfer shorts and torn vest, Blake was soon there with his hand out. 'Thank you, Marya.' Stupid me, I should have hidden it but why should I care what Watty has to say, and handed over my phone without a word and not too much regret.

'This is difficult, we know,' Blake said and on that basis Evan could have freaked out for all our sakes and everyone would have understood but he acted as if nothing could have disconcerted us less. Either Blake was going to stand there forever when I nodded instead of making a big deal, or give up and walk away which he didn't.

'These things are hard at first,' Blake said and I stuck it out by not answering. Evan gave him the usual silent treatment. There was a real chance the stand-off would last until the stars came out but it was getting chilly and Blake's concern suddenly cooled.

He tapped his surfer shorts pocket with my phone and said, 'There's a meeting at the art building in half an hour. See you there.'

We could have stayed looking at the fading light on the lake while everyone moved off with towels and baskets on their arms but instead followed them up the hill at a brisk clip.

'He's got no right to take our stuff,' Evan said.

'Too late. You should have spoken to Mum when you had the chance.'

'That Carl's got it coming to him,' Evan snarled.

'He was trying to help,' I said. 'Being without electronics might just change your life.'

'What about yours?' he said.

'Yeah, mine too, Evan.' And when I looked up my stomach turned over. Guthrie was way in front laughing with Sharrow but she soon fell behind to chat to Mo who adjusted her sunglasses to take in the glittery athletic body beside her in denim cut-offs and waspy T-shirt. Mo was genuinely stunned by her. It wasn't the reaction Sharrow was expecting and she started skipping along like a child. It was strange to watch her becoming younger while Mo turned into a frowning old lady.

Guthrie had gone on ahead and missed Sharrow skipping which was a relief. He caught up with my phone pinging away in Blake's pocket and I hoped the messages were from Dad and not Watty.

I was annoyed. Arcadia was just like primary school. Girls on one side of the path, boys on the other and I wanted to be anywhere but trudging along with slow, miserable Evan.

'That's my phone ringing,' I said.

'Too late,' Evan said. 'What's the meeting about?'

'To discuss the secret of dark matter.'

'No, it isn't,' he said.

'Did you know there's a theory that dark matter turns into dark energy? It's to do with gravity and the nature of space. Do you think lightness happens by accident?'

Evan sniffed. 'I prefer darkness.'

'No, you don't,' I said.

'I'm sure I said I did? Yep, I did.'

There was no light in my brother's brain but I tried.

'Hey, I didn't tell you Coco said I could stay with her in New York where she has an apartment. When we get back I'm going to ask Grandpa to buy me a ticket if I do well in my exams next year.' Something I'd been thinking about since Coco made the offer.

'Huh. She doesn't have an apartment in New York,' Evan said. 'Who would believe that?'

'She does.'

'You might be good at exams but really you're stupid.' Evan said. 'Yeah, you are. OK, so why did Blake say she was picked up living on the streets, taken in by a homeless charity who gave her a room and she begged to come here for respite to give her dreams a chance to flourish?'

More confused than usual, a frantic search began for reasons to convince myself he was wrong. Didn't the teachers say I had a good brain? Wasn't brilliant Shula a friend? Why would Coco lie about the apartment in new York? And why did I believe her?

'Mum says you look at the world through rose-tinted spectacles.' Evan's jaw tightened as if there was more but he wasn't going to reveal the details. 'Don't know why she said spectacles instead of glasses but that's exactly what she said. Yeah, and it's probably because the winery is full of hipsters in skinny jeans who talk like that all the time. Pass my spectacles, Lucien.'

'Stop being a know-all,' I said.

'Have to be with you for a sister. Who would fall for that?'

'So you really think I'm stupid?'

'Yeah, but don't beat yourself up. Coco was like, "Oh Evan we're going to be friends for the rest of our lives," but then said she'd rather be dead. See? We don't really know her.'

'She's had a hard time.'

'Yes,' Evan said.

'Blake told you she lived on the streets.'

'Yeah,' Evan said. 'Remember that time we slept on a railway bench when we missed the train coming back from Grandpa's?'

'Evan, that was years ago and lasted an hour. Poor Coco ate, slept, washed, did everything on the streets of New York and it was probably winter and she had no coat or warm shoes and was ignored by everyone walking by. No wonder she's not happy.'

'I'd love to do that.'

'Evan.'

'I would.

'Since when?'

'Not saying.'

'Is there anyone here you like?' I said.

'Yeah, but I'm not telling you.'

'OK, I'll guess. Constanza?'

'Shut it.' Evan narrowed his eyes and went into that dark place he goes to when he doesn't want to answer.

FORTY-TWO

The chilly evening and glow of yellow light on the wooden terrace lifted the surrounding green bushes and trees into a night time, hazy softness. We settled on the wooden floor at the side of the group circle and suddenly Carl came out of the shadows with Coco. Walking freely along, dragging an old blanket, she slung it over her shoulders and flopped down next to Guthrie.

Carl gave us a brief wave.

Evan frowned.

I smiled.

Guthrie nodded and I looked away.

'The consequences of our culture's addiction to porn hasn't been evaluated.' Blake woke us all up. For some reason he directed the words at Sharrow sitting opposite and her relaxed smile grew bigger as we listened.

'The dehumanising effect can't be underestimated,' Blake said.

A few people nodded and I glanced at Evan who leaned back on his elbows to gaze at the darkening sky.

'We're talking about a form of propaganda that's used by aggressors to make big money,' Sharrow said in borrowed speak.

'Good point.' Blake went on. 'When we become aware that females in porn lack any human qualities and the men who watch it when questioned say their girlfriends, wives, mothers, sisters are different, they fool themselves into believing the performers are doing it because they love it, rather than because they lack financial alternatives. The language used to describe them gives the game away.' He paused and looked at Sharrow.

'It's been proved that men who watch porn lack the respect that comes from understanding females they're not related to or going out with,' she said and we all looked at her. 'We're going to play a little game now.'

We are?

'This is going to be fun,' she said and reached for the brown bag at her feet and took out a bundle of bright scarves. 'We'll start with the guys,' she said. 'Please stand in the middle.'

Were we going to play hide and seek?

First up was Tomas, followed by Sun God who coughed briefly. Carl didn't know what to do when he got there and Blake gestured to Guthrie to hurry up. Faintly surprised by the we-know-nothing, lost guys standing in the middle of the circle waiting for instruction, Guthrie joined them with an 'everyone's looking at me and I don't care because I'm the master of the universe', kind of way. Then Evan got up and Carl waved him over to stand beside him with a huge, friendly gesture. Adding drama to the drama because much as he disliked him Evan couldn't refuse.

'Make sure you can't see.' Sharrow handed out the scarves and watched as they arranged them to cover their eyes.

Blake was the last to take a scarf and windmilled it round his face in record time.

'Now girls,' Sharrow swung up. 'Stand nearby, please.'

With hands on her heart, Sanvi squealed, eager to start the game while the rest of us patted hair behind our ears, pulled down T-shirts and let the idea sink in that we were all going to be blindfolded and left to free fall into each other. But that wasn't the case. We weren't given scarves.

'Spread out in front of the guys,' Sharrow said. 'They can't see you. Good. Stay there. Great. Don't move a muscle. Quiet everyone.'

I positioned myself opposite Evan with Carl nearby, far away from Guthrie.

'OK, guys take a few steps to the side,' Sharrow said. 'Now stop.'

It happened, Guthrie was practically in front of me. Just a few breaths away and the sudden electricity shot me to bits.

'When you feel someone close, reach out, guys,' Sharrow said. 'Let her take your hand to her chin, gently touch her features and try to guess who it is.'

With a bold, blue and white striped scarf tied haphazardly to his face, Guthrie swayed back and forth. I hoped he wouldn't sense it was me and his arms moved, trawling the air. I leaned as far back as I could until the deep flat space between us opened up a fault line.

I caught Sharrow nodding to me and took his warm hand in mine and laid his fingers flat on my cheek. He stepped forward and I could smell the dull soap on his skin. For a second it felt like we were the only people in the world and I wanted to stay there breathing in his curious smile. The ghost that was me faded as the gentle hand stroked my lips, lingered and traced the outline of my face, the soft part of my ear and dent in my chin as if he already knew them.

'Say when you know who it is,' Sharrow said at last and Guthrie hesitated.

Strangest thing was I thought I heard him whisper my name and the next mysterious word sounded like something that belonged to me but this time a finger pressed into my cheekbone and the next moment, he said. 'Ma – Marr?' Like he knew it was me but wanted to tease the moment into the last possible drop of a joke, maybe to drive me nuts. 'Marya?'

When he whipped the scarf from his face and his eyes met mine, he laughed and nodded. People milled around, their game was over but we still played long and lovely looks.

'Knew it was,' he muttered. 'I could smell that coconut shampoo you use.'

The fantastic connection vanished in a second and we were back on earth, standing in front of each other. He touched my shoulder to end the encounter and that was it – over – he was gone and I was left undecided about what it meant and whether he felt anything at all.

'Guys that's what real flesh and blood feels like. Soft, yes, and in need of the same interest, gentleness and care you'll want to give your partners in future.'

Sharrow insisted we did it again. Scarves were tied. The guys twirled. We moved round and sidestepping the previous one, tried again with someone else. This time, Carl. Next time, Tomas. None felt like Guthrie.

The soft Spanish stars twinkled in the purple night and the game ended with the smell of roses in the air. The yellow light from the tiny kitchen illuminated the grainy wood terrace and all around everybody talked, laughed, closer than before. Constanza started singing and Carl did a slow, spooning dance with her while Evan and Coco linked arms.

I decided to brave it out with Guthrie who was leaning on the door to the store room, peeling an orange over a small plastic bin.

'The game made us all a bit more human which I guess was the point?' I said.

'Yeah.' He rubbed his hands on the sides of his jeans and acted like he knew I was nervous when he narrowed his eyes. 'It's good without phones.'

'I'd forgotten,' I said and looked away, confused. 'What are we?' I asked, meaning us but it came out wrong.

'You don't have to take everything seriously.' Guthrie ate the orange after I turned it down, took my elbow and led me away from the door to sit beside him on the pushed back chairs. Like he had to look after me because I was being so pathetic.

FORTY-THREE

We sat there watching the others, hardly talking in a quiet, awkward way about different apps until Guthrie said, 'How's it going with Carl?'

What was he on about?

Sharrow shouted, 'Best collect our sleeping bags.' I totally froze and everything went quiet.

I didn't know what to do and when Guthrie stood up, I'm sure I turned pale or maybe green. The trance ended and it felt a bit like motion sickness as I followed him into the little, glowing room where the sleeping bags were in a heap on the floor. Constanza pulled out a red one, wrapped it round her and toddled off with a sly wink which I hoped Guthrie didn't see.

I soon found the one with extra padding that Mum said would keep me warm and Guthrie glanced at the pile and picked out a faded bronze, alpine number tied with old cord.

'Carl is just a friend,' I said.

'Sure,' Guthrie nodded. 'We're all friends aren't we?'

What was that supposed to mean?

'Over there,' he said which surprised me more than anything. I thought that was it, but no, we walked back into the night together. Unrolled the bags to sleep under the stars and this time I was next to him on the far side of the terrace near the cactus bushes, just before you get to the dark path leading to the loos.

In tattered sandals, torn T-shirt and jeans, Tomas was happy to continue throwing things at Sun God who ducked behind a tree. Someone turned off the yellow light and the cluster of quilted shapes on the terrace faded to black. I spied Evan sloping off with Coco, where to I had no idea and didn't care. It sounded like Carl was attempting to climb inside Lilla's bag with her already there but it might have been Mo, who squealed and laughed, they were so far away.

Settled in, flat on my back and surrounded by stars, I pulled up the top of the soft nylon and turned to look at Guthrie.

'Cosy enough?' he said and I nodded – but wasn't really. He knew it and shuffled closer. His head in line with mine. Our bodies touched through the fabric and I could feel him all along my left side. Not daring to move, hands on my stomach, the steady flow of warmth went through me while I brooded about what to say, how to begin – a hundred other things and stared doggedly at the twinkling sky, wishing he would speak. Disappointed when he closed his eyes, it was hard to tell if he was going to sleep or resting from the endless finger pointing stars.

There was nothing between the moon and me but fear. The kind that makes it hard to breathe normally because the night was so close to being ours.

From the age of seven I'd done nothing but read. Books were my passion. In books I lived a thousand lives, dreamt and explored like a bird set free beyond the wild nature of reality that couldn't be reached without them. Once I was in the Oxfam shop with my friend, Evie, who's brilliant at making things. While I touched and pulled out the second-hand books in a ruthless search for unknown worlds, she fidgeted with a hand-painted, wooden picture frame for 50p, bored to tears.

I felt sorry for her. Sorry for anyone who didn't love books but for all that and more, I was separate and lost in a sleeping bag next to Guthrie and *The Mill on the Floss* and everything I was into couldn't help me get out of my head and closer to him. Evie would have known what to do about Guthrie.

FORTY-FOUR

I was first to open my eyes to the chilly morning, hopeful Guthrie was there. He was, but totally dead to the world like the other dark shapes under the tall trees.

I fished a small pebble from the earth to hold up and blot out the sun rising from the distant hill and the details of every moment, word and look we've shared, zoomed back into my mind.

It was getting on. The dishevelled heap was still out of it and I couldn't lie there staring at him or the pebble in my hand for much longer. Feeling optimistic, I inched out of the bag to stretch my legs and find the toilet and heard someone in the kitchen filling the sink with water. The morning tinkles, clangs and whispers spread and by the time I came back, everyone on the terrace had discarded their sleeping bags and were getting themselves together.

There was no sign of Evan or Coco but I wasn't worried. Not until the dusty blue car came up the path and braked with a loud crunch. Serge got out and an apple rolled from his pocket to his feet. He stood there for a moment in old grey shirt and looked around. He spotted Blake slicing melon at the far table and hurried over. They talked briefly. Sharrow joined them and without a word to anyone they hurried to the car and climbed in.

Mo and I watched the car drive off and Evan appeared on the path in between the cactus bushes, grinning like crazy and looking as if he hadn't slept for a week. Bedraggled Coco was close behind in a similar state.

'What do you think they were up to?' Mo giggled. 'Hope you know Coco was pulled out of the lake before you came?'

'No, I didn't.'

'Yeah, that's what I heard. She says it's not true, won't talk about

162

it. I wish I could reach her.' Mo adjusted her sunglasses and pushed wet brown hair behind her ears. 'You having a good time?'

It took a while to answer. 'Can't complain. Did Coco try to kill herself?'

'I don't think so. She tried to swim to the other side but couldn't make it. Did you know Guthrie's dad's an alcoholic?' she said.

His dad's an alcoholic?

'Not that it's a reflection on him, eh?' Mo smiled. 'It's just like, my brain hangs on to things for no reason like they're important to remember when why would that be something I'd ever want to mention when it's none of my business?'

'Yeah,' I said. 'I look at someone and instead of seeing them gawp at all the things I know about them.'

'At home my bed has to be perfect,' she said. 'Clean pillows just so. Up here I'm happy to sleep on a board and don't care. Weird. Be careful.'

'About what?'

'Whatever it is you're worried about.'

Was I frowning? 'Oh, I'm OK.' I smiled in an unconvincing way.

I glanced at Guthrie who unzipped the sleeping bag and sat up. His eyes met mine for a second then travelled to Constanza on the terrace, all brown and beautiful in a skimpy, floral sundress as she tried to stuff a crumpled nylon ball into a drawstring bag without much success.

Mo's Welsh accent was magnetic in my ear as she told me about the drinks' business Guthrie's father once owned before he fell apart and lost everything in a bad investment. There was nothing surprising about what she said. The only mystery was how I managed to convince myself things had changed between us while trying to be oblivious to the sight of him craving another triumph in the shape of Constanza.

I stood there tormented until Evan put a hand on my shoulder, hair flopping on his darting-all-over-the-place eyes.

'Did you sleep?' he said.

'Yeah, you?' I smiled.

'Sort of.'

I didn't question him about Coco and Mo wandered off. The chat hadn't gone the way she planned because I wouldn't share my feelings. I watched her go and Coco threw her arms round us both and did one of Sanvi's swinging hugs. My hands hung down, motionless and blasts of lemony shampoo from both their heads filled my nose. Had they showered together? The thought made up for the idea that Coco was more troubled than I realised.

'I'm going.' I pointed to nowhere and trundled off, certain nobody would follow and the further I got along the path the easier it was to be away from their ordinary morning while my heart bounced from rage to sadness to something worse and back again.

What I needed was space. Time. Distraction. None of which were available in this suffocating atmosphere. A guy with spiky orange hair and pale skin walked past me eating popcorn and I turned to look at the lake.

Guthrie prefers Constanza. No more moon and starry evenings up there, I decided. That was it and out of control, I stumbled into a hidden place beside the lake and sank cross-legged on the warm ground to think in peace.

The blanket of silver water moved with glimmering hands that appeared to invite me in. My stomach was rumbling, the sun was growing hot but I didn't budge until a shuffling noise made me turn.

'So someone has found my best place? No, don't move. Stay there.' Dressed in an orange and blue kaftan, the poet from Lagos brightened when her sharp, black eyes landed on me. With grey dreadlocks and not a single wrinkle on her smooth face, a bobbing white bag bounced from her hip.

Light on her feet, she swung past me, dropped the bag and threw off her kaftan to stand proudly naked with shaking breasts.

'Whatever the problem, I run to this spot,' she said, scratching her neck.

I looked away but didn't need to. We were females together and she didn't care. Stepping out of her sandals, she strode down the bank with her hands clasped under her chin. 'By the time I leave I always feel better. You will, too. Sit still until I come back.'

Her name was Bolanile and she hurled herself into the lake and swam away with a big smile on her face. I sat in suspended animation watching her playing in the water and it felt like I was back in time with my grandmother by a beautiful, peaceful, unknown lake though no way would she have got naked in front of me. Old people don't have bodies in movies or on YouTube, do they?

When Bolanile got out I told her all about Guthrie. How he didn't know I liked him, why he was my favourite and how upset I was because I knew I didn't have a chance.

FORTY-FIVE

We found some shade under a tall evergreen tree where a cool breeze made it worth clearing the sharp twigs and stones to sit down on dry grass and crackling leaves. Trickles of water ran down Bolanile's wobbly neck from her wet, messy dreadlocks and spread out like a table cloth, the kaftan covered everything but her feet.

Buzzing things zoomed around us and one landed on the kaftan. I tried to melt into the tree trunk away from it but Bolanile wasn't fussed and gently brushed it off. The zinging in my ear was a nuisance and Bolanile waved a bent finger at me.

'Respite means nothing to you,' she said. 'You kids are all go, go, go.'

'That's not true,' I said. 'We sit around most of the time.' I reached into the bag for my phone to see what the time was but no, I remembered, Serge took it.

'When we were young school ended at two and we were over the streets playing catcher and ten-ten,' Bolanile said. 'Did what we wanted and no one asked where we'd been. There was no such thing as homework and porn, hah. I found an old book once when I was young about a newly discovered tribe with photos of bare-breasted women and half-naked men which I thought was extremely rude.'

Her face lit up when she looked at me. 'My god,' she giggled. 'I wrote a poem about those pictures when I was a kid but it wasn't until much later that I realised they were the only naked images on offer to the white man at the time and we were uncontrollable, aggressive, low-down, sexy savages to them.'

I'd never seen an old book like that and went back to having an imaginary chat with Guthrie.

'We had our problems. Life was hard,' she said. 'Our oil didn't help us much. The profits travelled further than we did. Every day was a struggle but from what I've seen of young people these days the pressures are ridiculous. Much worse than they were in my day growing up in Lagos. The violent images you see are impossible to remove from your minds. We didn't live like that. Mother Earth was part of us not something we needed to save.'

'I'm not obsessed with Guthrie,' I piped up and the bee took off.

'Well, he's all you've talked about. You mentioned you're here to mind your brother. You say he's doing fine but you're the one who's not doing so well. Am I right?'

I nodded. It was true.

'You know about Kito, the elephant who was brought up in a zoo?' Bolanile said.

I shook my head. 'I don't read newspapers.'

'Neither do I. Now listen. Kito was a baby elephant who learnt about the world by discovering what was around him in the zoo. He rubbed his trunk on the fences, scraped the earth beneath his feet, eyed the height of the grass and sniffed every weed in the man-made enclosure. The noises from the nearby caged animals were nothing to be afraid of because they were always kept separate. That zoo was everything Kito knew.'

Bolanile's voice grew soft and I strained to listen. 'One day a big, old, wild elephant was captured and they put him with Kito. The old elephant told of tall, waving coconut palms, abundant banana leaves, the salty smell of the sea and the thrill of trampling the vast jungle and lunging through spreading rivers at will. Kito, the zoo elephant, scoffed. He thought the old elephant was lying. There were no such places. No such feelings.'

A breeze ruffled the golden branches on the tree opposite and even though my mind was on Guthrie, I *was* listening and said, 'Natural life was outside Kito's experience then.' Thinking that was the end of it, but no.

167

'So it is with us,' Bolanile nodded. 'We live in the material world. We have our own learnt experiences and views about what is real. Like Kito, we get caught up in repetitive thoughts, ideas and actions that reveal the limits of our enclosures. As we move into the fifth dimension, the world is speeding up so fast, no one will be left untouched.'

I kind of imagined her to be my missing grandma until she said that and my brain sprang a leak. 'The fifth dimension?'

'The fourth dimension is imagined. You could put time there. The fifth is the spiritual realm. A magical, heavenly place that really exists. Each layer is a miracle. There is no suffering because fear is unknown and all of life is one. Look at your zoo. See it for what it is but be open to the places where light is beauty and beauty is truth.

'I came here when I was your age,' Bolanile said. 'There was some money, though not much left after I found my poor old mum, who was a clever shop keeper, dead from a painful bone disease. Her death nearly killed me and my guides instructed me to leave for Europe. Luck and a whole lot of love brought me here. The community had just started and I found another way of living. Still I go back every year. Every year without fail to reach inside the country that allowed my spirit to flower. Everything is wherever I am.' She paused. 'Now, enough of this. I need a nap.'

Even with my help, it took a while for her to stagger to a standing position while flicking away the odd bee. It was futile to ask for more. I was sorry our chat was over but her face was set in stone, her mind was made up. She looked suddenly older as her hand flapped away my arm. She didn't need my help. Walking beside her wasn't wanted and I stood back to give her space, hitched her white bag on my shoulder and followed her to the path where she stopped for a second and turned to me.

'Be the whole moon. Take your light from the sun. Refuse to change shape and fall into the shadows. Understand?'

I nodded.

'Pornography is much more dangerous than people realise,' Bolanile said. 'It's a form of psychological warfare that creates another kind of slavery. Violent fantasies add to the dark reality put into the future by way of the children. The invisible is becoming visible. See it, have the strength to move on and be thankful for what you know.'

Psychological warfare? Dark reality put into the future? The sensation of safety-pins springing open in my brain reminded me of the stories about the lizard people who rule the world. Is porn the easiest way of diverting our awareness from another beautiful and magical reality that exists just beyond our daily experience?

The moment the bare, hot, sandy earth opened wide in a dazzle and the effects of the cool breeze faded, the walk to the refectory in the afternoon sun felt more like a trek across a desert.

'Matter is created from energy. From the non-physical comes the information to enable the exquisite to form,' she said. 'You go out there and tell your Guthrie exactly what you want.'

Matter from energy. The exquisite to form. The sentences were linked somehow but my mind was still caught up with psychological warfare and dark reality, that is until she said, 'Your Guthrie.'

He wasn't mine but yes, I would tell him. I would but before I could do what she advised, I had to eat something, talk to Mum and open the gate to my cage, didn't I? By the look of her swinging kaftan and without me having to speak or explain, she flapped the back of her hand as if she understood how I was straining to make sense of it all.

'Keep your mind and heart open,' she said.

I was full of purpose, walking beside her but my blood was hotter than the air we breathed, it was so sticky and humid away from the water and I could tell she was struggling when we reached the wooden steps to the refectory where she stopped to hang an arm over the small rail.

'Eighty-eight,' she said. 'I'm not doing badly, am I? You run along now and forget about making do.' She took a deep breath and Serge appeared at the top of the steps and came down to help Bolanile. He made her laugh about something as he took her arm while I hurried off to get water from the jar and grab what was left of the brown rice and vegetables for lunch.

Serge's gentleness with Bolanile came as a surprise. Mum said he grew up in an ugly little town where old deaf pensioners are regularly beaten to death. I don't know whether she made that up but it was obvious Serge liked helping Bolanile and his patience was as impressive as the big smile on his face. He was being kind because that's who he is; a good guy like my dad.

I carried the bowl of food round the back and the kitchen smelt of roast potatoes and body odour mixed with perfume. In a white apron, Mum was busy wiping metal surfaces with a dishcloth. She stopped to pat her forehead with the back of a hand and, in the middle of washing dishes, a beady-eyed woman in a similar apron, promptly pulled the plug in the sink, turned to me and said, 'You can't eat in here.'

Unlike her, Mum was pleased to see me. 'I'll finish up later,' she told the co-worker, waved me to the wicker chairs outside the door and fell back, exhausted. 'Phew. I'll never get used to this heat.'

Working my way through the plate of food in my lap, a chunk of roast parsnip got stuck in my throat and I coughed. 'Mum, I can't stand it.'

'I know it's hot, honey, but the nights are cool and it's better than last summer when you babysat twice a week and stayed inside doing nothing.'

'Mum, I was reading my way through the Russians: Tolstoy, Dostoyevsky, Gogol, Turgenev, Solzhenitsyn.'

'Exactly.'

'Mum, reading isn't nothing. It's more than a life – it is life – all of life and I learnt more about Russia last summer than you can imagine.'

'You want to go home and read then? Is that it?'

'Mum, I want to get away from here.' I did and didn't at the same time.

'Well, I'm afraid you can't. The plane tickets aren't transferable and I can't afford to buy another one. I need to make a start on the mountain of sweet potatoes for dinner and that's after working all day doing breakfast and lunch while you've been enjoying yourself.'

She was in one of her rare, 'poor me' moods and blinked to stay awake while I finished off the rice and let the 'enjoying yourself' comment die a death.

'I can work in the kitchen and you can have a day off,' I said.

'Thank you, but no. I signed up for this so please don't ask to go home.'

Like Kito, the elephant, I was stuck in the third dimension where the wicker chairs, beating sun and sounds from the kitchen were solid pictures of the reality imprinted in my brain. Encoded by education, family, friends and our time in history when in fact something darker, more complex and magical was splitting everything I'd ever known.

'Bolanile says we're moving into the fifth dimension,' I said.

'Oh, does she?' Mum sighed. 'Well, that's nice. Pass me some water, sweetie.'

Why is it easier to talk to a stranger than your own Mum?

FORTY-SIX

One of those clammy afternoons you can't wait to be over, the sky felt heavy and even the bushes and trees sagged in the heat. Mum drank the water, refused another offer of help and dragged herself up from the chair. Time to get on with preparing dinner, she went back inside with a smile that had nothing else to say.

Why wouldn't she let me help her? Was it because the beady-eyed co-worker didn't want me in the kitchen? I didn't have a clue where to go. The hill or the dorms? They were the only choices.

I wandered round to the dining area. At one of the cleared tables under the bamboo roof, a few people were eyeing a maroon backpack on a vacant chair. It seemed no one knew who the owner was. An older man and woman were bent over their laptops, lost in their work and a trampy-looking guy was asleep on the floor.

There was nothing to do but have another glass of water and go back down the path the way I'd come. Without thinking, I flipped open my tote bag and hissed at myself. Inside was a small towel, brush for taming flyaway hair, sun cream, face wipes, deodorant, lip balm, waterproof mascara and tissues all jumbled up together but still no phone. The phone is my distraction. An impulsive full stop and it was annoying not to able to search for the fifth dimension when I had the urge.

Far too hot, I trudged up the hill to the art building, rubbing the sweating skin beneath my T-shirt which was no help at all because every bit of me was sticky. The barren path made me hunger for the noise and chaos of London. I felt lost and the no-man's empty scrubland in every direction added to the feeling of being dead to the world.

My heart twisted at the sight of the relaxed, disorderly group, half lying down in a circle on the wooden terrace. The on-going, daily challenge of Arcadia made me want to run not join them.

After rubbing a wet wipe across my face and moistening my lips with the rose-scented balm, I put on a smile. This was going to be difficult.

FORTY-SEVEN

The mood was sombre. The air smelt of paint and an annoying bird in the shadows of the building cawed non-stop.

An older woman with bubbly, blonde hair and plump body busting out of a yellow, tight tube dress, darted around the middle of the circle, arms in the air. Mum says it's a miracle what a bundle of female flesh can do. She was full of energy. I'd never seen her before and she paused to nod at me as if she knew what I was thinking, pointed to a space on the floor next to Evan and came to a stop in front of Constanza.

'That was great but next time remember to speak with flair and abundance,' she said.

Flair and abundance? Oh no. The group was in the middle of something important and turning my face from her, I slipped to the floor and tried to get comfortable between gobs of ancient paint.

'Keep your back straight,' she said. 'Use your hands. No need to shuffle and look at the ground.'

With a big smile, Constanza threw her head back and the woman turned her attention to Lilla. 'Are you sure you want to do this?'

Crouched in front of her, Lilla jumped up. Dressed in a thin, cotton, black dress, her mouth twitched. She was nervous. Some kind of therapy session was taking place and nobody but Evan flashed their wild eyes at me when I fake cleared my throat. I had the strong feeling Guthrie more than noticed me because he sort of stroked his furry face but because he didn't glance my way, I couldn't be sure. The uncertainty passed and it became one of those times where every cell in your body tingles with awareness of the guy you like so you have to concentrate harder than ever on what's going on. Afraid I would be asked to speak, I pulled up my knees and tried not to look uncomfortable in the sticky jeans and sweaty T-shirt by putting on an extra solemn face.

Relieved it was Lilla up there and not me, I watched her stare at the ground for a moment then take a deep breath. 'All my life I feel this – this, how you say, yes, no good. No beautiful. No clever. No enough.'

'Say it loud, Lilla,' the woman said. 'Act it out with your body.'

'OK. All time. This.' Pursing her lips, Lilla bent her head and cowered. Hugging herself tight, she folded inwards. Crushed into a ball.

'Walk around,' the woman ordered and Lilla whimpered as she snuck about in front of the group like a wounded cat then stood at the side with her head in her arms and I thought, *Yeah, I know that feeling,* and guessed everyone understood.

'Thank you. Now does anyone want to say how they feel watching Lilla?' the woman said. 'Go ahead, Mo.' She gestured in a theatrical way.

'Right.' Mo shifted the big sunglasses on her nose, stood up and pulled her T-shirt down to cover the elastic waist of a generous, knee-length, pink skirt. Sweet and motherly, she took her time before speaking.

'I do that,' Mo said. 'Close down when I get scared. Stressed. Feel sad. Thinking I'll never be anything much.' Hanging her head, Mo curled into herself. A perfect reflection of Lilla.

'All right?' Mo straightened.

The woman's voice grew louder. 'Yes, good. Now please walk.'

'Right then. Here we are. Now, see… Lilla's a really nice girl…' Mo began striding around. 'A strong, funny girl, who… look at her. I'm only saying she'd look good in a tea towel, in whatever she wears because it's true.'

Everyone laughed.

'And hell,' Mo sighed. 'She can speak Spanish and English. Some Italian. Who here can do that? Well, Constanza can speak Romanian which she says is close to Latin so that too and Italian. She's brilliant just like Lilla. Carl can do French and I can speak a bit of Welsh if you must know.'

Everyone laughed again.

'When Lilla talks about the garden she's making with her friends in Barcelona...' Mo said. 'I want to up sticks and go there now. If she isn't enough then no one is for heaven's sake because we all get down like that at times.'

Surprised and grateful, Lilla smiled like a baby.

'Anyone else?' the woman said and Carl jumped up.

'I see Lilla through a telephoto lens...' he said. 'And, like, yeah, I want to get even closer.'

'Relax and walk around, Carl,' the woman said and he patted his pony tail and grinned.

'I'm smitten. No, really.' Carl put on a shy face and winced his way across the creaking floorboards. 'Those big, expressive eyes. That giggle makes my soul leap, yeah.'

Everyone laughed.

'Thank you, Mo. Thank you, Carl. Now, Lilla, be the girl they see,' the woman said.

Full of anxiety and looking at her with disbelief, Lilla stretched and took a deep breath. One minute she was standing quietly at the side and the next, her arms were out doing everything to prove what an alert, confident, clever, pretty girl she really was. With all of us behind her, Lilla waggled her fingers at Carl and Mo to feel their love, shook her thick, black hair then started dancing like her body was on fire.

I came alive at the transformation. The way she moved was awesome. I'm sure Dad has done similar things with his offenders and though I didn't understand the full awareness and tuning into your body thing he mentioned by text, it definitely worked for Lilla.

In touch with herself but also part of the wildness of Arcadia at the same time, Guthrie saw my face and smiled. My fingers found a furrow between the floorboards and I looked down. One smile from him, the world righted itself and the solid wood turned to dust.

'Good. Well done. That's it for today,' the woman said and Lilla's madness faded.

'Wow.' Tomas fell backwards on the floor with his hands on his head as if the imaginary music Lilla danced to had damaged his ears.

Sharrow wiped away a tear.

The 'well done' felt like a death. It was over. I sat there disappointed as the bubbly woman bent down to speak to Blake then walked off towards the toilets in the bulging tube dress, sandals slopping across the floor in the tall, sure way I imagined an ancient Goddess would move.

Evan opened his mouth to speak. He looked at Coco whose eyes were travelling down a long, dark tunnel and changed his mind. Was she reliving the dancing at the friend's party where they were filmed? The stone cold look on her face was hard to get away from. Like doorways to a dark prison, her eyes drew me in until I could almost see the shackles on the bodies inside.

'Coco. Coco.' I leaned over and she slowly came back. 'You OK?' She didn't answer. 'Want to do something?'

'Go away,' she said.

I knelt forward and got up as gracefully as I could, full of emotion. There was no way to reach her but Evan stayed, saying nothing.

It took real nerve for Lilla to express her feelings. I envied her bravery but it had the opposite effect on Coco and with everyone else chatting and smiling, I suddenly realised our group had put down roots just like Blake said we would but underneath it all, there were still huge problems that refused to leave.

FORTY-EIGHT

Mid-August is the time the community members help out at a local farm for six days. Mum had an unexpected break from the kitchen and we took over the cooking, preparing meals for the twenty-five people who remained and ourselves.

Divided into three groups, Evan, Carl and Sharrow were responsible for the porridge, bread and fresh houmous and washed the peaches for breakfast. Guthrie, Lilla, Coco and Mo were the lunch group who made bean, chickpea and cauliflower stews, plus tomato, green pepper and lentil salads.

I was part of the dinner bunch with Tomas, Sanvi, Constanza and Blake so escaped the early morning start the breakfast crew had to suffer and avoided the midday heat in the kitchen, though boiling vats of brown rice, potatoes and quinoa was just as demanding.

Handed the recipes each morning, the absolute chaos of the first day changed into quick shrugs and we became efficient, smooth-running teams.

It's amazing what you learn when you work with someone you think you know. Take Tomas for example. Forget skinny and hopeless. He was an absolute powerhouse in the kitchen and whizzed around from fridge to stove checking rice as if doing something awesome while Blake slowly filled the sink to the top with water (what a waste) dabbling soap with his fingers before wandering off to find a cloth from the dining area which was already beside the stove.

Sanvi never trusted the first prod of the new potatoes was proof they could possibly be done until she'd forked and crumbled the lot and Constanza had her head down all the time, treating everything like quicksand, especially the quinoa which was easy to burn. I commanded the vegetable chopping board but slicing millions of onions, garlic and peppers, scooping skins and seeds to fling in the bin soon messed up the floor for miles around. I was far quicker at finding the dish cloth than slow, old Blake but less capable of enjoying cooking than the others.

Working as a team, we hardly had time to talk. If the meal was late it didn't matter because no one was in a rush. There was pressure but not the kind of pressure you get in a restaurant kitchen.

'Who made the fantastic houmous?' Coco said at lunch on the first morning when she saw Evan collecting up the plates. He grinned shyly, proud to admit it was him.

We had the craziest conversations about nothing.

'If I was God I wouldn't have these dents around the stem of green peppers,' Mo said. 'I mean, what's the point? Just make them square.'

'I'd make them grow already sliced,' Sharrow said.

'What about with blue spots?' Carl said. 'Compared to fish, vegetables are plain to look at,' and we laughed.

We swapped sessions a few times and by the end of the fourth day I could make a decent rye bread, bean stew, quinoa and vegetable dish in my sleep. It was the washing up that did me in. By the time the kitchen was clean and shiny in the evening, ready for the breakfast crew in the morning, I was exhausted. I don't know how Mum stuck it out day after day.

After finishing the last session and rampaging through the cleaning marathon to have a full evening to ourselves, the grinding sound of a motorbike shattered the peace. The odd noise was a shock to the senses. It was so out of place and the loud stories of mishaps over the past six days quietened down on our table outside the kitchen.

On the bench though, Guthrie, Sanvi and me were still laughing loudly with Tomas about how much he'd changed. With no sign of the nervous, awkward boy we met on the first day, he was becoming more gorgeous by the hour (yes, that thought occurred), and he reacted to our mocking smiles with humour.

'Imagine growing up here and never getting into a fight or having nightmares,' Tomas said.

'I need the buzz of the city and more girls than this.' Guthrie shook his head.

Too tired to take offence, the sound of his voice still had a traumatising effect but used to being around him now, there were few surprises left and whenever our eyes met there was a sympathetic distance that couldn't be misread. I liked him more than he liked me, hence the sudden interest in Tomas. No, not really. I still liked Guthrie best.

It was getting dark. The outside light came on as Serge lurched into view and I was glad Mum wasn't on the back of his wreck of a motorbike.

FORTY-NINE

In faded red shirt and worn backpack, Serge clunked to a stop in a pool of yellow light from the kitchen. Blake jumped up to admire the rattling bike. Carl and Mo tagged along behind and it was funny to watch how much the wannabe racers wanted to mess with the spluttering bike.

Serge pointed to the parts responsible for the knocking noise and kicked down the side to park. 'The combustion chamber's stressed,' he said and leaned the bike on its stand.

'You sure about that?' Mo said, showing off. 'Checked the pistons?'

'Yeah. Yeah.'

Scratching his chin, Blake eyed a rusty pipe with enthusiasm. Pony tail hanging down like a dead bird on his grey T-shirt, Carl nodded as if expecting the bike to reveal the reason for the problem if he just stared at it for long enough.

'I can't understand how you got it up here.' Mo shook her head.

'That's my job.' Serge swung his leg over, let go of the handlebars, came and emptied the backpack out on the table with Mo and Carl still hovering over the bike. We leaned in to grab a clattering phone and all I can say is, it was quite an emotional moment. Sanvi was so excited she ran off with hers and never came back.

'Don't worry. They are fully charged.' Serge smiled.

I glanced at Evan whose nose was practically coming out of the other side of the iPad screen and it was then I noticed Coco was missing. I saw her going to the toilets more than an hour ago before we sat down to eat.

The motorbike revved to life and with deep, choppy noises Serge whizzed off down the path with Carl and Mo staring after him and me thinking I hadn't asked where Mum was.

Maybe Coco had gone to the dorms for a rest? With no one up there she could sleep in peace. Weirdly, I had the strangest feeling that wasn't the case.

Scrolling through our messages, heads down, reading like crazy, the world turned deathly silent. Loaded with questions from Dad about what we were up to, there were also links to a new frontline service to reform offenders and cut crime which I ignored. There was a photo of Freddie learning to swim which might have been sweet if I actually knew him. Shula had already finished 'The controversial *Daniel Deronda.*' She thought it pretty tame, was halfway through *Adam Bede* which she preferred and couldn't wait to start *Middlemarch.*

There was no way I could catch up before school started and failing the George Elliot Summer Reading Challenge before I'd finished the first book was humiliating and embarrassing. A blue butterfly set up home on my shoulder. It was a welcome interruption from the *you're hopeless,* voices in my head and as the butterfly stepped over the ridge of my sleeve and walked down my arm before fluttering off, I glanced at the messages from Watty which I'd left until last.

'Shula said you were away so I've given your cream bun to someone more appreciative.'

Really? Good, then.

'Stay away little girl.'

I will.

'Consider yourself deleted,' was the last one from Watty.

There could have been a long, painful twisting in my gut as I looked at the nearby darkening trees and beyond them at the grey bushes, but all I felt was relief. Bye-bye, Watty.

Turning my attention to the white, budget smartphone in the middle of the table no one had claimed, I said, 'That must be Coco's?' There was no reply so I grabbed it, climbed out from the bench to find her and stopped suddenly when a rumbling louder than an earth tremor started up in the path beyond the trees.

Sharrow looked around. It sounded like a tractor crashed into something. Someone yelled. Blake began running and we followed.

FIFTY

When you think someone might die and they do, it's no less of a shock. A driver in blue overalls knelt over Coco as Blake shouted, 'No. Please God, no.'

Poised on full alert, the sudden calm inside was eons away from the panic and screams like something out of a horror movie coming from beside me. I put my arm around Constanza who crumpled up, yelling. Everyone cried in disbelief, turned away or rushed to hug each other while I stood there mesmerised by the pleated spindles of the spinning wheels and rivulets of blood coming from her curly matted hair. The tractor was on its side and the crushed girl underneath had blood pouring from her head.

The story hovered between Spanish and English until we learnt that in an attempt to swerve out of her way, the tractor hit a boulder and crashed down sideways on top of her.

The mangled figure in a tie-dyed dress was dead and her white, budget smartphone was ringing in my hand.

I pressed answer and a male voice said, 'Where have you been you fucking bitch?'

FIFTY-ONE

'It's Coco's phone,' I whispered and handed it to Sharrow with the guy yelling his head off at a dead girl who couldn't hear and she talked to the guy, whoever he was, in a quiet, patient voice while I stood there crying. Heartbroken. Poor, lovely Coco was dead and if she'd been here, the nasty guy would have yelled at her like that.

With real understanding for an angry man she didn't know, Sharrow finished the call, put the phone in her pocket, took hold of the driver's arm and said, 'It's not your fault.' They hugged and Blake ushered us back to the table outside the kitchen where I couldn't stop shaking, furious with myself. Why didn't I run and find her the moment I noticed she was missing? I'd sensed something was wrong and shouldn't have carried on sitting there. Who was that horrible guy?

Sun God, Tomas and Guthrie went to fetch blankets. Carl found a space under a nearby tree and stayed there with his head in his hands while Blake said things like, 'We'll miss her.'

Staring into the yellow light outside the window; the kind of light that slows the mind, Evan lay an arm around my shoulder as we listened to vehicles zooming up the hidden path and coming to stop a few metres away. We sat shivering at the sound of every unknown voice. Never asking who the people were who came and went until the air grew silent and the familiar, unseen crickets screeched louder than the noise of the truck that took Coco's body away.

Coco was dead and I rewound the moment again and again when I could have jumped from the table and gone to look for her. I wanted her to come back and tell me it was an accident, not suicide. Why her? Why?

The woman busting out of her tube dress who did the session

185

where Lilla stopped acting scared, arrived soon after the blankets which Guthrie dropped on the table with a smile. Mo passed them round and Evan tucked a blue one over us both but I didn't want the suffocating thing and shrugged it off to glance at Lilla, all small and broken in the pink blanket opposite. Nearby, Constanza couldn't stop crying.

China and cutlery clinked as the woman put hot mugs of tea on the table and spooned sugar for those who wanted some. Oat biscuits appeared from nowhere and a late-night feast broke out. I hadn't drunk tea since we'd arrived and wondered whether in times of emergency the vegan community were allowed to have milk but no, the white liquid was made from fresh almonds and tasted nice.

'Hemp milk is better,' the nameless woman said. 'But we've run out.'

'She's lying. It's in the roll-ups.' Sun God made a joke and Guthrie smiled.

'I'm sure it was an accident,' Tomas said and we went quiet. The woman in the tube dress shook her head.

'It's hard to miss the sound of a tractor hereabouts,' she said. 'Coco ran in front of him last week, the driver said, which is why he was going slowly. Only this time he hit the boulder when he swerved out of her way and you know the rest.'

We stayed like that for most of the night. Sad, confused, half alive and stunned, trying to make sense of something that refused to be understood.

The white, budget smartphone became part of the moon, blankets and tea that stayed fresh in my mind every hour that passed and whenever the dark path flashed into view with the red tractor that spun Coco's life from this world to the next, the figure lying smashed and bloody under a massive tyre always came as a shock and started me shaking again.

'You couldn't have done anything.' Guthrie leaned across the table and touched my wet cheek. 'She maybe would have walked into the water if she didn't want to be found.'

Nothing was understandable. Hot tears came rolling down my face and a life's worth of hurt poured out because Guthrie had noticed. Evan went red and tried to move when Guthrie slipped in beside me and folded us both into his furry arms and face.

Hours later we all crashed out under the stars and slept like babies until the sun was high in the sky.

FIFTY-TWO

The sun rose and fell and we walked around and slept at odd times as if we hadn't noticed. Everything hummed from a long way away. The paths and buildings, the bushes and grass were flimsy reproductions of reality and the illusion we were solid was the only thing that was true.

One minute she was here and the next she was gone. Coco was gone and wouldn't ever call me English girl again.

Over the next two days, Guthrie watched over me. I don't know why he followed me around but he did and I suspect Blake or Sharrow were responsible for asking him to make sure I was OK. He didn't have to because we all looked out for each other.

'You only had a mouthful of rice,' Guthrie said.

'I can't swallow anything,' I said.

'Yeah, you can.'

He was right, I could, and it was strange how much easier it was to bother with him right there.

There were times I stopped worrying about Coco. Stopped worrying about Evan, too. His spots flared up but Constanza stayed close, warm and kind. The times I stopped worrying didn't last long and even though after a while everyone seemed back to normal, we weren't and would never be. The sight of Coco lying there and the guy swearing in my ear was always there.

Going over every second of that evening was normal until Sharrow made huge bowls of popcorn and Guthrie laughed at my greedy face. I laughed at him laughing. It made a refreshing change from all the aching and crying and on the morning of the fourth day we went to the meeting room because a woman had flown in from New York to take Coco home and wanted to talk to us.

She was called Serenity and by chance the name suited her because she was a calm, composed lady with big, warm, dark blue eyes that matched the shade of her dungarees.

Me and Guthrie were discussing body bags, wondering if airlines preferred them because they were easier to transport and much cheaper than coffins. I hoped Coco would be carried home in a hard, wooden box and if not, needed to know if a bag would keep her safe.

'The thing is, how thick are they? Can you feel the body through the bag?' I said and Guthrie frowned as he typed the question into his phone. For some weird reason there was actually a signal.

It might seem like an odd conversation to be having when Serenity pulled up the chair in front of us but we'd got into the habit of discussing things like that because our minds wanted answers; any answers to any questions and we became obsessed with details. The whys were important and though I still fancied Guthrie like crazy, we'd become friends instead.

It was astonishing how easily we switched from talking about something remote like salted popcorn versus sweet then back to the material used to make body bags (thick plastic that's heat sealed to prevent leakage) but Blake said it was the brain's way of coping with trauma. I knew that. Dad told me that but it didn't help. Nothing helped though it didn't feel wrong that Serenity was on the verge of a smile whenever she glanced at Blake and it probably helped her and us when she started talking about Coco.

'The damage began when she was a kid of nine and filmed by a predator obsessed with little girls.'

'She said she was eleven,' I gasped.

'No.' Serenity looked at Blake again and this time she frowned. 'Coco was just nine. She was forced to watch and take part in porn non-stop after that and was taking money for sex by the time she was twelve. The conversations Coco had with all of you good people weren't the ones she was having with herself.'

'Yeah, I know,' Evan said and we all looked at him.

'Go on,' Serenity said.

'Her mum worked three jobs to pay for her dad's medication for the terminal illness he died from. The family had nothing. She was ill, too, in the end, her mum. No one could help until you lot told Coco about the respite course. Said you had your doubts but she convinced you it was right and your charity funded her.'

'Yes,' Serenity said. 'This was the last resort. The original predator gave her presents, was affectionate and listened to her problems, forged a bond to ensure her silence then stole her innocence. Perpetrators call it breaking in but let's not forget the damage done to them by hardcore porn and the interests of big businesses to profit from that abuse. Did she say anything else?'

'Loads about her sad, druggy, younger sister. They found her dead on the street. She was in it as well. Coco loved her grandpa. He was in prison. Stole stuff to help her mum.' Evan shivered and looked down. 'By the lake once, she took off all her clothes and danced around. Told me to have a good look because it was a real female body that cruel bastards had passed round for fun. People don't want to know how bad it is out there. She made me promise to give up porn because it gets into your blood without you really knowing what it's doing.'

Lovely little Coco. How could she be gone? I put my arm around Evan and squeezed him tight. A big tear fell down his cheek. Finally, he admitted he watched porn but it took a little angel like Coco to convince him to stop. In between the crying and fluttering of sad words that filled the hall, Serenity got up and went and stood beside Evan.

I started fantasising she was going to congratulate him for speaking out but she stayed there, silent as the day, and just stared ahead.

We all gazed at the plain woman with hands in the pockets of her blue dungarees and I glanced at the stage then out of the window at the barren landscape, aware that Evan had changed and Serenity was somehow marking it. Yet she'd just arrived. Could she feel us getting closer to understanding him the longer she stood there?

Evan wasn't the same when the talk ended.

Serenity touched his shoulder, waited for him to get up and walked with him to the door. Upright with a steady gaze, instead of confusion, doubt, fear and shame in dark eyes fixed on the gaps between the chairs, there was gratitude on Evan's face all the way into the sunshine.

It's true; the biggest things happen in the quietest moments. There are a thousand ways to live a life and he'd chosen his future.

FIFTY-THREE

Mum came back and wanted to go over everything but we were done by then and didn't want to discuss Coco anymore. We were sitting on the single bed along with the opened, silver suitcase in her tidy room at the guest house which was cool and smelt of real wax polish from the tin on the side.

Mum fished out the new T-shirts she'd bought from a trip to town.

'You'll like this,' she said and the navy T-shirt in her hand forced a shrug which she took to be approval as she dropped it on my shoulder.

'Well?'

'Yeah. Thanks,' I said in a vague, dismissive way. To be honest, the last thing I needed was another dark, no words, sensible T-shirt (I'm not paying money to advertise their products or whims, is what Mum says) but then she flung a pink, dress-length T-shirt at me which was perfect. She knew we were sad and still shocked and Coco was never far from our minds but stressed the importance of grabbing every opportunity to try and feel better.

'Life goes on,' she said. 'We must be grateful for that.'

I don't think Mum noticed how much Evan had changed because he was being quiet as always, and it was easy to assume the tanned, spot-free, clean-shaven face was the result of proper sleep, good food, clean air and sunshine when, in fact, he was ankle-deep in understanding how lucky he was to be free of porn.

Mum passed Evan another white T-shirt he didn't care about and would forget to wear, while I folded mine carefully, grateful to have something clean to put on. I still had no idea what the community did with their dirty clothes and had so far only washed my underwear.

'Have you got any soap powder?' I asked.

Mum frowned. 'There's loads in the kitchen. Now listen, we must talk about this girl's death.'

'We've done all that.' I said. 'I'll get some.'

'Not until we go over what happened.'

'I don't need to do any washing,' Evan said. *When, exactly, did he ever need to do any washing?*

'We've been through it a hundred times,' I said but Mum didn't believe me, got a bit fussed, looked in the small mirror, pulled the elastic band from her heat-frizzed hair and flipped it on her wrist.

'It's important to say how you feel,' she said.

'Mum!'

She was being annoying and fiddled around with two, braided friendship bracelets on her wrist before bunching the messy bundle of hair on top of her head and letting it go.

'Just a minute,' she said and unzipped the side of an orange bag to produce three, organic washing powder sachets. 'I forgot I had these.'

'Who gave you those friendship bracelets?' Evan said.

Mum went all girly. 'I don't know. What does it matter? They're only bracelets, Evan.'

I knew he was thinking the same thing as me. In a week we were going home and Serge would be left behind so there was no need to worry about him.

Mum gave up asking about Coco and we went back to the dorms with three, new T-shirts each. The skimpy, white, thin-strap, sleeveless one felt pretty good with the oh-so-faded jeans because my arms had gone as brown as Evan's face and later that evening it felt as if the distant fairy lights up at the auditorium were twinkling just for me.

The first person I saw was Sanvi, who was leaving for India in the morning with her father. She'd disappeared with her phone the moment Serge handed them over and missed seeing or hearing about Coco's death until the following morning, having spent the night with family friends in the community accommodation that none of us have seen or visited.

Smiling in that special way of hers in the half darkness, Sanvi was leaning against the brick arch of the pizza area to one side of the tables and benches. The shops were closed, the green ping-pong table in the corner glowed under the yellow light and it was strange because Guthrie, Blake and Sharrow weren't there.

Looking amazing in a short, blue spotted dress that transformed Constanza from scruffy to gorgeous, I gave her an exaggerated, admiring glance and she laughed.

Sanvi poured orange juice and Sun God, I mean Josh, handed out the full glasses. He looked more like a Greek god than ever and was enjoying being the waiter. All the girls were aware of his strong, muscly arms as he plonked the glasses on the table. The next day he had a lift to a festival in Portugal, where a job was waiting for him and we wouldn't see him or Sanvi again.

'I've never spoken to you,' I said.

With a startled face, Lilla joked, 'Me, also. Never. No.'

Sun God lit up. 'OK. Why not?' and stood back with hands on his hips.

'Because she fancies you,' Evan piped up and back in London it would have been hard to stop myself from strangling him but I didn't because this was Arcadia and it was true.

Unperturbed, Sun God ran a hand through his thick black hair. Girls fancying him was sooo normal for him. 'OK. Well, you can have an illegal beer then. We got some from town.'

'No, thanks. I can't stand the taste,' I said. Too laid back to deny I fancied him and far too interested in his reaction to deny it.

'Wait a while and we'll get some spirits and cans for the real party in the forest.' Sun God grinned. 'You missed the last one.'

'Yeah?' Evan was mystified and so was I.

'I could do with a beer.' The huge grin on Tomas's face, stuck there since his time with Janice, spread even wider when Carl thumped his back as if the bottles were hidden in his old, green T-shirt and the fist pumping would release them.

'Me too. Thanks,' Carl said.

'We've got some candles for later.' Pleased with himself, Sun God sucked in his perfect cheeks, fished a plastic opener from his jeans' pocket and hurried to pop the tops off two, large beer bottles that were hidden underneath the pizza counter.

The pungent smell spiked the air as he whooshed the beers to the table. 'There you go.'

With already wet lips, Mo grinned between sips. 'Ooh, that's nice, that is. Bit warm but tasty.'

Evan ignored my surprised face and lifted the bottle to his mouth as if the bitter taste was welcome and he was used to drinking.

'Malted beers are toffee flavoured,' Sun God said. 'Sure you don't want one?'

'Yeah, she's sure.' Guthrie's hands were suddenly on my shoulders and he added, 'If Blake or Sharrow catch you drinking, there will be trouble.'

'Hey, relax man,' Sun God said. 'They're not here and we're having a couple of beers to say adios amigos.'

The group's urge to have fun died with one glance from Guthrie's serious face and Sun God threw his arms in the air, ducked out of the half-light coming from the ping-pong table and strutted towards the distant stage of the auditorium where soft music had started playing.

Guthrie leaned over the counter to see how many beers Sun God had stashed away underneath the bar. Pulling out a plastic bag crammed with clinking bottles answered the question and Sanvi raised her eyebrows at the fuss he was making. It was clear by their reaction that Tomas and Carl felt the same way and they glanced at Guthrie as if he had the problem, not Sun God.

Without a hint of embarrassment, Guthrie marched into the darkness with the clanking bag of bottles and I caught up with him before he reached the lake.

'There aren't enough beers to cause any harm,' I said and he stopped.

'Yeah, have a few beers and vodka, why not? It's fun getting dehydrated and throwing up but no problem, you'll be all right in the morning when Josh has gone.'

'Josh?'

'You don't know his name?' Guthrie said.

'I sort of do but keep forgetting.' *He'll always to be Sun God to me.*

'You're sweet, Marya,' Guthrie sighed. 'Don't you see? He wants to have a drunken party but on his own it would be sad so everyone has to join in and he'll be fine because he's a drinker but who's going to watch out for your wasted brother or wrecked Tomas when they're out of it on the floor? How will it reflect on the community? On Blake and Sharrow?'

'You're right.'

'I live with my dad in a rubbish flat in Archway with nothing but ketchup and empty vodka bottles in the cupboards. I get home and he's usually asleep on the dirty sofa, newspapers on his face, snoring.'

'That's terrible,' I said. 'Where's your mum?'

'She left when I was two. Dad works nights in the security office of a closed factory, looking at blank screens. If I can't wake him up to get a couple of quid for a box of chicken and chips, I run down to my friends in the basement flat who happen to be lesbians. They feed me all the time. There's a girl, Paulette, from down the road who used to go there after school as well. She stopped coming so much when she got into porn and my friends racked their brains how to help her. We sit around for hours coming up with ways to distract Paulette. Talking's no use. She just laughs. All the stuff we're doing here is what my friends have said all along about porn.'

'What nice women,' I said.

'Yeah, the best. They paid for me to come and find ways to help Paulette. I thought I'd died and gone to heaven when I got here. All this space and sunshine. Peace, you know? The food keeps coming. The countryside is amazing. Honestly, it was so incredible that first day, I just wanted to love everyone.'

'That's so cute.'

He squeezed my arm.

I meant to say something else but instead this came out: 'Do your friends watch lesbian porn?'

'Nah. They hate it. Most of it's made by men and they don't want to be manipulated. Some of their friends watch feminist porn.'

'You sure you're not into it? What about that time in the lake?'

The bottles clinked as Guthrie slung an arm around my shoulder. 'Hey, lovely one.' He kissed my cheek. No one has ever called me *lovely one* before. My stomach jumped. We shuffled along the path, bottles clanking the darkness until we found the open sky and moon on a silver, grassy bank and plumped down. Tremendous beams between the trees shone like a thousand arrows and the perfect setting made us hug our knees and stare out, transfixed.

'I was in the lake with Coco once,' Guthrie said after a while and stared at me until I nodded. 'We did everything but have sex because you know – no condoms, and...'

'I get it.'

'We were being silly – it wasn't serious. She wanted to play around, she said, but now I know there was more.' He looked sad.

'There's so many things I want to ask her,' I said. 'Now I can't. It feels wrong to be here without her. That's what gets me.'

'I keep expecting to see her.' His eyes crinkled and he crossed his legs.

'Me, too,' I said and he smiled.

'I'll be back at sixth form college soon and spending every spare nanosecond at my neighbour's because I want to study physics, not mess around. I know. Yeah. It's a hard subject and I'm going to have to hold back from the girls a bit to get my head in the right place for exams next year, aren't I?'

'Not if you're honest with us, no. I'll still like you.'

OMG. *Did that really come out of my mouth?*

'How come you're so accepting, Marya?'

'Me?'

'Tell me.'

'Tell you what?' His intense eyes were getting scary and my heart started moving around like it needed to escape my body.

'Everything you've never told anyone.' Warmth radiated from his smiling face.

I fell back on the grass and looked up at the millions of stars that already knew all my secrets and instead of answering, said, 'Wanna go skinny dipping?'

The atmosphere flagged. I'd destroyed it.

'No. Let's find Evan.' Guthrie gathered the plastic bag of bottles from the long grass, tied it tight, swung it high and sent the cannonball of clinking glass into the darkness with a loud splash that toned out the yell inside me. *No, let's not go.*

FIFTY-FOUR

*W*hat have you got to lose? Talk to him. Tell him everything, I thought as we walked back towards the tables and the rest of the group. This time he didn't look at me, touch my arm or call me *lovely one*.

'Why physics?' I said at last.

'Right. OK. Well, I couldn't get a handle on physics at all until my neighbours hired a tutor for me before GCSEs.' He perked up. 'The guy who came to the basement was a retired university professor with foul breath but really got me into using my imagination to solve problems. Physics is the basis of astronomy, oceanography, all kinds of interesting subjects, not just subatomic particles and the study of galaxies.'

Guthrie was suddenly excited and that feeling where everything is possible and all you have to do is reach into the ether and grab it with both hands, returned.

We gazed futures full of fun and excitement into each other's eyes and I said, 'Yeah and their discoveries are leading to technologies we can't even imagine.'

'Quantum physics studies the bridges from what we know, which is hardly anything, to what is impossible to even get your head around.' Guthrie smiled.

'I was going to do English.' I almost touched his arm.

I am going to do English. Why am I lying?

'But I might change my mind after this trip,' I said. *Liar.* 'And do an extra A Level in cosmology or something at night school.'

Shut up. I don't know where that idea came from but it sounded good. 'If that's possible, because what's more interesting than our universe and how it came about?' I was becoming an idiot in front of my own eyes and needed to take control of the situation, but how, when just looking at him, sandpapered my brain and made me say things I hadn't thought about before?

'Cosmology? Wow.'

'Not really. I'm going to do English. It's my best subject.' He was thrilled by the admission and twisted right round on one foot and did a little tap. Being big and sturdy made the dainty gesture look extra silly but it was on purpose. He was making fun of me and the gentle twist and tap defined how happy I was. How happy we both were.

'Dark energy, dark matter and quasars, though. What are they about?' I wanted to match his enthusiasm and keep him talking. 'Those sad kids who watch porn don't know what they're missing out on.'

My eyes stalked the unknown energy in the sky, stars and watching moon as we strolled, side by side, hunched up and ready for something magnificent to happen.

Serious face seriously on, I said, 'Viewing the latest tangled up body parts just doesn't compare with the mysteries of our world.'

'Let's not dumb sex down too much,' he said and I was going to say I was talking about porn, not sex, when he pointed to the empty pulled out benches with lonely, yellow light on the green ping-pong table, scruffy basket of bats on top which forced me to lighten up.

'Maybe they're all having sex?' I really should stop this. He must have thought I was crazy for it.

'Wait, I know where they are.' Guthrie took my hand and hurried me back to the path.

To be honest, I didn't care where we were going. He was the only thing on my mind. Throwing the bottles in the lake was a bit extreme, but hey, if my dad was an alcoholic I might have done the same thing and the others probably wouldn't find it hard to forgive him.

Guthrie's desire to study physics was impressive and the fact he came here and fell in love with Arcadia and all the girls, was natural and easy to understand as long as his warm hand remained wrapped round mine.

We trudged along for a while in silence and flashes of moonlight streaked my no longer white trainers. The lovely night was enough to make me want to move to Archway which isn't too far from Lewisham and I began to imagine him becoming my boyfriend and seeing him every weekend.

In the pitch black, the sound of tinny music broke through the noise in my head. A creature scurried through the bushes and Guthrie dropped my hand when the outline of a solitary dancing figure came whirling round the bend. When he twisted aside his pony tail to rearrange huge black headphones, we realised it was Carl and as he got closer, the killer moves changed with the beat. He began singing out of tune and was so full of craziness it was hilarious to watch.

The night was his. He owned the music. Eyes closed and jumping, Carl was happily wrecked. I felt like an intruder watching him bouncing around and had no right to be there but at the same time my heart leapt. Who grooves down a midnight path in the middle of nowhere on their own? He does and if you put the scene on social media it would get a million hits.

'Nice footwork,' Guthrie muttered and Carl was practically in our faces before he spotted us and lashed out. So busy falling back, yelling, in a state of confusion, he looked clinically insane and it took a few seconds to coil his body back to normal, remove the headphones and flip the music off in his pocket.

'I thought you were trees, man.'

'Where you going?' I asked.

'To have it out with Coco.' With one eye shut, he looked up at the stars and dark trees as if they could hear him, grabbed his head and stumbled like he'd been let out of a car at the side of a busy road after suffering from motion sickness.

Guthrie stuck an arm out and caught him. I grabbed an elbow and Carl insisted on leading the way to the exact spot which I wouldn't have known. There were no dents on the path.

No tyre marks or traces of blood that we could make out in the dark. Nothing but newly raked earth to distinguish the tidying up the community had done. It was just a piece of ground. A piece of ground where a terrible memory was buried.

'You should have stuck with me. I wouldn't have let you die,' Carl said to the still air and struggled to pull away until we let go. Maybe he didn't make it clear enough because he said it again. 'I wouldn't have let you die, Coco.'

Grief is love and we stood there listening to Carl shout abuse at the dark universe. Our silence made him a bit irate after a while and he kept turning round and snarling as if her death was our fault. Why weren't we yelling? He didn't understand and we stared at the lake and the trees until the danger of him doing something stupid passed and the sheer impossibility of remaining upright stormed his knees and he fell, muttering something unintelligible to the raked earth.

Finally, he laid back with hands on his heart, headphones round his neck and we carried on standing there with time ticking by until Guthrie leaned on the boulder the tractor hit, and said, 'Goodnight, Carl. Goodbye, Coco.'

It was the closest thing to a funeral we would get.

FIFTY-FIVE

All too aware of the fact that Carl was unlikely to move for hours after he insisted on staying where he was, we gave up and started again for the mysterious party hut where the rest of the group were maybe still hanging out.

This time Guthrie didn't take my hand and we didn't talk about Carl or Coco. Nothing with a capital letter. Down the track we went and I'd never seen so many silver pennies of moonlight on the path before.

They somehow lit our way and I said, 'Do you think Carl's going to be all right without a blanket?'

'I'll go back and check on him in an hour,' Guthrie said. The track turned into a series of overgrown, foot-wide patches through rustling bushes and we climbed a sharp incline to find a wooden hut that resembled an out of place, large garden shed, complete with an old green pipe and rake lined up by the door.

There wasn't a sound coming from inside and I suspected Guthrie might have used the party story as a ploy to get me there. I needn't have got so excited. He flung the door open and four, tea light candles on an empty tin of catering size beans, fluttered. There was a strong smell of wood and beer. Crushed cans littered the floor and with their backs to us, Tomas was flinging peanuts at Sun God (I mean Josh), who was swigging vodka straight from the bottle and forcing him to wait his turn.

Unbelievably at peace, Constanza and Evan were asleep in each other's arms in the far corner and they floated into my eyes in a fairy dream of a blue and white, spotted dress and bare, brown limbs flecked with candle light. Their closed eyes and shining, sun-drenched smiles only a tease apart.

To witness Evan asleep with a girl in the corner of a smelly hut, halfway up a hill in Spain – I couldn't even put that into words. The only person I had to contend with then was myself and I was determined to do that no matter what.

FIFTY-SIX

With her tiny shape leaning on the splintered wall, Lilla was mostly out of it and it took several minutes for Guthrie to get her feet to connect with the rest of her body. She had no idea where she was, and going forward, pulled loose, groping the air for clues as he helped her to the door.

'Here. This way, Lilla,' Guthrie said and scowled at Sun God who was too stupefied to notice. As soon as the door closed, I heard Lilla chucking up outside and realised the silence in the hut was due to the lack of music. Asleep beside the lake, Carl's iPod was out of range.

From his Buddha-like position on the floor, Sun God's arm wobbled a bottle of vodka at me and Tomas nodded me to go ahead. Because I couldn't just stand there, I took a sip. It smelt of air, tasted of nothing, not even water but landed in my stomach like a bullet. Despite the enormous implications of drinking after everything Guthrie had said, I wanted to shake off the fact I knew he wouldn't be back. If he couldn't look after Carl and I didn't need him then he'd spend the rest of the night taking care of Lilla. That's the kind of good guy he was. Well, that's what I told myself and stopped caring about anything except what I needed to say.

No more spinning around the subject. It had to come out.

Missing Guthrie was hard to push away and I almost sipped too much vodka but Tomas reached to grab the bottle back. In amazement at the small amount of alcohol left, he waved the liquid at the wooden ceiling to make sure and looked at me, surprised I was still standing there.

I sat down between them on the rough, uneven floor, eyes on the ingrained dirt in the grooves between the planks and took in the empty, folded plastic bag Sun God had tucked under his calf. Arcadia isn't overrun with plastic bags so I guessed he was keeping the precious cargo safe. What was harder to understand was what I was doing with them. I didn't know and neither did they. The look that passed between the guys was confusion mixed with curiosity, knowing I was there on false pretences and wasn't much of a drinker.

'Don't ever sleep on a feather pillow or duvet,' Sun God said. 'Got that?' I nodded and he passed me the vodka.

'Geese wander around in a daze after being plucked by those animals,' he said. 'They let them run around flapping their bare wings covered in blood.' Sun God ran his strong, brown hands through his thick black hair and with pure hatred on his face went on. 'Then they slaughter them for meat and people swallow their pain and fear with cranberry and apple sauce. Geese mate for life and mourn when their partner dies. Don't get me going about foie gras and the pipes they shove down their throats to fatten them up.'

I wasn't going to and Tomas yawned. This wasn't news to either of us. I felt sorry for the defenceless geese. In a split second every hurt done to all the animals in the world sped through me. I was furious and wanted my cat on my lap as the vodka warmed my throat. The small candles fluttered in the corner and the shadows of moving arms patterned the wall like killers searching for a goose to butcher.

I'd seen the inside of a filthy factory farm on YouTube. The injured, stressed, often deformed chickens lived and died in confined spaces without a glimpse of sunshine. It was enough to put anyone off meat. The workers also suffered injuries from repetitive tasks in unhealthy conditions as well as respiratory problems from airborne diseases. I knew factory farming was increasing to meet demand and when the full impact of the methane emissions, dispersal of waste and pollution was explained, I vowed to give up dairy as well as meat but haven't quite managed it yet.

'Go on,' Sun God goaded me. 'Say what's on your mind.'

'I will then. Porn's a totally, stupid, ridiculous waste of time.

Nobody needs it.' This was a strange thing for me to say because it had nothing to do with geese but I couldn't stop. 'Porn is a form of factory farming where bound up kids are left in shock and pain with no way to fight back. Where subsequent viewings force kids, like geese, to succumb and grow weaker, leaving them hanging through the bars of big business while what's left of their flesh is used for work place filler.'

'Yay, mate, you got that right,' Sun God said but Tomas rubbed his eyes, more concerned with the almost empty bottle he placed between his knees.

I turned around. Evan was still fast asleep. I didn't intend saying anything else but the fire in my throat spread to my mouth and what with the admiration on Sun God's face, it really had to come out.

'Was it right for the parents to sit in the garden drinking coffee thinking us kids were OK, not knowing Maddie, my friend in junior school, had hardcore porn on the TV in her bedroom upstairs while the party music was still playing?'

'Na, that wasn't right but it happens.' Sun God raised his eyebrows and Tomas leaned forward to listen, elbows sliding from his jeans.

'How hardcore was it?'

'I don't know enough about porn to tell you but it was vile and Maddie forced the five of us; three girls and two boys who were only eleven, to dance around to the music while watching an actual girl's body being ripped apart from behind.'

'Pretty hardcore then,' Tomas said. 'How old was the girl?'

'About the same age as us,' I said. 'It was Maddie's bedroom. Her TV and she couldn't stop giggling. She hit us with a pillow because we didn't think it was funny. A sort of fight started and I couldn't breathe. Couldn't move. I was so scared when one of the boys pushed her on the bed, I tried to get out but the other boy locked the door and when he raped her, I didn't see because my face was in my hands. I heard them though. Maddie was crying, telling him to stop but got up afterwards and pretended she was fine. Told us not to say anything because her parents would kill her and it was nothing, they'd done it before. We didn't believe her. He just did up his pants and looked at us girls huddled together and then we heard someone coming up the stairs. His mate unlocked the door. We ran for it and no one ever knew. When they saw our faces, the parents thought we'd been watching a horror film. Mum finished her tea. Didn't say a word. No one asked. They just assumed that's what we'd been doing. The next day was the last of primary school and we ended up at different secondaries. I saw Maddie once after that and she said if I ever told anyone what happened, she'd say I was a liar. That's what got me. The other girls said they weren't there when I tried talking to them.'

The feeling of revulsion came back. I'd never stopped obsessing about it and was so lost in the pink bedroom, pillows on the floor, remembering the dazed smile on Maddie's crying face I'd kept secret for all those years, I didn't notice Guthrie standing behind me, just inside the door.

I didn't know Evan and Constanza were wide awake and heard it all. I glanced at Tomas who couldn't stop blinking while Sun God frowned, tried to focus, flipped the empty bottle over by mistake and said, 'That's shit.' And I didn't know if he was angry about the lack of vodka or reacting to what I'd said.

I carried that incident with me the whole of my life and it was the oddest thing because once I told everyone I couldn't imagine why it had been such a major part of my life.

Two seconds later, gentle Guthrie pulled me upright and hugged me tight. It was an insistent, warm, Sanvi-like forever hug that pushed everything else out. Somehow Tomas and Sun God managed to join in and Evan and Constanza took their turn to rub my arm, touch my hand and caress my hair. The compassionate, hopeful, loving spirit of Arcadia was in the group hug and nothing that lay ahead until the end of time, mattered more than the steady relief of their love.

They say you can feel your soul leap during prayer, meditation, certain songs and special dreams but they don't tell you how incredible it can be for a problem to suddenly be heard and understood.

FIFTY-SEVEN

When Carl stumbled through the door with a sobered-up Lilla, he had no idea what was going on. All of us burrowing into each other must have looked weird.

'What did I miss?' His mouth hung open and he unplugged the headphones and rolled into the room with music raging from his pocket. Amazing song after amazing song bounced out of his chest and all the candles flickered. Spellbound by the sudden electronica, me and Evan grinned at each other and everyone joined in to that great song by The Waterboys: *The Whole of the Moon*. The one Mum loves. A song that isn't about a lover's eyes, the way she looks at him, her incredible beauty or the way she moves, but celebrates her magnificence as a person: 'I saw the crescent, you saw the whole of the moon.' Cutting loose and yelling, pointing at each other, bursting with energy, we sang along. Lilla kicked off her sandals. She had terrible rhythm but that didn't stop her moving in an extreme case of beat avoidance.

Arms out, heads back, we were the song and it almost became a competition who could sing the loudest and make the biggest fool of themselves.

Evan's whole life weaved in and out of my mind. The time he stood at the window looking at the rain because Mum was late coming back from the shops and he wouldn't believe the buses were probably packed and nothing bad had happened. Evan's wild, frightened face when his friend was taken to hospital with pneumonia and nearly died flashed right past, and the morning he said, 'I'm going to rape a girl, kill her and then kill myself,' settled for a moment as I watched him belting his heart out with life-giving sweetness, arm in arm with Constanza.

From one thing comes another and Evan and Constanza faded as Guthrie swished me into him and we slipped alone into a secret lake where slow water swept us into a dream.

FIFTY-EIGHT

Sharrow had an engaging but efficient expression on her face when she opened the door. Her wide smile said she wasn't going to make a fuss but her steely, blue eyes proved the opposite was true. Either way, I didn't care because I was happier than I ever thought possible and Guthrie and me couldn't stop. Even if Mum walked in on us I would have carried on kissing him.

'OK, guys,' Sharrow said and Guthrie reluctantly looked over.

'Sorry to bust it up but you know… need to get going. There's a hike this morning. Remember?' With a cheery smile, she glanced at the empty vodka bottle on the floor, crushed cans scattered round the hut and each of us in turn, surprised we weren't as drunk as the debris suggested.

I let Guthrie go, we linked arms instead and though Sharrow was calm on the surface and used to allowing people to be themselves, she couldn't resist following Tomas and Sun God around as they picked up the dribbling cans and dropped them in the plastic bag.

'Look,' she said. 'We expected things to go astray at some point but alcohol never solved a single problem and if this happens again there will be serious consequences.'

By the look on Sun God's face he'd already left for the festival in Portugal with more fun and loud music in his shrug than there was for anything that was likely to happen in Arcadia. He didn't care and hadn't changed. 'Sure. Sure,' he said while we stayed quiet.

The birds were waking up as we stepped into the fresh, earthy smell of damp grass and the brightening sky was shot through with the promise of another boiling hot day. Hand in hand, me and Guthrie lagged behind the others. Up ahead crunching the path, Evan turned to glance at me for a brief second with a look that said,

'I always knew *you* were the one with the problem.' What would he say about Maddie when we when we were alone? He probably remembered the party because I was so excited I hardly slept the night before and he was jealous he wasn't invited and had to stay home. It bothered me because I didn't want Evan to tell Mum because she'd tell Dad who would go to the police. For certain.

It was easy to imagine how my life could fall apart as a result and I tried not to think about being questioned. The shame of telling on Maddie. The wait for the knock on the door and fear of walking the streets in case I bumped into Vernon Wood. He and his mates could alter everything about my so-called bright future and would it change anything? Vernon was already in trouble with the police and if Maddie denied the whole thing and the others refused to admit it was true what would happen to me then?

When we sat down for breakfast at the art building, the dazzle on the dried grass and trees beyond the cool table was the kind of sunshine you want to kiss. It was perfect, the food smelt of raspberry jam and we were all bleary eyed but somehow wide awake. I needed to persuade Evan to keep quiet and watched him gaze at the palettes, brushes and boards lined up, clean and ready to use and knew his mind was on what happened to Maddie. He knows her brother.

The floor had been swept. A couple of unrolled sleeping bags rested under the nearest tree. The art building looked like the most romantic place on earth with paintings of cactus, bright leaves and trees on every surface. I looked at Guthrie. He got it and when he glanced at Evan's confused face, patted my back in a *there, there* way.

Yellow bra poking out of her unbuttoned blue and white, spotted dress, Constanza was happily talking to Tomas who didn't look as brand new as she did but was enjoying himself. Everything I'd said was an easy part of the lovely atmosphere. I was the same as them with a similar problem and we were all part of the new morning on the terrace.

Lilla was shy after throwing up from drinking too much a few hours ago, but looked up now and then to smile at me and Guthrie because we couldn't leave each other alone.

Not deviating from the serious job of cramming as much bread, leftover rice and tomatoes into his mouth, Carl was a mess. His greasy jeans were torn, the leaked pony tail was crawling all over his face but the way his bright eyes focused on Lilla made him appear totally with it.

When Guthrie went to shower and Evan, who was chewing melon like a greedy child, juice dripping down his chin, shifted into his space beside me, I knew he was going to ask about Maddie.

'Keep your mouth shut about it,' I said.

Evan frowned. 'What you don't realise is, that guy's going to get killed.'

'You don't know him.' I was shocked.

'Yeah, I do. It was Vernon Wood, wasn't it?'

I looked down. He was right but I didn't give in. I couldn't. He lives in the next road and his name and whole family cover all the evil done down our way.

'Stop saying you're going to kill someone, Evan,' I said. 'Please. There's nothing you can do about it.'

'Everything OK?' Blake squeezed up opposite to make room for a man I'd never seen before. Tall and friendly, older than Blake with a thick black beard from chin to sideburns, he thumped a bowl of porridge on the table and dropped two clinking spoons.

'Andrew, my life partner,' Blake said proudly and the guy grinned.

'Hey, everyone. Good to meet you at last,' Andrew said with a cool American accent.

'Hi Andrew,' we said. Evan's surprise was obvious but we were all thinking the same thing: *Oh, so Blake's gay. Right.* That's how astonishing the information was, and when Andrew took a huge jar of vegan chocolate spread from the backpack on his shoulder and flipped open the lid, the smell was so good it made me giggle.

'Come on. Dig in. Don't be shy,' Andrew said and all the

wonderful things about Arcadia were underlined by the sudden smooth taste of chocolate on stiff rye bread.

I thought Sanvi had already left, but no, this was her and Sun God's last meal. Soon the table filled with chat about train times, flights, coaches and donations to the second hand clothes shop.

Sun God smiled at me. Too good looking to be true in fresh white T-shirt and denim cut-offs, I tried to avert my eyes but couldn't. If not for him I wouldn't have said what I did and was grateful but still didn't know anything about him.

It was on the tip of my tongue to ask what his story was. 'Where do you live?' I asked instead.

His bright blue eyes darkened and he turned away. 'I'm not sure.'

The chance to ask why he wasn't sure, passed, he was too busy eating and Mo came up the track with a small brown bird cupped in her hand. Sun God was the first out of his seat. When Mo stroked the tiny limp head with tears running from beneath her sunglasses, I thought he might cry, too. So that's why she wasn't in the hut last night. Mo's back was wet with sweat so I jumped up to fetch her some water.

'The sparrow's seriously sick. We have to keep the broken wing close to the body until we can get some vet tape to stick it down,' Mo explained. Lilla, Tomas, Carl and Constanza abandoned adding spread to their food and crowded round, clucking at the sparrow while Evan licked smears of chocolate from his lips. Clearly, Vernon Wood was the last thing on his mind.

FIFTY-NINE

We waved Sun God off after breakfast. He had an all-day ride with three guys on their way to the same festival in Portugal. A much older man with grey curls flattened by a blue headband, issued instructions about bags and water bottles and like a well-behaved child who couldn't wait to get going, Sun God obeyed.

Squashed into the back of the yellow Renault, Sun God shouted, 'Seeya,' without a care in the world, eyes on the blue and green distant hills as the car pulled away in the sunshine and vanished into the shimmering emptiness.

He took my secret with him. A secret he'd probably never think about again and none of us knew what twisted his heart apart from factory-farmed geese. He never said why he was there. He didn't have to. No one asked and now he was gone. Arcadia wouldn't be the same without him.

Ten minutes later after loads of hugs, we waited outside the dorms to wave goodbye to the proper taxi with sign, taking Sanvi and her serious-looking dad to the station. He talked to the Spanish driver about the route to the city while Sanvi dragged her backpack between her legs, suitcase already on the seat beside her.

Serge wasn't driving the taxi which was weird. I thought that was his job?

Sanvi pointed to herself. 'Don't forget to read my blog.' I nodded but didn't know anything about it and frowned.

'Blake's got the link,' Sanvi said and there behind me was Guthrie, fresh and clean and smelling of soap. He put an arm around my waist for a second and touched my hand. The world drifted by as we stood there in silence, no boundary between us. The driver started the car.

Sharrow showed up and kissed Sanvi goodbye through the open window.

'Thank you for being an important part of the group. Safe trip,' she said.

Suddenly it was 11am, the car drove off, lovely Sanvi was gone and I was really tired.

Sharrow wasn't pleased when Evan insisted on staying behind. 'I'm sorry you're not hiking.'

He shrugged and glanced at pretty Constanza and when Sharrow turned round he took the chance to slope off. Lucky him.

'OK, don't forget the sun cream and fill your water bottles,' Sharrow told the rest of us. 'Guthrie this is yours.' She handed him a small, white, sealed envelope which he buried in the back pocket of his jeans. I guessed it was a letter from home but didn't ask.

'Blake's going to drive up with the food and meet us on the hill for lunch,' Sharrow said. 'Grab your stuff and be back here in half an hour.'

Hill? Oh, no. It would be hard enough crawling up the stairs to the sweaty dorm without a long trek up a boiling hot hill afterwards. I wished I had the nerve to pull out like Evan.

Letting go of my hand, Guthrie bumped me sideways to wake me up. Tired with bloodshot eyes, it was obvious he was also in two minds about the trek. 'We could stay behind.'

'No, see, I'm not used to being the difficult kid,' I said.

'I could do with a sleep, too,' he said.

'The sleep thing sounds nice.' I played with his furry hand and we locked fingers. 'OK, so I'll like shower and get my stuff. We're going.' And I ran off, looking forward to cleaning up and changing into my new, pink T-shirt dress.

SIXTY

Drenched in sweat, it's a wonder any of us made it up the hill after a night without sleep. Turning the last corner of the winding path that stretched into infinity was a real effort in the sickening heat and when Sharrow said, 'That's it. You made it,' I doubted it was true.

The landscape was exactly the same as every other bend we'd shuffled round and I sipped the last few drops of the warm water, feeling a bit sucked in like the bottle but no, we had arrived. Breathing hard, we followed Sharrow the last few steps through bulging bushes to a shady, flat area where Blake was on a bright red cloth with a grey cooler, open box of food beside him.

'Hey there,' he called.

My knees flaked at the sight of cold water and oranges. Guthrie just stood there, eyes popping at the radiant valley and hills falling into the distance all around.

'Not something you see in Archway,' I said.

'Or Lewisham.' Guthrie looked at me with a touch of scorn. We fetched bottles of water from the cooler and rubbed damp, hard, icy glass over our skin until the coolness stung. Then we started on the oranges and I could tell Guthrie was yearning for the surrounding landscape to stay within reach of his eyes as we pitched our backpacks a little further away from the others.

Evan settled himself near Constanza, and I hoped he wasn't going to talk about Maddie's party to Blake who didn't know anything about it. Along with Sharrow, he wasn't there when I spilt the beans and though no one had mentioned it this morning, I knew they would. It seemed now wasn't the time though, because Evan was carefully picking jewel-red drops from a pomegranate as if they might fly away and opposite him, Blake was busy pushing reluctant bottles further down the lumps of ice in the cooler.

You'd think we were half-starved by the way we consumed vegan cheese, bread, fat tomatoes and bits of juicy orange stuck hard to our fingers and faces. There was a dream-like rhythm to the sound of a car coming up the hill and when it came to a stop, two birds flew out of the trees and shaggy-haired Paulo, co-founder of Arcadia, came through the bushes, hand in hand with a smaller, female version of himself except Odell, his partner, had flaming, dyed red hair and a sweeter, friendlier expression.

There was nothing casual about Blake and Sharrow's reaction as they rushed to collect forgotten cushions from the car to make them comfortable under the tree and soon everyone was making a fuss, offering water and oranges.

As soon as we finished eating, me and Guthrie left them to enjoy the visit and snuck off down the path for some time alone but I wasn't in the mood for exploring the woods and didn't want to get any closer to the sheer drop beyond the trees. 'Let's stay here,' I said.

There was a brooding, burning look in Guthrie's brown eyes when he frowned. 'Sharrow said there's a hut round here somewhere.'

'When did she say that?'

'This morning. Not long after she gave me this.' He took the folded white envelope from the back pocket of his jeans and handed it to me. I opened it and looked at him for so long, he took the envelope back.

'Bad move,' I said.

'OK. That's fine.' He bent down and kissed my forehead.

'I mean, just giving me condoms – like that. Why did Sharrow give them to you?'

'To keep you safe, I guess. What do you want to do, Marya?' His gentle eyes scanned my face and it felt like this was the closest we would ever get. Maybe the best memory I took home with me and would later regret unless I said it like it was.

'In the lake we did everything but that.'

'Yeah.' He grinned and lowered his eyes.

'But afterwards you hardly noticed me. Didn't speak. It was like I'd imagined something special happened.'

'Yeah, it was awkward,' he said without looking up. 'I thought it might ruin our friendship and didn't want that to happen.'

I went suddenly cold. 'But we weren't friends then.'

'It felt like we were,' he said.

'No, it didn't. You wanted to keep your options open.'

'Not really.'

'Yeah, really, and what about Coco? She liked you didn't she?'

'I don't think she was that into me after a fling with Carl,' Guthrie said. 'Blake had to have a serious talk with her because one night she threw herself at him. I miss her. She was great.'

'I keep thinking I can see her coming down the path,' I said.

'I know.' He gave me a little glance and a smile.

'You liked Sanvi?'

'Yeah, she's was a real friend.'

'More than that?' I said and he shrugged.

'You've watched a lot of porn, haven't you?' This time he shook his head with disgust and his face hardened.

'Are you having a go at me?'

'No, why would I?'

'Look, Marya, I don't know what this is about but if you're scared I get it. OK?'

'You said you're here because the girl who goes to your neighbours after school, Paulette, yeah, was into porn and they paid for you to come and find ways to help her. But it's you who's addicted to porn, isn't it?'

He said nothing for a while, looked angry and drew back. I was thinking I want this to be different but didn't know how to alter the sudden coldness between us. We were close and I'd ruined everything.

'You've got a real problem, Marya,' he said and stomped off.

I shouted and in the end he turned round all helpless and hurt. I felt sorry for him. With glazed and tired eyes, even his limp arms looked sad when he wrapped them around himself. Close behind, I followed him as he wandered back down the path like that — protecting himself. On through wild, yellow and white ragged flowers, we climbed a bank, careful not to fall into a ditch and found a quiet place with smooth grass to sit. Still uncomfortable and silent but together.

'There's lots of way of saying what I really mean but this is the best.' I shifted over to touch his cheek and then did what they do in the movies with a full-on soft kiss that would make anyone watching, blush.

'Woah.' Guthrie was the first to pull away. 'You sure?' I was and he knew it but he held me at arm's length, gripped my shoulders to make certain I couldn't get any closer and spoke rapidly.

'You're on to me. So, OK, I'll tell you. Then it's up to you.'

'Don't if you don't want to.' I wanted to carry on kissing him. It felt so good.

Guthrie made no attempt to answer, turned away and slumped flat on his back on the pale grass, hands on chest and the hardest part was waiting and watching him gaze at the aimless blue sky with not a single word coming from his mouth. I left a small space between us and did the same. Just lay there and looked up. Unreal bright leaves glittered in green and yellow peaks above my head, stuck oddly to the sky like a kid's collage and I had the sense there was something I was supposed to do. Something I was supposed to say but had no idea what it was.

It felt like the spell I was under would break at any minute if he didn't speak. I was nervous, gripped the firm ground and turned to watch the blank expression on his face soften when he closed his eyes for a moment then looked at me, maybe wondering what to say.

I smiled the kind of patient smile I give Evan. He held back and because I didn't have the right words to prompt him, the harsh headachy heat of the hot afternoon settled on me like a stuffy blanket.

'Going over it in my head all the time is stupid so I'm just going to tell you. OK?' Guthrie sighed.

'OK,' I said, not daring to look.

'My dad gets angry a lot,' he said. 'He medicates with alcohol and I do the same with porn,' Guthrie said.

I kept quiet and he went on. 'Temptation is always just a click away. I still give it some now and then but not being able to watch it in Arcadia has dampened the craving. Compared to how sick I was, I'm fixed but I'm not. Not yet. Not at all. Really. You should know that weak pig is still me but I've never hurt a girl or pushed her into anything. I haven't. Honest.'

'Hey.' I grabbed his arm but he picked my fingers off one by one with a sharp glint in his eye that said, *Behave. Don't distract me.*

'I've been with girls I don't even like or find attractive. None of it was healthy. It was just a ridiculous front but I didn't care. I just marked random girls out for taking and dived in for fun. There was no respect. No feeling. Nothing.'

This maybe shouldn't have been happening when his little lie about Paulette was really a whopper to hide his addiction, but the more he told me who he was, the more I fell for him. He had his own private relationship with honesty and I thought coming clean was his challenge. I was wrong. There was more.

Guthrie was flying blind when he said, 'My best mate, Ali, fell in love and I was jealous of him and his girlfriend. How she made him feel was all he ever went on about. Waiting in line for lunch or the bus, they looked like they lived on their own little island. Just the two of them. They didn't need anyone else. I felt small next to them and sort of knew I didn't want to risk looking stupid by ever getting to know a girl I was scared of.'

'Why be scared though?'

'Clever girls are way beyond a guy like me.'

'Well, that was unexpected,' I said.

222

'Was it?' Guthrie laughed.

The air went clammy and humid again like the sudden rush of love that passed through me. There was something important I wanted to tell him but there was no need.

'Right now I like you more than ever,' he said.

There was no stopping us then. No going back from the dream that had already happened.

Like drowning, I was swimming. He touched my face and I turned. Skin dabbled against skin and the whole universe egged me on.

SIXTY-ONE

Lying back naked afterwards all I could think was, *Wow, so that's what all the fuss in the world is about. I sooo get it now.*

When I sat up on the grass, I was dazed, amazed and elated but the slight muscle ache in my side suddenly turned into an all-over horrific sweat at the sight of hundreds of red bumps on my arms. There were fire balls on my legs, shoulders and neck and sickening bulbs on the backs of my hands. Everywhere but my face while his furry skin was untouched.

Guthrie went wild. 'Oh my god. Sorry.'

Embarrassed, I pulled on the crumpled T-shirt dress and couldn't believe the state of me. 'Are they ant bites? Mosquitoes? What?'

No insects buzzed or hovered nearby. There was nothing to blame but for some reason I couldn't keep still. 'What happened?' There were so many bites it was difficult to see where they started and ended and Guthrie peered in. 'Do they itch?'

Unhinged by the feeling of a thousand, hot drills piercing my skin, I didn't know how to describe the horror. 'What are they?' So much for our hush-hush disappearance. Now everyone would know what we'd been doing. What should have been the most romantic day of my life had turned into a nightmare.

'I'll get Sharrow,' Guthrie said. 'Don't scratch. You'll make it worse.'

'No. No. I don't want anyone to see. Don't.' I wailed and made a fantastic effort not to completely lose it.

Wanting to help, Guthrie reached out but dared not touch me in case it hurt. 'OK. Don't worry. We'll go down and find a doctor.'

'What doctor?' I thought he'd gone crazy. 'This isn't Archway.'

'I heard someone say there's a doctor here,' Guthrie said. 'She's one of the community members.'

'Is her surgery next to the dry cleaners?' I yelled.

He smiled. 'Are you OK to walk?'

Doing a stupid dance, I flipped my feet up to look. There was nothing but grass and dirt on the soles and I stood there, tears stinging my face, trying not to scratch myself to death.

'We'll take it slow,' Guthrie said and the thought of hiking all the way down the hill in the boiling hot sun was too much.

'I can't go anywhere. I don't want anyone to see me,' I said and he scrabbled in the grass until he found my flip-flops, carefully brushed the dry earth away and laid them on the ground in front of me while my body burned and the skin between my fingers began to itch like mad.

Guthrie took one long look and said. 'Blake came in a car. I'm going to get him. Don't move.'

'NO,' I shouted as he disappeared through the rustling bushes but he didn't turn round. There was no way Blake could tell every part of my body was covered in bites if he couldn't see them. He might believe I was only sitting there when attacked by bugs and not lying flat out naked with Guthrie. But this was Arcadia. A place where, in the end, pretence is impossible and the inability to carry on with old ways of living will always find you out.

'Ah, Marya.' Blake arrived first and grinned while Guthrie stood back, embarrassed, hands in the pockets of his jeans. 'You're not the first and won't be the last to get eaten by mozzies. My car's just over there. Here. It stings at first.' He handed me a pen thing which I rolled over the back of my hand first to see if it worked. Sticky and cool, the liquid provided immediate relief but I would need a hundred of them to stop everywhere from itching.

'The huts are the best place to mess around for that reason,' Blake said to Guthrie who tried to look as if none of this had anything to do with him and failed badly. Hunched up and awkward, he stared at me but because Blake treated it like an ordinary occurrence, I began to feel better and the pen soothed my arms and ankles while the excruciating itching on my thighs and stomach continued as we headed to the messy car which was deep in used coffee cups, smudged CDs, grit and pebbles.

We looked out of the open windows until Blake pulled up outside the refectory and said, 'I won't be a minute.' He ran off up the steps and I couldn't believe we were left sitting there.

'Where's he gone?' Guthrie said and I shook my head, crossly.

'How would I know?' The car seat was melting into my back and what with the burning sun streaming through the open dirty window, the extreme discomfort of the itchy bites and Guthrie's long, drawn, worried face, it felt like we might have to wait for hours but then Mum appeared with Blake and my heart was pounding so much I could barely breathe. The surprise made me jerk the T-shirt down to cover my knees as if that would hide all the bites.

Reading the situation in less than a second, she got in a bit of a tizz. 'Oh for goodness' sake.' And turned to Blake. 'Can you drop us at the guest house?' Then she nodded at Guthrie and ignored us all the way up the track and down the tarmac road in the direction of the exit.

It wasn't the best introduction but Blake tried to lighten things by telling us about the time he got out of the sea after a dive, climbed onto a boat and found a scorpion in his hair. 'I was doubled up trying to untangle it, tripped and knocked over a bucket of knives above me. A sharp one flew into my face – hence the scar,' he said.

Mum tutted and we said nothing. So that's how he got the scar? A knife attacked him.

'Mum, you didn't say hello to Guthrie.'

'Sorry.' She turned around without a smile and looked at him for a second. 'Hi Guthrie.' It was hard to know what she was thinking but I imagine it was something along the lines of, *The sooner I see the back of you the better.*

'Hi Marya's mum,' Guthrie said and grinned. Trust him not to mind.

The car stopped outside the guest house and I kissed Guthrie on the cheek as the door opened. 'Won't be long,' I said.

'I'll wait at the refectory,' Guthrie said.

'No need,' Mum nodded. 'Marya can let you know when she's right again.' I could have killed her. Since when did she think it was OK to take over?

The car left with him looking back at me. The parched heat went with him and the shade of the trees, nearby blossoms and Mum's cool room in the guest house belonged to another country. A country I'd forgotten existed with curtains, real beds, space to breathe and a bathroom with flushing loo.

'Have a cold shower, Marya,' she said. 'And I'll find the bite lotion. I'm sure there's something of mine you can wear. That boy didn't have a lot to say.'

'Mum, I already told you his name's Guthrie.'

'Oh, yes. Guthrie. Hmm.' She looked agitated but I didn't ask why because I knew.

Once I'd washed, covered myself in soothing cream and put on a not too bad, yellow T-shirt of Mum's, she made tea with a secret kettle hidden in the chest of drawers.

'I wasn't sure what Arcadia was all about when we got here,' Mum said, ignoring the question that was clearly on her mind about what I was doing to get in such a state. 'I knew about the eco-sustainable, organic and vegan side but wasn't sure what these people's relationships amounted to.'

'They have hook-ups,' I said.

'Not really. They have relationships but not traditional ones. For example They have temporary marriages.'

'That's a hook-up, Mum.'

'Not quite. Here it's a conscious liaison.'

'Mum, I don't want to know what they do.' I was scared this would lead to the question she was desperate to ask.

'Just hear me out,' she said and perched on the double bed

opposite. 'Or they have a two-year or five-year marriage with a ceremony and vows that can be repeated, rewritten or ended depending on the desires of the couple in question. They form much deeper connections because they have to live with each other and the lack of conflict and lies between couples is the basis of Arcadia. There's no disappearing so problems have to be faced. What do you think?'

Our eyes met. I thought of mentioning Vernon Wood and Maddie but the moment passed. 'Sounds stressful.' I couldn't wait to finish the tea and get back to Guthrie, not have a heart-to-heart with my supercool Mum. Her obsession with porn has changed into a preoccupation with relationships and I didn't know which was worse.

'Do you know about Attachment Theory?' she said at last.

'No and I don't want to know but you're going to tell me anyway.'

'I had a message from your dad when we were at the other farm,' she said.

'Yeah? And?'

'He sounded fed up,' Mum said. 'According to Attachment Theory he fits perfectly into a certain category. I can't remember which one but he is a bit of a commitment-phobe. Independent. To tell you the truth I don't think it's working out with that woman.'

My heart leapt. 'Is Dad coming home?'

She fiddled with the friendship bracelets on her wrist and got up to fill the mug with more water from the kettle. Me saying that maybe made her think I was right and she said, 'I don't know what he wants to do.'

We went outside and sat in the shade for almost an hour and the faded wicker chairs creaked whenever we moved. The distant hills turned misty and all the time I imagined my dad coming home from work and me and Mum in the kitchen, chatting and laughing about nothing at all just like we used to. It was a tentative hope, not a solid one, but the dreaming made it feel possible and all the while Mum rattled on about how we're pre-programmed to seek attachments with others and our relationships depend on how secure our bonds were with our primary caregiver.

Mum had to go back to work but insisted I stay where I was and spend the night there instead of wrapped in an uncomfortable nylon and polyester sleeping bag outside or in the sweaty dorm. The angry-looking wheals on my skin had shrunk to red spots. I felt better and wanted to go but she wouldn't hear of it.

Fiddling with my phone proved how desperate I was to speak to Guthrie but with no signal there was no hope of reaching him.

'There's plenty of time to catch up,' Mum said. 'He's not going anywhere. I'll bring food back when I finish work and we can talk some more. We rarely get the chance to spend time together these days.' She loved me being there and I didn't have the heart to object.

I wondered what Guthrie was doing and whether he was missing me like I was missing him.

The dusty blue car came up the track and Serge jumped out in a hurry. He left the door open and strode towards us with a paper bag. 'Croissants from the bakery in town. Don't tell anyone,' he laughed. 'But they're made with real butter.'

The fresh, floury, fluffy in the middle pastry with slithers of real chocolate melted in my mouth. There was nothing more satisfying than fishing out the last of the toasted almonds from the paper bag and pouring the crumbs down my throat.

Mum wanted to make more tea but Serge needed to get going so I was left on the wicker chair in awe at the sunset. The orange and purple sky matched the fiery effort to believe what happened to Maddie would eventually vanish from my memory.

SIXTY-TWO

The next morning at the refectory when breakfast was almost over, I downloaded my messages and had to close my eyes more than once to remain calm. It was like I couldn't relate to normal things anymore because I'd practically become part of the trees and pebbly paths, an inhabitant of the fifth dimension with no memory of the taste of cheddar cheese.

There were a few Arcadians left at the next table in colourful dungarees, cut-offs and bright cotton dresses who were deep in conversation about Carl Jung and the true meaning of synchronicity while I sat on my own munching toasted rye bread and guess what? Yep, houmous.

I was listening. It was interesting but I turned away to read Watty's message first. 'Does this remind you of anyone?' I thought he said he deleted me after I didn't reply last time? He must be bored or in need of someone to harass because there was picture of a naked backside on its own without even an elbow in the corner to show it belonged to an actual person. It was supposed to be amusing and make me laugh but I couldn't warm to the joke and flinched.

'Don't send me pictures,' I replied and deleted it.

I tried to digest Shula's opinion: '*Middlemarch* blows the rest of Eliot's novels away. All that compromise is a lesson for us. Living in such strangulating and conventional times was the road to hell for women.' I hadn't finished reading *The Mill on the Floss* so just stared at the words. Weren't these times just as strangulating?

It made me sick to think about what everyone in the group had been through and I knew when back to London, life would rush past like a runaway train and the Arcadian way of seeing and living in the world would be drowned out by the latest news and never ending stresses. Why drag my feet?

'Mum,' I said.

She raised her eyebrows at the serious tone and swallowed a lump of porridge. 'What, honey?'

'Do you remember that time I went to Maddie's party in primary school?'

'Yes, What about it?' Mum frowned.

Feeling like I was wading through mud, my stomach rolled ahead of my body but if I didn't tell her then I'd never be able to do it. I had to keep going. 'All us kids were up in her bedroom.'

'Yes. You went to watch a film.'

'Yeah, a hardcore porn film and it turned violent when Vernon Wood pushed Maddie on the bed and raped her with the music still playing.'

It wasn't just any old silence that started up when Mum looked at me. It was possibly radioactive. 'All those years ago,' she said. 'You didn't say a word. And you? What were you doing?'

'I screamed and hid my face in my hands. Maddie laughed afterwards. She was too scared to do anything else. We heard someone coming. Sam unlocked the door to let us out and we ran away.' My mind went back to shoving our way down the stairs, bumping into the handrail and felt sick. Just as sick as I felt then.

Having a stoic for a mother is sometimes useful because they listen carefully and think before speaking. 'That poor girl. I'm glad it wasn't you but witnessing it was trauma enough. Thank you for telling me, honey. It was brave of you.'

I smiled and my eyes filled with tears. She reached across the table and said, 'I remember you all crashing into the garden. You looked as if you'd been up to no good then disappeared into the kitchen for juice. I didn't think anything of it – never occurred to me anything bad had happened. You know Vernon was interviewed by the police when he was twelve for attacking a girl in Hilly Fields?'

I shook my head.

'They let him ago because he spun such a good tale about how a crowd of them were mucking about behind the trees and when his mates backed him up that nothing happened, her mum withdrew the accusation because it got too much. That scumbag is well known. So are his friends.'

'You're not going to make me tell the police?'

'I'm not going to make you do anything, sweetie, but I will have a word with Dad. Don't worry, he won't make you do anything either.'

No fuss, no drama. My mum is the best.

SIXTY-THREE

I was stupidly happy when I got to the sunny art building and was about to ask Guthrie for his hand in marriage when I spotted Lilla kneeling beside him outlining a drawing with a pencil.

No one looked up from their work apart from Evan who gazed at me like a surprised teacher who'd forgotten I existed.

Someone had cut Carl's hair and it hung in a kind of a flat bob around his chin. The pony tail suited him better and he waved as I crossed the wooden terrace to talk to Guthrie.

'Marya, what happen? You have all over.' Lilla pointed the pencil at the bites on my arms then turned her attention to my legs. 'Lot of them.'

Guthrie sat bold upright and smiled. 'Hey, you're here. You OK?'

'Yeah. The cream helped. I got bitten, Lilla, but Guthrie saved me.' We all laughed. It was obvious that wasn't the case and he jumped up, took my elbow and led me away.

'Later, Lilla,' he said and she scribbled all over the drawing and dropped the pad on the grass with a sulk but when I turned round Tomas came to sit beside her and she was smiling again.

Surprised not to find a rickety table and emerald jug and glasses behind the shadowy building where we went hand in hand, the long grass, trees, flowery shrubs and silvery pool looked a bit sad without them. The loss made the dense foliage appear less magical but we found a spot by a tree to stand and talk. No way was I going to tempt fate by collapsing into the grass.

Guthrie leaned back against the tree trunk while I eyed the flying insects with suspicion. 'What did your mum say?'

'Nothing. She was cool. I finally told her what happened with the girl who was raped in primary school.'

'And…'

'She took it in. Didn't say much. Like I said she was cool and now I feel like I kicked a boulder into the lake and it's floated away. Like I really didn't think that was going to happen.'

'It's gone. Come here.'

We kissed under the tree and kissed again. Then went back to join the others. Later that day we all trudged to the refectory for a special dinner for Sharrow's daughter's birthday. We didn't know she had a kid.

'Her name's Lulu and she's five.' Sharrow's face burst with pride and we wondered who the dad was but no one asked.

'Guthrie and me are going out,' I told Evan on the way down.

'Where you going?' he sneered.

'Don't be an idiot,' I said and glanced at Guthrie behind us chatting to Blake.

'Well, since you haven't noticed, me and Constanza are getting it on as well,' Evan said, all sweaty with shirt half off and hair in his eyes.

'What? I thought you were just cuddling friends.'

'That, too,' Evan said with the kind of swagger a guy has when he's happy. 'She might come to London soon.'

'Where she going to stay?'

'Dunno,' he said but I could see he did and suspected it was Mum who didn't know which wasn't something I didn't want to get into when he looked so pleased with himself.

As soon as my phone got a signal I texted Dad, Shula and Watty. 'I've got a boyfriend. His name's Guthrie and he lives in Archway.'

For some reason Watty didn't reply but Dad and Shula said the same thing. 'WOW.'

'I got my exam results,' Evan shouted and pulled a face.

'Good news?' I said, fearing the worst.

'How come I only got a D for geography? I'm bad at maths but got a C. That's not fair.'

'You'll have to drop out like Bill Gates,' I said and he nodded.

'I'm getting a job. Dad knows. I've already told Mum.'

Evan handed the phone to me and the results weren't that bad. 'You did well in chemistry,' I said and a figure crept up behind him. It was Constanza.

'I look after you, Ev,' she said and plonked an arm around his shoulder. We climbed the steps to the refectory which was decorated with low-hanging bright balloons and it was especially weird to imagine Evan going to work and never catching the bus to school with me ever again.

The lights came on and a crowd of kids I've never seen before began screeching their heads off and Lulu, Sharrow's cute daughter with huge black eyes and thick, glossy hair, in yellow dungarees and Wonder Woman helmet, started singing happy birthday to herself and everyone joined in.

Guthrie left early the next morning on a cheap flight to Luton where his neighbours were going to meet him and drive to Archway. It was hard to say goodbye but as he doesn't live too far away, I wasn't worried about seeing him again though I minded being stranded in Arcadia for a few days without him.

'Keep away from the mozzies in Lewisham,' he said and kiss, kiss, kissed me.

Serge took him to the station and came back for Carl who was leaving for France.

With his body half out of the car window, Carl shouted, 'See you next year.' His clipped hair had got even shorter overnight and made him look quite ordinary.

'You coming back for a third time?' I said.

'If I can. I'm not cured yet.' He laughed. 'My parents will pay for more respite when they see how hard I've tried to get off porn this summer.'

He loved Arcadia and we loved him.

'Message me,' he said as the car drove away and before we were swallowed by the morning sun, the rest of us collected our swimmers and plunged into the lake.

The terrace up at the art building was quieter than ever afterwards, and the hours passed slowly. I stared at the cactus bushes and the track leading to the compost loos and everywhere I looked I could see Coco, Sun God, Sanvi, Carl and Guthrie. The shooting stars that night were an eye-popping reminder of how demented the summer had been and when I gazed at the full moon it felt like we knew each other and a kind of divine energy rushed right through me.

I told Tomas and he said, 'The moon reflected your own light coming from a place of abundant love. It was nuggety. Yeah?'

The word nuggety didn't quite pin-point the magnificent feeling but I was grateful he understood. 'Thanks. Yeah.'

Something was up with Tomas when the group thinned out the next morning and no one knew what it was until Lilla said he'd lost his phone. We were ordinary teenagers again and no one mentioned leaving Arcadia as we hunted the art building for it. In the end Constanza went off and found the phone on a bush near the lake wrapped in one of Tomas's ratty T-shirts and when she handed it over he had no memory of leaving it there.

'Keep your glasses on,' he told Mo when she couldn't believe he'd forgotten taking it with him when we went swimming.

'Don't you worry I'll keep them on,' she said. 'But I'm taking the responsible hat off for good when I get home, I can tell you. My brother doesn't know it yet but his new sofa's for me and I'm moving in with him.'

'Ahhh, that's great.' Tomas threw his arms round her and a wet kiss landed on her cheek which she found repulsive.

'I haven't got time for nonsense.' Mo pushed him off.

There was no big party to wish the rest of us goodbye. One by one people arrived from all over the world for Yoga, Meditation, How To Start An Eco-community and Heal Yourself courses. They searched the trees, hills and lake for photo ops to prove their new-found inner peace, and it felt like we knew who they were, watching them react to Arcadia like stowaways coming up from the dark and into the light, just as we had done.

During the long, hot walk to the refectory to download messages, Lilla announced she was staying in Arcadia.

'But of course,' she said, despite never mentioning her aunt was a member and if the summer worked out she would remain here for good.

'I'm coming back one day,' Evan said. 'So I'll see you then.'

'…Maybe it can happen,' Constanza agreed.

'I'll be in Swansea if ever you want to visit,' Mo said and Tomas gave Lilla one of Sanvi's long swaying hugs.

'I'm not sure I'll be able to cope with Birmingham after this,' Tomas said. 'I might take off and go see Carl in France.'

'You lucky you have home,' Constanza said and we all turned to look at her.

'You don't have a home?' Tomas said.

'Yes, but no good.'

'Where you going then?' Mo said.

'I think about it.' Constanza shook her head. 'Maybe see friend.'

I didn't know much about her and had left Evan alone when they were getting close so didn't like to ask what her plans were. Evan looked troubled and they fell behind to talk while the rest of us carried on down the hill with the sun burning into our necks.

We were leaving in the morning and every step reminded me of Coco. Whenever I turned around or looked up at the wide blue sky, I expected to see her tiny body in a tie-dyed dress come round the bend but when those soulful eyes looked at me there was no fear, no shame, no guilt left.

SIXTY-FOUR

It's wrong to think adults don't change. They do and when we got home, Mum was like a different person. As soon as we arrived in anonymous, noisy, wet London with non-stop traffic drilling holes in my head, it was the end of August and she ran up the stairs and got straight on the phone to Serge.

I mean she last spoke to him that morning at the station before we caught the train to Malaga. Why the rush?

It was nine o'clock at night. The bags were still in the hall and Mum only came back down the stairs when the pizza delivery arrived. Anyway, instead of being slow to say what was going on, she came straight out with it without hesitating for a single second.

'I can't put up with London for much longer.'

By then I'd cuddled Tickle half to death and Evan had told Jeremy what a cool summer we had as he headed out of the door to the hospital, and the next minute Dad was there.

He never comes late. A bit of mushroom flopped on my knee when he walked into the kitchen, I was so surprised, and with a mouth full of stringy, delicious cheese (I'm giving up dairy for good soon. Honest), it was hard but I managed to swallow and said, 'Hey Dad, what you doing here?' before reaching out for a hug.

'He wants to move back in,' Mum said.

I nearly chucked the whole lot up. Trust me when I say I wasn't expecting that. Evan was grinning his head off and Tickle started moving his tail back and forward under the table as I fell back in the chair.

Then Mum dropped another bombshell. 'As for Arcadia…'

The beautiful word was full of sunshine and bounced trees and light into the kitchen along with a silver lake until she added, 'I'm going to live there with Serge.'

They'd sorted it all out between them and me and Evan didn't have a clue. It felt like she was waving a gun at us.

'Not for a little while though,' Mum said. 'I have to hand in my notice at Wolf's Winery. We have to sort out the finances and the community members have to approve me becoming one of them which might take some time. Serge has a little house on the far side of the hill and we're going to see what happens.'

'Shell's moving in with her sister in case you're wondering,' Dad smiled. 'She couldn't stand my snoring. Plus there's a guy with a chocolate Labrador she prefers to me. The dog, not him. Obviously.'

That's how crazy parents can get during your teenage years. He'd just rented a nice flat, bought a new sofa, introduced us kids to the new 'friend' and in the blink of an eye it was all over. They really have no idea what they're doing.

'I'll be back and forth,' Mum said. 'This is still your home. We're still your parents.'

Dad finished off the rest of the pizza even though he'd already had a curry. I made coffee. Evan washed up and it all felt the same. Only it wasn't.

The next few days were confusing bordering on weird. I couldn't imagine not having Mum around and much as I love Dad and wanted him back it was hard to believe it would only be him in the house. And what if he met someone else? What if it didn't work out with Serge in Arcadia? Would they swap around again?

Walking down the High St. the next day to meet Shula, I noticed three lush trees I hadn't seen before, stopped to look at them with Arcadian eyes and bumped smack bang into Watty. Hands full, he was rushing to the post office and nearly dropped the lot.

'Whoa, babe, you look good,' he said and stood over me with an intense stare, sort of sucking me in.

'Must be because of my boyfriend,' I smiled and rolled my eyes to heaven. 'Why the surprise? I said I had a boyfriend.'

'Woah, no joke? Hope he's good at it and you'll give me a go next.' And vanished.

What did I ever see in him?

On the way back from Shula's house where I told her everything, even what Vernon Wood did (she wasn't surprised), Watty saw me before I saw him and appeared at the door of the cafe with an aubergine held between his legs. Angled crudely, he pointed and waved the thing at me, laughing like crazy.

Sad idiot. I couldn't be arsed to say anything and swanned past with my nose in the air.

*

'Nobody's life is normal,' Evan said when we scrunched up on his bed to scroll through Sanvi's blogs on his iPad. 'I wish Hilly Fields would turn into Arcadia. Wouldn't that be great?'

'Yeah, I guess,' I said. 'But what about the weather?'

There was a thick, grey sky full of rain outside. This was still supposed to be summer and we badly missed everyone while listening to Mum and Dad downstairs going through all the bills spread out on the kitchen table.

Tickle got into the action by jumping on my lap and walked around for a bit before settling down. I stroked his soft neck and we carried on reading about the water retention system, things about the flora and fauna we hadn't taken in at all, and looked at thousands of photos of the landscape. None of our group were recognisable because of the detailed information about our course, why porn is used as a coping mechanism and the long-term, indisputable benefits of quitting. Sanvi had gone to town explaining the dangers and I was full of admiration for her hard work.

The doorbell went and I leaned forward to listen to Mum's footsteps down the hall but couldn't make out who it was.

'Evan,' she called. 'Your friend's here. Come in, sweetie. You're soaked.'

Surprised, he jumped up and so did I. He doesn't have any friends called Sweetie. We stopped on the landing to see a damp-looking Constanza in a summer dress, flip-flops, see-though nylon mac and backpack over her shoulder.

If there's one thing Evan's good at it's not saying the right thing. 'Oh, no,' he said and Constanza started crying.

'Now, don't,' Mum said. 'He's done nothing but talk about you since we got back. Evan? Evan.'

We ended up on the sofa drinking tea and Evan put a gentle arm around her and this angry brother who wanted to rape a girl, kill her and then kill himself had the softest, warmest, kindest but slightly nervous expression on his face which made it clear wherever he'd travelled he'd reached the right place.

Mum made Constanza have the last chocolate biscuit. Dad barely batted an eyelid, smiled, grunted and went back to sorting out the bills in the kitchen. Only this time he put the radio on and a voice blared out: 'Experts say one in ten young men have been left impotent after an addiction to porn.'

And no one took a blind bit of notice except for Evan who shook his head. 'It should be banned. That stuff rewires your brain.'

He actually said that.

'No, don't worry, Constanza, you can share Marya's room until you find somewhere,' Mum said.

I grinned. 'Well, yeah.' And the voice on the radio faded, low music drifted out and Guthrie banged the door, right on time.

On the dripping wet doorstep, he gave me a big kiss before we even got inside then waved a really fine, second-hand copy of *Middlemarch* in my face and every skin-prickly hormone rushed right in.

It wasn't porn that scared me now... it was love.

ACKNOWLEDGMENTS

The statement, 'I want to rape a girl, kill her and then kill myself,' was made by an angry teenage boy to his mother. Thanks to that young, ordinary, quiet young man, the idea brewing in my mind for almost a decade was able to clearly form. Nothing else is based on real conversations or events. The characters are completely fictitious. However, the harmful effects of pornography are increasingly evident and the novel was created thanks to parents and teenagers brave enough to open up.

Huge thanks to my agent, Charlie Viney, for many years of clear-eyed judgement, enthusiasm and support. To his and my surprise and unlike my last six books, a traditional publisher didn't step up for this 'remarkable novel.'

I will never stop thanking Shannon Cullen who skilfully edited *Guantanamo Boy* and *The Glass Collector*. Her work will always underline mine.

The Whole of the Moon wouldn't exist without the extraordinary professor of sociology and women's studies, Gail Dines, and her book, *Pornland*. I was lucky to spend a few hours with her and her husband in Australia some years ago and can't recommend her work highly enough.

I am forever grateful to the widely differing eco-communities I've visited: Damanhur, Tamera and Findhorn, none have a Respite From Porn course (as far as I'm aware there's no such thing). Their unique, alternative, peaceful and loving ways of living continue to inspire. Thank you to the boundary-pushing writer and filmmaker, Betsy Pool, husband Eddie and daughter, Olivia, for sharing their home and lighting the way. Thanks also to the lovely people I spent two weeks with in Brazil.

A big thank you to talented writer and editor, Lucy Popescu, who managed to read and give feedback on the story when incredibly busy. I took your helpful words on board.

To my many beautiful and true friends, I can't thank you enough and along with my wonderful family, especially my adult son, I love you all. Your kindness, patience and suggestions become more precious with each passing day.

ABOUT THE AUTHOR

ANNA PERERA
www.AnnaPerera.com

Born in London to an Irish Catholic mother and Buddhist Sri Lankan father, Anna Perera taught English in two London schools, spent a few years in charge of a unit for excluded teenage boys, gained an MA in Writing for Children and has published six books, including the critically acclaimed *Guantanamo Boy*. Translated into more than a dozen languages, the novel was shortlisted for the Costa Children's Book Award, Branford Boase, and numerous other awards including a nomination for the Carnegie Medal. The novel was adapted into a sell-out play in London and regional theatres. *The Glass Collector* was also nominated for the Carnegie Medal.

Anna give talks, delivers creative writing workshops for schools in Britain and abroad, has been a judge for The Young Muslim Writers

Awards and the Jhalak Prize and helps run a book club for refugees and asylum seekers.

Guantanamo Boy
Reviews

'This powerful and humane book shows that hatred is never an answer, and proves the pointlessness of torture and the danger of thinking of anyone as 'other.'
— Nicolette Jones — Children's Book Of The Week — Sunday Times

'Perera has a warm, sympathetic style which makes it possible to keep reading when the going gets tough.'
— The Observer

'One of her greatest achievements is to make the frightening monotony of the two years in which he suffers so full of suspense.'
— Kate Kellaway - The Observer

'An excellent novel . . . superb.'
— Amanda Craig — The Times

'Extremely powerful, and the descriptions of torture are genuinely harrowing.'
— S.F. Said — The Guardian

'Timely, gritty fiction.'
— Times Review

'Could it happen? It has happened. That's why teenagers should read this book.'
— Irish Times

'The argument is as well balanced as the moral outrage is palpable.'
— Financial Times

'Rising star: Anna Perera. Her novel highlights the teenagers sent to the camp as it tugs readers into its vivid nightmare journey.'
— *Boyd Tonkin — The Independent*

'Guantanamo Boy's ability to deal with difficult issues surrounding the camp makes it a compelling read for people of all ages and a remarkable achievement.'
— *politics.co.uk*

Printed in Great Britain
by Amazon

80520944R00149